BOOK THREE OF THE ECOSYSTEM SERIES

HOUSE *of* EARTH, HOUSE *of* STONE

JOSHUA DAVID BELLIN

House of Earth, House of Stone

Cover and interior design by Damonza
The Line of the Queens by Jessica Khoury

For the future

BOOK ONE
SWORD

Ours is a landscape aswarm with ghosts.
We live in an afterworld, struggling to
imagine what we've already lost.

—Anthony Doerr,
"Phantoms and Prey" (2010)

DOMINIQUE STANDS IN *the brood chamber.*

*She is a child of seven, and her world is falling apart—
her mother and father and baby brother dead, the only home
she's ever known turned alien and hostile. She had a pet
for a time, a cat named Leo, but just this month he tried
to tear her throat out, and the women who watch over her
hacked him to pieces before her eyes. When the bad things
started, when she was five years old, the grown-ups walked the
campus with rifles at their shoulders and handguns at their
hips; from her bedroom high in the Cathedral, she heard the
sound of gunfire echoing deep into the night. But she hasn't
heard that sound for months, and now the men and women
carry whatever weapons they can lay their hands on: knives
and sharpened stakes and the meat cleavers with which the
women turned poor rabid Leo into a pile of blood and fur
and purple guts. When they were done with him, they washed
the bloody pawprints from her bedroom floor with mops and
buckets of water.*

*Dominique's eyes scan the brood chamber, the golden
waxy floor and walls with their six sides. She's never been
here before, though she's known of it since she was a girl of
three. Her parents told her about it, and about the creature
that once dwelled here: the queen bee, the one who was going
to save the world and make the flowers bloom again. The
one who, they told her, carried a part of Dominique inside*

its body. That's why they named it after her: Apis dominica, Dominique's bee. She was fascinated by the idea of sharing a part of her body with a bee, but when her parents finally showed her pictures of it, she found herself repulsed by the creature, an enormous insect the size of her baby brother before he died. Before the birds with feathers the color of a robin's red breast swooped down from the sky and snatched him from her mother's arms—her father was dead by then— and carried him off into the trees. Her mother screamed and ran after them, then clutched Dominique's face to her chest as the bloodbirds began to feed.

The brood chamber echoes her steps as she walks to the center, where the pictures she saw showed the queen wrapped in something like golden threads. Dominique shudders as she reaches down to touch the soft, gummy wax of the chamber's floor.

"Mommy," she says. "I wish you were here."

There's a book her mother used to read to her, a book about a girl her age who grew up close to the university. The girl's name was Rachel, and she was a girl who loved and worried about the world, which in her own time—long before the rise of the Ecosystem—was becoming treacherous and wild. Rachel grew up to be a scientist like Dominique's mother and father, but she sickened and died, just like Dominique's father sickened and died when the queen bee stung him and Dominique's mother sickened and died when the pretty pink flower in the garden bit her on the ankle. Ever since then, Dominique hasn't wanted to look at that book, with its cover picture of a monarch butterfly hovering over Rachel's shoulder. She wonders whether that's what happens to people who care for the world, that they sicken and die at the world's touch. She tries not to think about what might become of her when she grows up, if she grows up at all. The thought scares her so.

But there's one thing that scares Dominique more than anything else, and it's why she's come to this room today. It's something her mother said as she lay dying in her bedroom in the Cathedral, her skin drained of its beautiful brown color and her eyes cavernous as a skull's. She told Dominique that she loved her, and that Dominique must be strong once she was gone. And then she told her that, because Dominique shared part of her body with the queen bee, she must visit this place, and learn if there was anything she could do to stop the Ecosystem now that the queen was dead. She must be prepared, her mother told her, to make a sacrifice—a big word for a hard choice—to save the world her mother and father and little brother had known and loved.

"Will you do that, Dominique?" her mother asked, her breath whistling through the empty space where her teeth had been.

"Yes, Mommy," she answered, and held her mother's hand while she died.

But she knows now that she didn't mean it. She said it only because her mother was dying, and she was trying to be strong for her. Now that Dominique's here, in this shiny, empty room that once housed a monster, she knows that the sacrifice is too great. Even to save the world, she knows it's something she simply can't do.

"I'm not ready," she says to the silence of the brood chamber. "I'm not ready to be queen."

My DREAMS HAVE been like that lately.

For the past few days, at least. Since we returned from the site of my former village. Since I learned of the fate of Miriam, and of the war she plans to launch against us.

I've not slept much in that time. The queen before me, Celestina, told me that women of our bloodline don't need to sleep at all, but in that, as in so much else, she was wrong. Queens can go without sleep for longer than most people, that's true. But depriving ourselves of rest over lengthy periods of time weakens us, clouds our minds. Makes us less able to communicate with the Ecosystem. And now more than ever, I need the Ecosystem to listen to me, to talk to me. To tell me what to do.

I visit the brood chamber multiple times during the day, and sometimes at night. It's there that my dreams of the little girl who would become the first queen of the city are strongest, and this convinces me that they're more than dreams—that somehow, in this chamber, the blood I share with Queen Dominica connects me to her mind, her memories. Some of the things I see in my dreams—rifles and cell phones, fluffy cats without the red eyes and curved fangs of the fell-cats that inhabit my world—are totally foreign to me, yet when I see them through Dominique's eyes, I know their names and purposes. When I lay my head on the floor where Dominique stood nearly two hundred years ago, I'm joined not just to the Ecosystem but to *her*, the seven-year-old girl who would overcome her reluctance and accept the sacrifice, the giving of herself in exchange for her people's safety. I feel her fear, her resolve. When I wake and find the questions I want to ask ready-formed on my lips, I feel her so strongly in the room with me, I expect her to answer.

But she never does.

How did you do it? I ask of her. *How were you brave enough? How did you know that your strength, your will, wouldn't fail?*

I rise from the floor after my dreams have dissipated, stretch out my arms so the Ecosystem can grasp the silver bracelets I wear at my wrists. I draw comfort from the wild, and I provide it with comfort in turn. I try to push my awareness past the black web that blocks all light, the tangled strands of power that hold the village in thrall and that will soon begin their march toward the City of the Queens. I never succeed. Something stands in my way—the dark queen, I tell myself. It could just as easily be me.

My own mother died years ago, when I was less than three. My father's body lies beneath tons of soil in the dark queen's lair. My best friend, my only friend, if she's alive, is trapped within the strands of the queen's web. And the dark queen herself—Miriam, the girl I treated so shamefully when she was mine to teach—is planning an assault on our city that will complete the work of destruction the Ecosystem began when Dominique was a child.

I need allies. I have none. So I call on another enemy who should have been a friend. Another friend whom my own faults turned into an enemy.

HE ENTERS THE throne room with the limping gait he'll never recover from. I healed his broken leg the best I could, but the dark queen had gotten to him first, and she knotted his bones so tightly it might have killed him to undo her spell. When I laid hands on his twisted thigh and slowly straightened it, my mind flashed with an image of her solid black eyes and streaming black hair, and though it was only a vision, it took the breath from my lungs and nearly stripped the strength from my own legs.

"You wanted to see me," Isaac says in the listless voice he's used ever since we returned from the village. When, that is, he talks to me at all.

"I need your help," I say.

He shrugs, only one of his shoulders lifting. I could have healed his left arm—the one whose use he lost on our first trip into the Ecosystem—but I refrained. He surrendered it willingly in an attempt to save the girl he loves, and as soon as I touched it, I knew that giving it back to him would violate the queen's compact, the sacrificial bargain that keeps my power and the Ecosystem's in balance.

"I know you must hate me," I say.

He shrugs again.

"I need information from you," I say, deciding I'd best keep this about business. "You were with Miriam the longest, and you know her better than anyone. From what I can tell, she never ... exposed you to anything, infected you like she did Levi and Gideon and Dinah. So you should be able to report on her plans."

"I've got nothing to report," he says. "She didn't let me in on her secrets."

"Did you hear her say anything, though?" I press. "Anything at all? She must have talked: to Levi, or to...."

"To who?" he says, with a touch of anger. "Her urthwyrms? She was barely human. She looked at me, and it was like she was looking right through me. Like she didn't even know me...."

I turn away so I don't have to watch his tears. But that doesn't help, because I can still feel his pain, can see as if through his eyes the cold black stare of the girl he was supposed to marry. The girl I could have helped, could have healed, but instead....

"I'm sorry, Isaac," I say. "But I need to know."

His tears take a long time to end. I wish I'd had the sense to hold this interview somewhere else—in Celestina's garden, or in one of the Cathedral's common rooms. Anywhere other than this sterile silver chamber gleaming with candles, where I sit on a throne I've hardly earned and the only boy I've ever kissed stands crying at my feet. I consider stepping down from the raised platform to put us on the same level, but I tell myself it's better if I don't come too close to him.

"She kept saying you took it from her," Isaac says at last.

I cock my head. "Do you know what she meant?"

"No idea." He refuses to meet my eye. "At first, I thought she meant that she knew ... that she knew about...."

About me and him. About how we'd betrayed her—kissed at the swamp, revealed our feelings for each other the day he told me he was going to marry her. When I visited the dark queen's brood chamber, she said something similar: *You took it from me. Now I will take it back.* I assumed the same thing Isaac did: that Miriam was accusing me of stealing her betrothed. Now, I'm not so sure. "That's all she said?"

Another shrug. "She said a lot of things that didn't make sense. She said it belonged to her. She said she'd show you, she'd show everyone. It was all crazy stuff. I couldn't make out half of what she said anyway. Her voice...."

He shudders. I don't blame him. I heard her voice.

"But there's one thing..." he says.

"Yes?"

For the first time, his eyes meet mine. "I could be wrong about this. It was dark down there, and Levi kept crawling around and pushing me, and Miriam would...." He takes a deep breath. "Anyway, one time when she was talking, I heard another voice. Or I thought I did. I couldn't see anyone else in the room, and it was so soft I could barely make it out. But it wasn't Levi. It seemed like it came from somewhere else. Deeper down. Like someone was ... buried, or something."

The word *buried* makes me think of my father, crushed by a cave-in near the dark queen's brood chamber. "One of the villagers?" I ask.

"They were all trapped outside the room," he says. "The ones that weren't dead."

"The voice," I say carefully. "Could you tell if it was a woman's, or a man's?"

"I told you, I could barely hear it."

"So you don't know what it said."

He shakes his head.

"All right." It's not much to go on, but it gives me an idea. "Thank you, Isaac," I say. "You've helped a lot."

My words sound stilted, formal. I rise, hoping he'll take the cue and go.

He doesn't. "Are you going to attack her?"

"Not if I can help it."

"But if she tries to take the city, then you'll…."

"I'll defend it."

"Even if it means killing Miriam."

"Isaac," I say, as gently as I can, "you know that Miriam might already be gone."

His jaw tightens; he swallows. "I thought you were supposed to be some kind of queen," he says. "So heal her."

"Oh, Isaac," I say. "I can't heal the dead."

His eyes lock with mine. They're the only thing about his face that hasn't utterly changed since his wedding day. His cheeks are gaunt, his hair long and unruly from the time he spent in the dark queen's lair. But his eyes, soft and brown, gaze at me not with the reproach I expect but in supplication. As if I *could* raise the dead, if only I tried hard enough.

But I can't. Even a queen can't bring the dead back to life. And I know of no cure for the anguish I see in him, either.

"Thank you again for your help," I say curtly. "My guards will escort you out."

WHEN ISAAC'S SAFELY gone, I leave the throne room and head for the council house exit. The glass eyes of previous queens, including Dominica and my great-grandmother Leonida, stare down at me as I walk past their windows. The panel that was to have commemorated Celestina's mother Estella remains unfinished, her figure sketched in but her face a blank of transparent glass. The windows that might have commemorated other women of queenly blood—my mother and grandmother, Celestina herself, and the line of Dominica's youngest daughter, Divina— were never built and never will be.

Cold rain greets me when I step out onto the queen's grounds. It's not yet midday, but the sky is the color of ash. I keep wondering if the recent spell of freakish weather—freezing rain for a solid week—is an effect of the dark queen's power, but then I get a hold of myself. Surely she can't be so strong as that? Surely the strands of her web can't reach into the clouds?

I close my eyes and summon my chief housekeeper— Celestina's chief housekeeper. She appears within minutes, laboring across the pavement that separates the council chamber from the queen's residence. I don't fully under-stand how this works, but there's some sort of mental connection between the queen and her domestics, just as there is between the queen and the Ecosystem. I seem to have inherited that connection along with everything else when Celestina fled the city and I assumed the throne.

The housekeeper takes some time to cross the pave-stones. She's very old—a crone, to use one of Angelica's favorite words—though I don't know exactly how old. I don't know her name either, or if, like the maids she over-sees, she gave her name up when she entered the queen's service. She's solid through the midsection, a woman who's been with child, but her right hip rises steeply higher than her left, giving her a stiff, lurching gait. I'd fix the imbal-ance in a trifle, if her habitually sour face didn't caution me against it.

The old woman curtsies painfully before me. "Your Majesty."

"I need to talk to Aurelia," I say. "And I could use a coat or something."

She frowns. She never speaks out of turn—in fact, she hardly speaks at all—but I suspect she's annoyed by my refusal to wear the elaborate gowns and hairstyles of my predecessor. The pockets of her apron bulge with canisters and powders I'm sure she'd love to slather all over my face, but I've resisted her hints thus far. I won't even consent to have my nails painted. It would be a wasted effort, as I've taken to biting them to the quick.

"Your Majesty," she says, and curtsies again before handing me her shawl and hobbling off to find the captain of the city guard.

I sigh and drape the lacy thing over my hair and shoul-ders. I don't know if I'll ever get used to ordering people around, but the sad reality is, the queen's retainers won't act without my say-so. If I could break them of their habit of calling me "Your Majesty" and "Queen Sarah," I'd do it, but I've pretty much given up on that. Thankfully, most of them refrain from calling me "Your Highness," which I can barely stand when I feel so low.

The rain falls harder as I make my circuit of the city grounds, and within minutes, the shawl is soaked through. I cast it aside and bow my head, letting my hair absorb the force of the raindrops.

To look at the city, one would hardly know we're preparing for war. There are no troops mustering on the open spaces or guarding the gates before the Cathedral, no weapons piling up in the outbuildings. I've ordered the gardens' produce to be moved to indoor storage cellars, but if the city's besieged, we'll soon starve. I've also consulted with the engineering corps, learning the rudiments of the underground pipes that bring water into and out of the city, but whether these can withstand a prolonged cold spell, those who maintain their upkeep can't say. These deficits aren't my fault—the City of the Queens was a university, never meant to be an armed fortress—but still, if the city falls, it'll be my responsibility. I wish I could rely on my trusty urthwyrm, the one that brought me and Isaac back from the dark queen's lair, but the poor thing would freeze solid if it were to venture from the underground warren where I keep it quartered.

Still, we're not quite as defenseless as we appear. As queen, I command the Ecosystem in the vicinity of my realm, and those creatures that can withstand the cold—warhogs and bloodbirds, prowler monkeys and more—will come to our aid if I call them. I've been experimenting with a defensive barrier, a living hedge such as the one

Miriam built around the village, and though my power pales beside hers, I haven't given up hope that my seedlings will take root and grow. The men and women of the queen's guard, though small in number, are steadfast in spirit; the residents of the city, if untrained, are stalwart. One of the last lessons I learned from my grandfather was this: those who defend the thing they love are able to call on reserves of strength they never knew they possessed. Were it not so, the human race couldn't have made it through the Ecosystem's initial assault.

Against all that, there's Miriam, whose power over life and death is so great, it'll take more than love to defeat her. It'll take a miracle, and in my almost eighteen years on this earth, I've found true miracles to be the rarest of visitors.

Footsteps ringing across the ice-slicked paving stones make me look up to see Aurelia approaching, her head held high in defiance of the stinging droplets. An ageless woman who's served as captain of the city guard since the start of Queen Estella's twenty-year reign, she lost two of her soldiers on the mission that recovered Isaac. Though she approved my plan at the time, I've gotten the feeling ever since that she's holding a grudge. She treats me with brusque courtesy, but no more.

"Your Majesty," she says, bowing instead of curtsying. The crest of spiky hair atop her head is frozen stiff.

"Any progress with the outer defenses?" I ask.

"The wall goes up," she reports noncommittally. "It's not secure."

I nod. My wyrm's last act before going underground was to level the empty buildings that used to house the university's students. With the rubble, we've been piecing together a wall, but it won't be strong enough to stop the queen's forces unless I can bind it with something that grows. "And the scouts?"

"They're unable to approach the village," she says. "The black web has spread eastward toward the city over the past day, and we believe it conceals the main host of the dark queen's army."

"That's a safe assumption," I say. "How close has it come?"

"If its pace holds steady, it will reach our gates within a week."

The news isn't entirely unexpected, but still, my heart slams against my chest at Aurelia's words. "You're sure?"

"At its present pace," she repeats. "Less if it quickens."

I search her eyes for a glimmer of sympathy, but there's none. I take a deep breath and try to still my racing heart. "Aurelia...."

"My Queen?"

"Years ago," I say. "At the time of the Great Rupture. With the Brotherhood, and Delilah...."

Her face flinches at the name of the lost queen, but she says nothing.

"Did the city guard keep any records about her and her followers?" I continue. "Any testimony in the archives? I could use whatever you've got."

She remains stony-faced. "There are no records."

"You're telling me something as significant as an attempted revolution took place, and no one thought to write it down? In a city that used to be a university?"

Her gaze hardens, becoming almost insolent. "The queen at that time—"

"Was my great-grandmother," I say. "And Delilah's cousin. I can't believe she didn't have anything to say about a member of her own family challenging her reign."

"If Queen Leonida had anything to say," Aurelia answers, enunciating each syllable as if it's a chip of ice on her tongue, "her words are lost to history."

I study her face, which has settled back into flinty opacity. I suspect she's lying, or at least, that there's more to this story than she's willing to tell. The tale I heard from my father was this: barred from the throne by her cousin, the young Delilah conspired with other members of the community to seek Leonida's overthrow. When the plot was uncovered, she and her followers fled the City of the Queens to establish the village where I was born. There, a man named Malachi—Chief Sensor before my grandfather Aaron—founded a secret society, the Brotherhood of the Sensorship, which held the village in a grip of terror that resulted in many deaths.

Yet there were gaps in the story my father couldn't or wouldn't fill in: what became of Delilah once the Brotherhood took power, what chastened Malachi and his brethren into ceding oversight of the village to the line of Wardens. What role my grandfather, who was only a boy when he left the city, played in all of this. Now that a dark queen has arisen in the village, one determined to take back the city of her ancestor's birth, I long to know the full story of those early days.

But I'm pretty sure I'm not going to get it from Aurelia, not without using my power to strip it from her mind, and that's something I refuse to do. She faces me impatiently, every line of her body indicating that she's

17

eager to free herself from my company. A spent work crew chooses that moment to straggle by, their clothes and hands sooty gray from the rain-mixed rubble, which gives me the excuse I need to dismiss her.

"All right," I say. "I want you to double the crews on the wall. I'll see if I can get some friendly creatures to help out. And I expect immediate reports if the status of Miriam's army changes."

She bows stiffly before departing. "My Queen."

I watch her stride off, her back braced against the wind. I consider visiting the library in hopes of finding the records Aurelia won't admit to, but something tells me that if they exist, they won't be housed there. I close my eyes and picture the sprouts I've planted beneath my defensive wall, the slow-growing seeds of life so much weaker than Miriam's approaching web. When Celestina showed me the world known only to the queens, I marveled at the power I held in my hands, a power I'd never guessed was mine. Now I feel like the child I was when my grandfather first opened the Ecosystem's secrets to me, the only difference being that I have only days, not years, to learn all that I must know.

With a feeling of dread weighing down my steps, I return to the brood chamber, and to my dreams of the girl who would be queen.

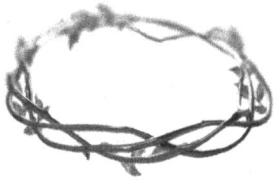

EVENING FINDS ME in the highest tower of the Cathedral. There's a small room here whose original purpose I don't know: bare stone decorated only by arched windows that face in each of the four directions. It might once have served as a watchtower, a storage space, or a mere ornament. From this vantage, I can look out on any point of the city, whether that be the artificial lake with ice knitting in its shallows, the distant cemetery whose grave markers stand against whitened grass, or the inadequate barrier where ant-size people labor against the freezing rain, assisted by wild jackalasses I've recruited to haul the blocks of stone into position. Beyond, I can see the towering trees of the Ecosystem, their crowns concealing the distant darkness of which Aurelia spoke.

I shiver with more than cold. There's a polite knock at the door, and I turn my attention from the unappealing vista. "Come in."

I smile when the door opens to reveal seven-year-old Rebecca, the only apprentice Sensor to survive the trek to the City of the Queens. She lost the use of her legs in the urthwyrm attack at Miriam and Isaac's wedding, but recovered her mobility thanks to my father's healing touch. After all these weeks, it still amazes me to see her walking—and running, and skipping—as if she never lost a day. She's not even winded from the long climb upstairs.

"Hi, Sarah," she says. "You look tired."

That's something I've always liked about Rebecca: she says what's on her mind. Not like everyone else in the city, who are either afraid to tell the truth for fear of offending their queen or, just as likely, lying brazenly to my face.

"I am a little tired," I say. "There's been a lot on my mind."

"So it's true what Gideon said?" she asks. "You're the queen now?"

"Is that bad?"

She sizes me up. "You don't look like a queen," she says. "But I like you better that way."

I laugh and hold out a hand to her. She joins me at the westward-facing window, which I've left open to the frigid air. Rebecca's eyes grow wide as she takes in the view from hundreds of feet above the ground.

"I need your help," I say. "Something only a Sensor can do."

"I'm not—"

"An apprentice can do it too," I reassure her. I feel the anxiety rising from her skin, and I let a soothing wave flow from my hand to hers. "You know there's trouble in the village."

"Gideon told me."

"Did he tell you about Miriam?"

"A little." She cranes her neck, as if she could see the village from here. "He told me she's sick."

"Not only that," I say. "She's very angry, so angry she wants to … to hurt people here in the city. And it's my job to stop her."

"If you can't," she says, "will people die?" She says

nothing of her parents, who fell in an attack by Miriam's creatures on our way to the City of the Queens.

"I'm afraid so, dear one," I say, using her mother's pet name for her. "That's why I need you. I know I don't look like it, but I *am* the queen, and I'm asking for your help."

She lets go of my hand, leans her head out the window with her eyes closed. I feel her sending out filaments of Sensation, probing the Ecosystem's mind. I doubt she can Sense much from here, especially with Miriam's web strangling the forest's life. Then she gasps, a sharp intake of breath through her nose, and when she draws her head back inside, her dark eyes are clear and focused. "What do you need me to do?"

I smile at her. "Did you ever dream you were a bird?"

"I guess so...."

"Then watch this."

With the power Celestina unlocked in me, I reach out to the Ecosystem, call it to my aid. It's only a minute before a fat bloodbird lands on the windowsill, its feathers slicked with rain. The bird searches us with keen black eyes, casually burps a bubble of blood. Rebecca recoils from the stink, but when I extend a hand, the bird hops onto the silver bracelet at my wrist.

"I need you to be my eyes," I say to Rebecca, while the bird preens its feathers, smearing them with blood. "I can't spy on Miriam's army without her knowing I'm watching. But you can do it through our friend here."

Rebecca's face pinches with doubt. "I can't Sense things that far away."

"You won't need to," I promise her. "Your mind will

be connected to the bird's, and all you'll have to do is report what it sees."

"You can do that?" she asks.

I touch her hand, let my power flow from the bird to her. Her eyes widen as the connection is established. "How did you…?"

"I told you I was queen," I say.

She smiles nervously, closes her eyes. With my hands binding the two, I coax Rebecca's thought and the bloodbird's into closer and closer alignment. The bird cocks its head, shifts on its perch. Merging with a human being is a new experience for it, too. But a Sensor's mind is linked to every living thing in the Ecosystem, and all I'm doing is making the link stronger. Within seconds, the bird settles, and I let it hop onto the windowsill as I release Rebecca's hand.

"Now listen carefully," I say to the two of them. "You're going to fly west, as fast as you can. When you see the dark queen's army, stop and wait for me to tell you what to do."

The girl steps to the window with her arms outstretched, but it's the bird that spreads its wings and drops into space. Rebecca's eyes remain closed, her face expressionless: she's no more afraid of the fall than a fledgling on its first flight. She's silent for a short time, the only signs of life being her quiet breaths and the movement of her eyes under their lids. Then she speaks, with an odd croaking quality beneath her child's voice.

"We see the forest," she says. "It rushes beneath us as we steer into a driving gale."

"Good," I say. "Hold that course. Tell me when you see the treetops darken as if with cloud."

"The wind is against our wings," she says. "We will be there as soon as we can, Your Majesty."

"Now, stop that," I say. "You know my name is Sarah."

A small smile crosses her lips before smoothing away like a ripple on a pond's surface. Her closed eyes flick back and forth, keeping pace with the bloodbird's wing beats. From time to time, her eyes' restless motion ceases as the bird glides. I wait for the creature to reach its goal, and my own heart pulses in sync with the pattern of its flight.

The leaden clouds have faded to dusk when Rebecca speaks again. "We are here."

"What do you see?"

"The trees toss as if in torment," she says, her face tightening with momentary pain. "It is not the wind. Boughs fall, and the earth shakes."

"Lower yourself to roost," I instruct. "But stay hidden. Not too close to the ground."

There's a pause as the bird dives. I feel it light on a branch within the canopy, and I know it would take only the smallest effort on my part to see what it sees. But I can't risk it. Its eyes aren't the only ones watching.

"We see darkness," the hushed words fall from Rebecca's lips. "Darkness, and creatures moving within."

"Human creatures?"

Her closed eyes scan the scene before her. "Human, yes. But wearing halters of black around their necks."

"Is my ... is my father one of them?"

There's another long pause, then the croaking voice

speaks again. "The healer named Gabriel is not among the dark queen's forces."

So he's truly gone. I don't know if it brings me comfort to know that he died before the queen had a chance to make him her slave. "What about Leah? Is she there?"

Rebecca's eyes move rapidly beneath their lids. "We see the woman named Leah. A leash is about her neck. Her eyes are black."

Sorrow and anger war within me at the thought of my best friend's debasement. If she arrives at the city gates animated by the dark queen's power, how will I fight her? How will I bring myself to kill her if I must? "I need to know how many people there are," I say to Rebecca, trying to calm my thoughts.

"Too many for us to count," she says, and I'm not sure whether that's her or the bird talking. Bloodbirds can't count past three, the highest number of hatchlings in a single brood. "The human creatures are not alone. Foul things walk among them, and some fly above."

"What about urthwyrms?" I ask. "Do you see any of them?"

She shakes her head in a strange way, tipping it like a bird's. "No wyrms travel with the dark queen's army."

"Are you sure?" I can't believe the queen would leave a host of urthwyrms behind to defend an empty village when such an irresistible force might be brought against the city. "Look harder. They might be underground, using the same tunnels they dug to approach the village."

"They are creatures of great power, too mighty to hide from our eyes," Rebecca says. "The ground would surge upward in ruts and hummocks if they traveled beneath. There are no wyrms among the dark queen's … wait."

She's silent for another long spell, as if watching while the queen's army passes beneath her. I'm tempted to tell her to fly away, but I know this might be the only chance I'm going to get to spy on Miriam: the closer she comes to the city, the riskier it'll be for both me and my agents to scout her movements. I wait anxiously while the bird views whatever's parading beneath it, and Rebecca translates the images from its eyes into speech.

"Something comes up behind the main body of the enemy," she says at last. "Something powerful, yet wrapped in darkness. We have never seen its like. It has not dwelled on this earth before, we think."

"What is it?" I ask.

"We do not know its name," she answers. "But its work is death."

She shivers. I can no longer resist peeking at what the bird sees, and when I do, a wall of blackness rises in my sight, with a huge, shambling shape moving as if it's part of the dark. Before I can make out what it is, a black rope uncoils from the mass of shadows with the speed of a striking snake.

"Rebecca!" I shout. "Get out of there. I order you—"

It's too late.

Rebecca's body goes rigid, a scream that sounds like a bird's dying cry forming in her throat before being abruptly cut off. She slides to the stone and lies still for the briefest of moments before her body convulses, her back arching and her neck straining. I drop to the floor, attempt to lay hands on her, but something with the bite of a whip erupts from her mouth and throws me against the wall. Dazed, I watch as she rises to her knees, then jerks fully upright as if pulled by invisible strings.

She turns to me, her eyes opening. Their orbs are solid black.

"You have failed, seed of Leonida," she says, but her voice is that of the dark queen, hollow and cold. "And now, you have delivered another life into my hands."

"Miriam," I say. "If you want to fight someone, fight me. Rebecca is innocent. You...." *You used to love her,* I want to say, but the thought has barely entered my mind when Rebecca's mouth issues a stream of mocking laughter. She takes a step toward the open window, flexing her legs as if to test their strength.

"The girl can walk, I see," the dark queen says. "But can she fly?"

"Don't!" I scream.

I leap to block the western window, but my enemy deceives me. Rebecca's arms spread like wings before she throws herself at the eastern-facing window, shattering the panes of glass. For a split-second, her small figure hangs in the void. The child doesn't even scream as she plummets to the ground five hundred feet below.

Leah told me once that to heal people, you have to know them as they are. You can't pretend they're who you want them to be. That might help keep them alive, but it'll always prevent you from making them whole.

I brood on that advice as I sit by Rebecca's bedside.

The littlest Sensor rests under the healers' care, unconscious but alive. Bloodbirds caught her before she hit the ground. Her face and arms are cut by glass, but the dark queen's presence has abandoned her—departing her body, I assume, to avoid the impact of the fall. I've scanned the girl's mind, and it's undamaged. I haven't checked her memories, maybe because I hope she remembers nothing at all.

For my part, I hope I remember everything. Isaac will never forgive me—I'll never forgive myself—but if the time comes, I'll need those memories to help me do what must be done.

It's LONG PAST midnight when I leave Rebecca's bedside and return to my residence. Caleb and Noah will watch over her through the rest of the night. I weighed their inexperience against their pleas to help out, and decided that Rebecca was best left in the hands of healers who know and love her.

The first-floor windows of the queen's house cast misty bands of candlelight. Something glistens by the front door, something that's not rain. I freeze with a feeling other than cold when I see it's Aurelia, her silver tunic catching the warmer yellow light. I've no energy for more bad news, much less for another quarrel or lecture.

"My Queen," she says, bowing. "Is the girl recovered?"

"She will be."

The captain of the guard nods but makes no move to go. I wonder what the protocol is in such circumstances, whether I can summarily dismiss her without further blemish to our relationship. Not willing to risk it, I let her into the front hall, where she stands dripping. She must have been waiting a long time.

"Do you have a report?" I ask.

"The wall strengthens," she says. "The beasts of the wild do the work of many people. And something new grows from the soil at the wall's base."

"I know," I say. "I finally got it working. Because of ... because of Rebecca."

She nods again as if she understands. Maybe she does. The fury I felt at the youngest Sensor's narrow escape from death lent power to my hands, and when I sank my fingers deep into the swampy ground, the seeds heard at last and came to me. At their accelerated rate of growth, they might be ready when the dark queen's army arrives.

Aurelia follows me down the hallway to the sitting room beside my bedchamber. She's never entered this house in my presence, and I'm struck by the hesitant quality of her steps, so unlike the proud, haughty demeanor she showed me earlier today. I ignore the mud she tracks on the carpet and let her trail me to the richly furnished room, where she drops into a chair by the fireplace.

I sit facing her. The fire crackles, but aside from that, there's not a sound. The old housekeeper hobbles in with a silver tray bearing a late supper. She frowns at the muddy footprints, but exits with a short harrumph when I wave her off. It occurs to me that I'm not the only one who's exhausted by this past week's labors; the stark shadows from the hearth accentuate the lines of Aurelia's face, making her appear pale and gaunt. Maybe she just needs a few minutes' rest, the warmth of the fire.

When the minutes stretch on, though, I grow impatient. "Is there any more news?"

She shakes her head. "The scouts report no change in the dark queen's advance."

"Then I'll say goodnight."

She looks up at me when I stand, but fails to do the same. "My Queen...."

"I'm tired, Aurelia," I say. "It's not that I wouldn't love to sit and chat, but unless you have a good reason to be here…."

She lowers her gaze. I've never seen the woman so uncomfortable, so timorous. Her hands twist around each other like a raw recruit's before a very unforgiving master.

"I've spoken with my lieutenants," she says in a near-whisper. "They don't approve of what I'm about to tell you. But after what happened today, with the girl…."

I return to my seat. Aurelia continues to wring her hands, refusing to look me in the eye. "What is it?" I ask.

"There are traditions," she answers. "Traditions preserved by the captain of the guard, passed down by word of mouth from the time of the Great Rupture. We're sworn to secrecy, and even now, I risk my position by talking to you."

She gives me an imploring glance, but I'm too angry for pity.

"You know something about Delilah," I say.

She nods.

"And yet you've let me face her heir, twice, without that knowledge. You approved my mission to her village, and we suffered losses—my father, as well as your own guards—when the information you've kept from me might have benefited us. Just today, when I asked you directly if you knew anything, you insisted you didn't."

"You asked if there were records," she mutters. "Technically, I spoke the truth."

"Technically?" I snap. "A child almost died, and you're talking about technicalities?"

She lowers her head again. Warmed by the fire and freed of ice, even her rusty crest of hair seems to droop.

"*Technically*, I could have you removed from your post for withholding vital intelligence from a queen of the realm," I say. "I could have you locked in a cell, or banished from the city, or handed over to the dark queen for her to mete out justice." I don't know how much of this is true, but Aurelia doesn't dispute any of it. "Who would stop me?"

She looks up, her face miserable. The rain has dried, so what I see on her cheeks must be tears.

"I could also do this," I say, and clench my hand into a fist.

Aurelia clutches her tunic just above her heart. She tries to maintain an upright posture, but I squeeze tighter, and she doubles over. "My Queen—"

"That's right," I say. "I *am* your queen. Yet you show me no respect. You've never forgiven me for taking Celestina's place, even though she was the one who abandoned the city while I'm the one who stayed."

"It's … not that," she gasps. "Not the reason.…"

"Then *what*?" I demand. "What are you hiding from me, Aurelia? What are you so afraid of?"

"You … see too much," she chokes out. "You … suspect.…"

She can't go on. I rise to stand above her as she falls to the carpet, catching herself with a single hand. The other is knotted in her chest. "This is the dark queen's power.…"

"We're the same," I say. "Deep down, our power is exactly the same. There's nothing she won't do, no life she won't barter to serve her ends. Why should I be any different?"

Aurelia's face is ready to burst. I let her go and turn my back as she collapses on the carpet, shuddering to draw breath.

"But I *am* different," I say. "I don't demand your blood. All I ask is that you tell me the truth."

Shakily, she climbs back into her chair. Her eyes are red with burst vessels, but I can heal those easily enough. When I take my own seat, she meets my gaze fully and speaks. Her voice, hoarse at first, regains its strength as she proceeds.

"The guard has existed since the dawn of the Ecosystem," she says. "In the days before Dominica came, we were commissioned from among the students and laborers of this university to do battle against the creatures of the wild. At first, we fought them with guns, and when our ammunition was expended, we fought them with knives, and when our blades dulled and broke, we fought them with our bare hands. We died in great numbers, and we would have died out entirely, along with those we sought to protect, had the line of the queens not arisen. In recent years, our work has become largely … ceremonial," she says with a rueful smile, touching the fabric of her elaborately embroidered tunic. "Yet we have ever been proud of our service to the city, and we swore that we would not see it threatened again, whether by the Ecosystem or by human hands."

"Get to the point, Captain," I say. "It's late, and the dark queen's army is on the march."

She gives me a hard look that's much more like the

Aurelia I know. "Be patient, My Queen. It is difficult to tell of these things."

I tamp down my edginess and wait.

"At the time of the insurgency led by Delilah and Malachi," she goes on, "Leonida revived the guard as a fighting force. Though it grieved us to turn our strength against our own people, we were convinced that the city's fate depended on our remaining loyal to our queen. Thus we threw our weight against the rebels as your great-grandmother Leonida decreed, and having overcome them, we held them in dungeons deep beneath the queen's grounds until the day of their trial and subsequent banishment."

"Banishment?" I say. "My father told me that the Sensors left on their own."

She smiles the way Celestina used to when I revealed my abysmal ignorance of the world's ways, and the flush I feel in my cheeks isn't just from the fire.

"Your father was a great healer," she says. "But he was neither strategist nor warrior. He never questioned the history that was deemed suitable for public consumption: that a revolt that would have plunged this city into a second chaos had been averted without bloodshed or retribution. The guard knew better. We knew that to end the threat, there could be no glimmer of mercy shown toward those who had fostered the breach, be they friends or family, spouses or children. And so, My Queen"—she gazes at me with an expression of mingled sternness and sorrow—"we showed none."

I mull this over while Aurelia turns her head to stare into the fire. I'm loath to disturb her reverie, but her words trouble me in ways I'm not quite able to articulate. "You would have needed the support of the queens to maintain a lie that big," I say slowly. "Starting with my great-grandmother. If she was only trying to protect the city, why would she want to keep the true story from coming out?"

Aurelia looks back at me, and I see I've asked the right question—or the wrong one, judging from the torment in her eyes. When she speaks, her words are a whisper.

"There is a deeper truth to this story that even the captain of the guard is not privy to," she says. "A truth that survives only in rumors of shameful deeds committed by Queen Leonida herself. The full truth lives, if at all, in the memory of one woman alone—a woman of power so great it terrified even a fellow queen."

She fixes me with reddened eyes as she says this. At first, I don't understand what she means, but then I recall what my father told me about Celestina's mother Estella, how she feared that my mother might return to the city to take the throne from her. She bred urthwyrms to prevent that from happening, and when my mother fell into their path, she put her plan into effect. Those same wyrms were the ones that destroyed my village, then went on to become the dark queen's deadliest pets. "Are you telling me that Leonida ordered the guard to kill her cousin?" I say. "To kill Delilah?"

Shame shuts down Aurelia's face again, but she manages to answer.

"I do not know what became of the lost queen," she says. "All I know for a certainty are the words she spoke to the sole visitor she was allowed during her imprisonment. With these words, she passes out of the city's memory, and it may be that this is why the captain of the guard has preserved her words so faithfully for almost a hundred years."

"What were they?" I ask.

She hesitates before answering, and fear flickers across her face.

"No more lies, Aurelia," I say. "Enough people have died already."

She lets out a heavy breath. "I have held this secret for many years," she says. "It may be that the time has come to speak the lost queen's words aloud, and that you are the very one meant to hear them."

She stands and goes to the window. I watch icy droplets slide down the glass, veins of water turned to blood by the fire's glow. Aurelia refuses to look at me, and when she speaks, it's in a hollow voice, as if the dark queen is speaking through her.

"Delilah's words were a mother's plea," she says. "They were these: *What will become of Aaron? What will become of my son?*"

MY BRILLIANT PLAN to catch up on sleep is foiled by Aurelia' tale. Long after she's left my residence for her own quarters among the guard, I lie awake in the queen's bed, and for all its luxurious comfort, I find no respite from my racing thoughts.

Leonida was my great-grandmother. That much I knew. But so was Delilah. The two queens who fought for control of the city were both of my blood.

I think back to what Isaac told me in the throne room, the accusation Miriam repeated to both of us: *You took it from me. Now I will take it back.* And the voice he heard from beneath the ground, the voice he couldn't make out—could that have been Delilah's voice? A voice not heard in the city for almost a century, but now crying out from the earth where her bones lie buried?

No matter how many times I tell myself that *I'm* the one who's going crazy, I can't shake the thought from my mind. And no matter how many times I tell myself that Delilah—if it *is* Delilah—is wrong about me, I can't convince myself that she is.

I never took anything from her, not personally. But I'm Leonida's heir, the one who sits on the throne Delilah lusted for and lost. It spins my head to think of the circumstances by which the warring cousins' blood flows in equal measure through my veins. Aaron was Delilah's son,

Seraphina Leonida's daughter, and the two of them produced my mother—but how? How could the children of
rival queens have come together to bear a child? I've had
no access to Seraphina's life as I have to my grandfather's
and mother's; she died so long before I was born, I've never
thought to search the Ecosystem for her traces.

But now I need answers. And I'm running out of time
to get them.

I slip from bed and head down the hall. Stepping
lightly so as not to rouse the old woman whose snores issue
from the room across from mine, I approach the door that
leads to the brood chamber. I've left it ajar, as Celestina
had the only key and wasn't about to donate it to me when
she fled the city. Cold stone turns to freezing dirt as I take
the stairs that descend deep below the queen's residence. I
carry no candle, needing only the pull of the Ecosystem to
guide my steps.

When I enter the chamber and extend my arms for
the golden tendrils to catch hold of my bracelets, I feel
what I always do in this place: the thrill of the wild surging through my body, a thrill I can no longer distinguish
as mine or the Ecosystem's. There's no separation between
us anymore, no distance. I might not feel like a queen, but
I feel most like myself when I merge with the being I used
to consider my enemy.

"Show me my grandmother," I say to it, though
it needs no words of mine to know my will. "Show
me Seraphina."

The world opens before me, sensations running down
my arms and solidifying into visions before my eyes. As
with so many things, it was Celestina who taught me how

to search for moments hidden from human observers: if the Ecosystem witnessed it, if it was graven on the mind of the wild and not forgotten, it's there for me to find. I see the forest as it was before the dark queen's power took hold, with no shadow clouding the trees, no black web choking the life that thrives there. But that's not the only thing that's different: there are creatures I've never seen before, plants and trees and animals that have passed into memory through the constant wheeling of time. I'm seeing the woods, I realize, from years and years back, long before I was born, long before my mother was born. A young woman is visible in a forest glade where russet grass grows beneath trees with feathery leaves, a woman I recognize instantly by her golden hair and blue eyes.

Seraphina.

She walks barefoot on the grass, wearing not a queenly gown but a simple white shift cinched at the waist by a sash woven in a pattern of unfamiliar yellow flowers. Unlike a Sensor in the same circumstances, she makes no effort to hide herself from the Ecosystem, and thus its eyes—my eyes—drink her in at leisure, watching as she sits with no fear among the oddly garbed trees. She looks to be about the age my mother was when I was born, but she's been training as a pureskin for years. The Ecosystem of this time knows her as its future queen. It wouldn't dare harm her.

Then her head snaps up, her gaze focusing on a patch of the red-tipped grass that grows long and wild at the clearing's edge. I reorient my inner eyes to see what startled her, but there's nothing to see; the woods are empty of any intruder, any foreign presence. Seraphina stands and approaches the margin of the glade, her power rippling outward to identify what's trespassed on her privacy. Her eyes widen, and for another instant, I glimpse their startling blue. But then she waves a hand and all falls dark, and much as I entreat the Ecosystem to show me more of the scene, there's no more to show.

She cut the connection. Hid herself from the Ecosystem, preventing it from recording any more. Whatever she saw, she didn't want it to be available to other eyes—least of all, I suspect, to her mother's.

Was it my grandfather she saw? A Sensor, shielding himself from the Ecosystem, and thus invisible in my vision? Was this their first meeting?

"Show me more," I insist. "Show me another time."

The Ecosystem fumbles for a moment, disjointed images flashing by too quickly for me to make them out. Then a new vision asserts itself, and I'm no longer seeing the forest glade but the queen's own garden, the one behind my current residence. In its basic layout, it's the same garden where Celestina imparted her knowledge to me: the high hedge that encircles it, the terraced beds that descend from the back door haven't changed. But the details are different, the flowers predominantly blood-red in color, the silverbloom bushes that were Celestina's signature creation missing altogether. It's nighttime, but the moon illuminates two figures who sit on a bench near the garden's center: Seraphina, her face and figure showing that she's aged considerably since I first saw her, and a man with a powerful frame and long dark hair. He's facing away from me, but I have no doubt it's my grandfather. His brown hands rest atop Seraphina's pale ones, and as I watch, he leans toward her for a kiss.

Once again, the vision goes dark, and no efforts of mine avail to bring it back. I can easily guess what's happened: in the flush of passion, the two momentarily forgot to hide themselves, but Seraphina realized her error and wiped both herself and her lover from the Ecosystem's mind. I wonder whether that careless second was enough to doom her—whether it was witnessed by her mother on her nightly visits to the queen's brood chamber. When Seraphina was discovered with child, did Leonida know who the father was? And if so, when Seraphina died giving birth to Delilah's granddaughter, how did my grandpa spirit the girl away before Leonida could intercept him?

A secret passage, the answer comes to me. A way for him to get into and out of the garden, and for Seraphina to escape her mother's eyes when she wanted to meet him in the forest. How Seraphina hid it from the woman who ruled the Ecosystem is beyond my capacity to understand. But it's the only way.

"Show me," I murmur. "I need to see."

Once again, the Ecosystem hesitates, my inner vision briefly falling dark. When it brightens, I'm puzzled by what appears: the main gate to the city, the one in front of the Cathedral and close by the skirt of the forest. I'm about to redirect the Ecosystem when a figure standing on the pavestones catches my eye: a tall, black-haired woman with skin a touch darker than mine, who lifts her head bravely though her mouth is stretched in an unnatural grimace. At her side, a boy with skin like hers clutches her hand and glances anxiously at her face. The woman stares straight ahead, into the forest. Fifty or more men, women, and children cluster behind her, and on either side, lining

40

the way the group must walk, guards in golden uniforms trimmed with red sashes stand at rigid attention.

I've seen this vision before. It's the day my grand-father left the City of the Queens. When I first saw it during my training with Celestina, I had no idea that the woman who held his hand was Delilah, nor did I see the guards who hemmed her and the others in. Why does the Ecosystem show it to me now, when I asked it to reveal the passageway that enabled Aaron to visit Seraphina? What is it trying to tell me?

As I watch, there's movement among the ranks of the guard, and a pretty girl with blue eyes and golden hair pushes through the crush of bodies and throws herself at Aaron. He freezes as if stunned, then shakes loose from her embrace and pulls closer to his mother. When Delilah leans down to fend Seraphina off, I glimpse something I missed: a flash of pink at the woman's brown throat. Before I can get a good look at it, a figure with pale skin and a crimson dress rushes up behind the guard, and the next instant, the scene goes dark for good.

Leonida. She blinded the Ecosystem's eyes so it couldn't record her daughter's farewell—or, perhaps, so it couldn't retain the memory of Delilah's end. No matter how hard I beg, cajole, demand that it show me more, there's nothing more for it to show.

In desperation, I reach out toward the village, seek-ing to make contact with the dark queen. Now more than ever, I need to know what she knows, what she *is*—what spell gave birth to the web she sends against us, what malign fate grants her power over the living and the dead. I struggle and strain until the Ecosystem cries out for release, but all I see is darkness, a veil of black that blots out the whole world. I'm about to break the connection when a spark ignites within the void, turning my inner horizon to flame. I hear a woman scream, the answering cry of a child, then such pain descends upon me it's as if my actual body has been scorched by killing fire.

I wrench free of the vision, fall to the floor of the brood chamber. Exhaustion and grief make me too weak to rise. I've learned something of what happened in the past, but that doesn't change what's happening now. If it truly is my great-grandmother's spirit that has returned, I have to end the threat she poses to the city I rule. And that means that the body she inhabits, the body of a girl I might once have healed, must die.

"Dominique," I plead, and hear the echo of my own voice. "If you're listening, help me. Show me what to do."

I STAND BEHIND a parapet at the peak of the Cathedral. Cold rain stings my cheeks, the wind whips my hair. But nothing can tear my eyes from what lies before the gates.

If only something could.

The trees within view of the city are cloaked in darkness, as if the storm clouds have dripped down to blanket the land. Black vines twist around the trunks, hang heavily from the branches. Black rivulets seep across the earth like spilled ink. Moment by moment, the tide of night approaches nearer to our gates.

The dark queen's army has arrived.

The web that shrouds the forest is as thick as it was in my vision from the brood chamber, so thick I can't see the creatures, human and otherwise, that congregate in its shadows. But I can feel the queen's power emanating from below like a freezing gale, and I'm no longer so confident the wintry weather isn't her doing. She's holding her ranks in check for now—waiting for something, though I don't know what. Assessing our forces? Anticipating our surrender? Or does she simply want to multiply the fear that runs through the city, to make us quail like a helpless forest creature before she swoops down on us?

I turn to Aurelia. Her face is as resolute as ever, though the sleeplessness of the past several days makes her eyes bright as if with fever. Neither of us has seen much of our beds in that time.

"Are you ready?" I ask her, and hope my voice doesn't betray my anxiety.

She scans the ground below. "I would not have believed it," she murmurs.

"Believed what?"

"Such power," she says. "And anger. If Leonida were here to face her foe, what stratagem would she call on to save her city?"

"Probably not this one," I say. "But it's the best I've got."

I step up to the parapet as Aurelia signals to her troops below. They form ranks in neat order, though most of them are common citizens whose training consists of a mere week. Even with the large number who volunteered or were recruited to supplement the guard, I can't help thinking how pitifully few they are against the dark queen's forces. Nor can I help remembering that Isaac stands among them.

That was his idea, not mine. We haven't spoken since the day I questioned him in my throne room. Aurelia told me he presented himself at her post, insisting she add him to the city guard. I know she couldn't turn him down, not with our situation being as dire as it is. But I have grave misgivings about him being here, and not only because of the condition of his body. I'm not sure where his true allegiance lies, what he'd do to protect the girl he loves.

Or perhaps I fear what *I* would do to protect him.

I abandon my futile attempt to find his shaggy hair

in the mass below. Raising my arms, I call out in a voice that's amplified by the bloodbirds circling overhead.

"I am Sarah, queen of this city," I say. "I would speak with Delilah, daughter of Divina, as one queen to another."

The hush that falls over the forest is total, and while it lasts, I hear the thudding of my heart. I glance at Aurelia, whose frown suggests that, though she seconded my plan, she knew all along that it wouldn't work. The soldiers below try to maintain their postures, but I see breaches in discipline, a nervous glance here, a stepping out of line there. No one breaks and runs. That's a mercy, but I'm not convinced it'll last if I receive no answer.

At last, a screech emerges from the forest, and something dark separates itself from the deeper darkness and takes flight. At first I think it might be the shadowed form that assaulted my bloodbird spy, but as it rises above the trees, I see that it's much smaller, a bat-winged monstrosity with a body shaped like the creature that used to be called a lion. Its streaming mane surrounds a visage as mashed and rotten as spoiled fruit; its tail, curled and leathery, carries a barbed tip swollen with venom. The mane at first conceals its rider, whose own hair trails behind it in greater profusion than the beast's. When she reaches my height, she wheels her mount and shows me her face.

Miriam's face.

"Queen of the city," she repeats in a disdainful tone. "Where would you hold our parley?"

I point below. She peers at the spot, her frozen features and black eyes incapable of revealing her thoughts. Without a word, she angles her beast downward, toward the tent Aurelia's troops have set up in front of the city gates.

"Here goes nothing," I say to the captain of the guard, and raise my arms once more.

There's a sound like a hurricane, and the bird known as a gryphon rises from behind the Cathedral. Its black wings beat against the breeze as it positions itself above us; its naked head tilts so it can stare at us with blood-red eyes. I've never ridden one before, and I wouldn't do it now if not for the fact that gryphons are the only winged creatures in the Ecosystem large enough to carry two full-grown human beings over long distances. Unless, that is, Miriam has created something even larger.

I reach up toward the bird's talons, catching hold of the leather straps the ever-resourceful Gideon has created to secure the riders in place. Aurelia, her face determined, does the same. When I conceived this aerial entrance, I thought it might have the austere look of a queen and her second-in-command arriving on a battlefield to treat with the enemy. I even clothed myself in my one and only dress for the occasion, the silver gown I was given when I served Celestina. Now that we're airborne, however, I suspect that the two of us look as dignified as twin pieces of carrion dangling from the gryphon's claws. I sigh and, at a nod from Aurelia to show she's ready, signal the bird to start down.

It circles the battlefield, emulating its ancient ancestors' habit of lazily descending to retrieve carcasses slain by other creatures. Just before it reaches ground, I let go of the straps and land at a run on the grabgrass. Not too clumsily given the ankle-length dress, I tell myself, until I look to the side and see Aurelia dismount with considerably more poise. We'll have to discuss her technique later, if there is a later.

The dark queen sits astride her beast, watching us with black eyes, her face showing neither admiration nor amusement. She's wrapped in a black mantle that conceals what I saw in her brood chamber: the tattered remains of her wedding dress, the Sensor's token she wore on a string at her throat, the stone knife in her breast around which black blood oozed. When we approach, her mount kneels on its front legs, allowing her to slide from its back. The grabgrass coils expectantly at this foreign presence, but I command it to leave her alone.

"Your Majesty," I say, and perform a bow while Aurelia does the same.

"Your Majesty," she responds in the same mocking voice as before. "What petitions would you have me hear before your city is overrun?"

I say nothing, but gesture toward the tent. She strides there before me and Aurelia, her hair billowing behind her like a cloud of darkness. Gideon, who stands at attention outside the tent, draws back the front flap as we approach. His single eye lingers on the dark queen. I offered to restore his other eye, but he told me he's gotten used to its absence. From his grieved look, he'll never get used to seeing what's become of the girl he once knew as Miriam.

Inside the tent, two chairs have been set, along with candles to illuminate the interior and a brazier of coals to dry our wet clothing and hair. The chairs aren't quite thrones—that seemed excessive—but they're made of ornately carved wood and cushioned with soft white pads.

I offer my guest the finer of the two seats, and after a hesitation that makes it seem as if the implacable mask of the dark queen has momentarily slipped, she lowers herself into the chair. I take my own place, while Aurelia stands at my side.

In the light of the candles, I study my opponent. She's grown even thinner than the last time I saw her: her arms are nothing but bone, her face pinched and lined. The flesh around her eyes and mouth seems to have contracted, giving her a cadaverous look, while the blackness beneath her brows has spread outward to mar the brown of her cheeks. The eerily floating web of her hair behaves like an organism unto itself: it's constantly moving, reaching out tendrils and pulling them back even when her head is at rest. I wonder if that organism has grown inward as well, taking control of Miriam's mind and body, holding her in this state of living death.

"I see that you have brought your servant to witness our conference," the dark queen says. "I, too, retain such a servant."

A strand of hair uncoils from her head, extends itself to its full length and then, before my disbelieving eyes, continues to grow until it nudges the tent flap open. Gideon startles, but he wisely does nothing to disturb its progress. Within minutes, the appendage reels itself back in, and when it reenters the tent, a human form is held tightly in its loops. The living strand spins the prisoner around, and I see her face.

"Leah," I gasp.

It's her, and yet it's not her. The clothes she wears are hers, the cheery yellow dress she sewed herself. The rain has plastered her garment to a small, compact body that used to bristle with energy. Now her limbs seem slack, unresisting as the dark queen positions them at will. The prehensile strand makes her curtsy, then kneel at her mistress's feet. When she looks up, I see that her eyes, once so sharp and bright, have become like the queen's, nothing but black smears in a face devoid of all expression.

"They can be so useful, these handmaidens," the mouth that belonged to Miriam gibes. "So attentive to a queen's every need."

I try to control myself as the Leah-puppet caresses the dark queen's hair. My fingernails sink into the arms of my chair to stop me from leaping the space between us to clutch the throat of the evil creature that manipulates my friend.

"Your Majesty," I say, gritting my teeth in what I hope passes for a smile. "Your power is undeniable, your attendants rightfully loyal to their queen. You command a mighty army, far greater than any this world has known."

She inclines her head slightly, but her look shows she's not buying my canned civility.

"And yet, there is no need for one of your lineage to lead an army to our gates," I continue. "No need for two queens of the realm to squabble over what might be shared."

"Shared?" the word falls coldly from her lips.

"Indeed, shared," I say. "Shared, and strengthened through our joined labor. Just as we have shared this token of our common ancestry."

I reach inside the breast pocket of my dress and withdraw the serpent symbol I received many years after my mother's death—the same symbol I thought I glimpsed in my vision of Delilah's exile from the city. It belonged to her first, I'm sure of it, though I can't be sure how it was passed down to my mother. The pink stone flickers in the light of the candles, and though there's nothing in the black depths of the queen's eyes that makes me think she's moved by my appeal, there's no doubt she recognizes it, the physical sign of all that was taken from her.

"You were a healer," I say. "A powerful healer in the City of the Queens, long before I was born. You knew the ways of the Ecosystem as well as any of your generation, and you might have shared this knowledge had you been given a chance. You *did* share it with the people of your village, even when the Sensorship ordered that the ways of the healers be forgotten. Even then, you sought to preserve the seed of what you knew, what you were."

The dark queen's head tips as if she's listening to a sound from far off, a faint echo returning across the vale of years. Leah's hands have ceased their mindless stroking of the queen's hair, and she stands as if riveted by my tale, though her black eyes can't sharpen and tease as they used to. Everything I've said so far is guesswork based on what I've been shown by the Ecosystem and what I've learned of the village healers, but it seems my guesses come close to the truth.

"You were born a queen, Delilah," I say. "You were deprived of your birthright by your cousin, a woman of my blood. Perhaps she thought herself justified; perhaps she was merely afraid of what she did not understand. Either way, I accept responsibility for her acts, and I would atone for them if I could. I would welcome you back to the city of your birth, not as an enemy at the head of an invading force, but as an ally and fellow ruler, from whose wisdom I can learn much and from whose powers we can all benefit."

The queen says nothing, but her hand rises as if to touch the token. In the ensuing hush, I hear the crackling of coals and the pattering of raindrops on the tent. Aurelia stands motionless as a statue and makes no remonstrance at my peace offering, though I know she questions the point of these negotiations.

What is your endgame? she asked me when I told her what I planned to do. *Assuming she accepts, do you honestly expect to share the throne with a ghoul to the end of your days? And when you die, what then?*

I don't know, I answer her now. *I only know I can't stand the alternative.*

My thoughts are shattered when the dark queen throws back her head and laughs. It's a horrible, choking sound, more like the cawing of a ravener than the mirth of a human being. Leah's mouth opens in concert with her mistress's and spits out a strangled squawk. When the queen has had her laugh, her face returns to its icy mask, her eyes to their depthless malice.

"You think yourself wise, heir of Leonida," she hisses. "But there is much that you do not know. Seeds were planted long before you came into this world, and what grew from them cannot now be undone. You are of the blood of my enemy, and you must prepare yourself for your fate, or else die unprepared."

A strand of her hair lashes out, plucking the token from my fingers before I can react. Its pink is swallowed in the darkness of her bosom. With a flurry of black robes, she stands to leave, Leah trailing mechanically behind her.

"I am of your blood, too," I say as she reaches the tent's exit.

She spins to face me. I struggle to remember that this was once Miriam, a girl on the verge of marriage, plagued by doubts and fears I was too wrapped up in my own heartache to heed. She spits black blood at my feet, and I know that the dark queen's anger is too strong for reminiscence or appeal.

"I renounce our tie," she says. "I will permit you to live only long enough to see all that you love in ruins."

She wheels and exits the tent, dragging Leah's limp form behind her. I rush to the opening and see her striding rapidly across the grabgrass, which needs no bidding of mine to shy from her wrath. Mounting her beast with Leah behind her, she gives a bloodcurdling cry, and the abomination leaps into the air, its powerful wings propelling it toward the blackened forest. I lose sight of her in the darkness, but a cry much louder than hers erupts from the trees, as if every creature in her army has loosed its voice as one.

The Ecosystem is at war.

I'M ABOUT TO call for the gryphon when it swoops down from the sky and clutches me and my lieutenant in its talons, giving us no chance to grip the straps. We're soaring above the city in less time than it takes to blink, and I see the reason for the bird's haste.

A barrage of black tentacles explodes from the forest, pummeling the tent where we stood just moments before. A half-scream for Gideon is all I have time to emit before the old firestarter, with a speed belying his years, rolls beneath the flailing strands. When he rises, the red-hot poker from the brazier of coals swings from his fist, and he uses it to force the dark queen's web to retreat. He sprints for the gates just as my gryphon, having set me and Aurelia down within the city, catches him by the arms and rises out of his pursuer's reach.

The next instant, he lands beside me. I reach out instinctively to check on his condition, but this is Gideon, and I needn't have worried.

"Mistress Sarah," he says. "Are you harmed?"

"I'm fine," I say. "Take your position, and wait for my orders."

He runs off to assume his post at the head of the civilian soldiers. I've found that they respond better to him than to anyone in uniform.

"Aurelia!" I call, but she's right by my side.

"My Queen," she says calmly.

"You know the plan. No one leaves the city unless I say so."

She bows. I expect some commentary on my failed peace treaty—if only a knowing look—but she hustles off without any such display.

I call for the gryphon, which lands beside me and allows me to clamber onto its back. Then we're airborne again, rising so fast it makes my stomach drop. From our position hundreds of feet above the city, I look down at our defenses. The wall we've built rises to a height of over ten feet, constructed of stone that's nearly invisible beneath a covering of roots and vines. It looks like the ruins of a city torn apart by the Ecosystem, yet it's those same plants that hold the edifice together. Winged creatures like the dark queen's beast will be able to surmount it, but from what Rebecca reported when she mated her mind with the bloodbird's, the queen has opted mostly for a ground assault. If any of her forces take to the air, I've got bloodbirds of my own ready to meet them.

I direct the gryphon to climb even higher, where I can get a good vantage on the forest. The queen's legions have begun to emerge into what little light the cloudy day affords, and I see that the first line of attack consists of human figures, all of them moving in the sluggish way I observed with Leah. The bird dives closer at my command, and I confirm what I feared.

The faces are familiar to me, faces I've known all my life, though never with such blank expressions and lifeless eyes. There's Esther, the last Chief Sensor our village ever had, a middle-aged woman whom I would sometimes see in my dreams before I learned my mother's face. Her eyes are blacker than her hair now, and a strand of the dark queen's power binds her throat. There's Daniel, our longtime Chief Warden, who taught my father and mother—and, years later, Isaac—what little our village knew of the healer's art, the scraps of lore that must have been preserved from Delilah's time. Now he's simply another plaything at the whim of the dark queen's leash, shuffling forward with shoulders stooped and sightless eyes cast down on the ground. Behind him, I see the tall, willowy form of Beulah, the woman Leah loved so much she risked servitude to try to save her—but though Leah's much shorter form walks beside that of her beloved, there's no indication that either of them is aware of the other's presence. The men, women, and children who follow them are the same: bound by the dark queen's web, slaves of the dark queen's will. I have no time to count the villagers she sends against us, but I estimate the number to be four score at least.

A chill far deeper than wind or rain shoots through me. When I visited the queen's lair beneath the village, I saw bodies crushed and torn beyond recognition. Yet here they are, marching in lockstep toward a second slaughter. Has Delilah the power to reanimate the dead? If so, might she conjure my own father's broken form to fight against me?

I steer my bird higher. Not only to get a better view of the battlefield. To prevent myself from seeing too closely what comes next.

The marching figures nearest the city gates stumble, falling to their knees. Some of them flail feebly against the ground before lying still. Others struggle to rise, the queen's halters pulling against what traps them. Esther, by far the strongest of the villagers, manages to gain her feet for a moment, but then she's flipped onto her back, spread-eagled to the rain-slickened turf with blank eyes staring at the sky. She strains so hard her back arches, but the attack I've ordered can't be stopped: the muddy ground beneath her has been shoved aside by innumerable fingers of grabgrass, which clutch her body as tightly as ropes. She twitches for a moment longer before lying motionless beside the other prisoners. I try to detect her heartbeat, but the dark queen's hold over her blocks me from telling if she's alive.

Leah lies a few feet behind her. I draw a deep breath to steady myself, then instruct the grass to pry the ground open even wider beneath my friend's body. Carefully, as carefully as if I'm mending a doll made of sticks and straw, I wrap Leah's inert form in grabgrass, cover her nose and mouth so she won't breathe mud, seal her eyes lest she wake to find herself in darkness. The queen seems not to grasp what I'm doing, so I take my chance and pull Leah beneath the turf, then coax the grass to seal the hole where she lay. Delilah's anger blazes at me in a sudden scream, but it's too late for her to reclaim her servant: all she can do is release the halter around Leah's neck before it's devoured by the lawn. She was too confident, forgot that here, so close to the city, the Ecosystem answers to my command. Now that she's aroused, I can't risk the same procedure with anyone else for fear that the queen might snuff out their life before I'm done. But Leah, at least, is beyond her reach.

I speak quiet words of encouragement to the Ecosystem, urge the roots that lie beneath the sod to bear the body of my best friend under the city gates to the spot I've designated. Whether I can revive her there, whether separating her from the dark queen's power might have stolen the life I most wished to save, I can't think about until later.

Much later.

Dark shapes burst from the forest and gallop toward the city with the speed of maddened warhogs. Which is what they are—mostly. Their hindquarters are those of the giant pigs I've hunted in the forest, feasted on in the village. But their heads are distorted, the lower jaw long and tapered as a crocodont's, the tusks protruding like spears. Instead of front hooves, they have arms, wiry and simian, covered with fur the color of a prowler monkey's. They're too far away for me to see clearly, but I have no doubt their arms end in hands capable of grasping and climbing.

I take a quick glance at the city to make sure Aurelia and Gideon have obeyed my orders to keep their troops far from the front gate. Then I spring my next trap.

Miniature pain trees lined up outside the city gates take a synchronized breath and open their pores, releasing a blue cloud that hovers like mist in the rain. Normally these trees are the last thing I'd want so close to the city, but the day Rebecca almost died, I ordered work crews to plant saplings around the perimeter, then used all my power to hasten their growth. They're little more than six feet tall, but even at this pygmy size, I'll have to order my troops into a full retreat if the wind shifts.

The mist hits the approaching monsters full in the

face, and the first breath is enough to stop their headlong speed as if they've collided with a physical wall. Some collapse under the weight of their ungainly heads, while others wander without direction, arms tangling with legs until they drop as heavily as stones. No sooner have they landed than their almost-human hands reach out to drag their bodies toward the trees that have felled them. Their lungs are full of the pain trees' seductive scent, and they can't help craving another breath.

Now, I tell the trees. *Strike now, and finish them all.*

With a sound like a thousand bowstrings, the trees release their quills. The brutes' faces are tattooed with venomous stingers, but their only reaction is to open their mouths in a grotesque semblance of a smile and to drool in ecstasy, black tongues lolling. Within minutes, their lungs will cease to function, and the trees' roots will reap a reward of flesh and blood.

Over the sound of the queen's renewed fury, I breathe my own deep sigh of relief. A moment later, it turns to a gasp.

Five of the monsters have escaped the poison and are squirming up the side of the barrier, using vines for handholds. I was wrong to think their hands near-human; they're more like the hands of monkeys, impossibly nimble and fast. In a moment, the creatures will reach the top of the wall and enter the city.

"Aurelia!" I shout. Her face turns upward, and she immediately sees the danger. City archers release their own fusillade, and three of the five monsters thud to the ground riddled with arrows.

The remaining two creatures leap wildly to the

pavement and resume their galloping pace. Aurelia runs to intercept their charge, but before she can reach them, one of the monsters drives a tusk through a soldier's body and lifts him like a tattered flag on a standard. The beast flings the bloody form across the courtyard just before Gideon drives his poker through its back, and it sprawls at his feet.

Aurelia stands over the second invader, her sword black with its blood. I close my eyes and reach out to the human victim, but I know at once that he's beyond my power to heal. I know, too, that he's not Isaac, but that does nothing to stifle my rage.

I tug the gryphon's beak more roughly than I need to, and together we vault into the sky.

"Delilah!" I scream, my words torn by the wind. "I offered you a place in the city, a chance to rule in peace. Now I make another offer: surrender, and your life will be spared. Refuse, and suffer a second death."

The forest shakes with mocking laughter. The wind howls in my ears. For a second time, the dark queen's beast rises above the battlefield, and I see that she clutches a fistful of black threads in one hand, each of them trailing to the woods below. She cracks them like whips, and something dark moves in the shadow of the trees. Blinded by stinging rain, I can't determine what it is.

"You dare threaten me?" she jeers. "You dream that I can be sated by the blood of *one* of your servants? What will you do, then, when the streets of your city stink with corpses, and beasts yet more dire than these glut themselves on the bodies of the living?"

I've heard enough. I reach out to the bloodbirds flocking in the vicinity, direct them all at the queen in a swarm of crimson wings and razor beaks. They surround her in such numbers I lose sight of her astride her winged mount, and I kid myself that my allies will bring her tumbling to earth where I can deal with her at my leisure. I'm hardly surprised when a burst of black tendrils scatters the flock, most of the birds using their speed to escape but a few plummeting to the ground as masses of bloody feathers. The queen raises her arms, and for a wild moment I believe she's going to call lightning from the sky.

"Little queen," she chides. "If this is the best you can summon, I pity your vassals indeed."

She waves a hand, and the forest opens like a black mouth to vomit her brood.

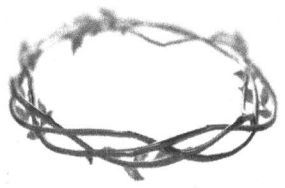

THERE ARE TOO many of them to count. Some walk on hind legs, though they're anything but human. By far the majority crawl on four, or slither across the ground, or fly with the speed of arrows toward the city. It comes to me that the first wave of her attack, the entranced villagers and hybrid warhogs, was nothing but a vanguard to try my strength. Seeing how little I have, she sends an army of thousands against us.

Brightly colored specks, too small for me to distinguish clearly from this height, are the first to reach the protective wall. They leap for it and cling there, and I realize that they're poison arrow frogs, using sucker-like feet to climb. They're joined by humanoid forms with porcine faces, nameless things that leap past my pain trees and clamber from stone to stone with the agility of fell-cats. Actual fell-cats leap in their wake, avid to slice flesh and bone with curved fangs that never stop growing. But even these predators are no match for the birds we call shrieks, small but deadly falcons that attack in swarms and pick their prey clean in seconds. A cloud of the black-masked raptors wheels above the city, then dives in their characteristic arrowhead formation, the tip sharpening as they fall.

"To cover!" I shout to my lieutenants. "Get everyone out of there!"

Aurelia and Gideon act at once, directing their troops

to retreat to the Cathedral and its outlying buildings. They wouldn't have nearly enough time to reach their goal if I didn't hurl the remaining bloodbirds in the path of the shrieks, the two flocks colliding in an explosion of black and red. The larger-bodied bloodbirds drag a few shrieks to the pavestones, where they use their heavy beaks to stab and rend. By far the greater number of shrieks dance around the attack, then turn and tear my legions to pieces while still in the sky. Every red-breasted bird that falls to the stones is a blow to my heart. I reach out to the shrieks, hoping against hope that I can use my power to weaken or at least divert them, but it's as I expected: I hold no bargain with the dark queen's forces, and they shrug off my commands like rain.

Come, I tell my gryphon. *Let's even the odds.*

The huge bird drops instantly into a dizzying nose-dive, and even with our senses attuned, I feel as if I'm going to be sick. It brakes sharply as it hits the main body of the shrieks, its massive wings sweeping scores of them from the sky. The bloodbirds rally at the gryphon's arrival, their raucous shouts filling the air. In a body, they drop on the shrieks that have fallen to the stone. I can't access the shrieks' minds, but I can imagine their terror as they look up at the armada of red that descends upon them.

I pull my gryphon upward once more to survey the scene. Most of my troops have gained the safety of the buildings, but a dozen soldiers at least have been downed by stray shrieks. The bloody puddles that surround them make me shudder as I recall the queen's words. At my command, the victorious bloodbirds lift wounded warriors from the pavement and fly with them to shelter. I assess the damage these fighters have suffered, then send pulses of healing power to those capable of receiving it. Those who are beyond healing I instruct my bloodbirds to carry nonetheless, to clear the streets before the next wave of predators arrives.

It's not long in coming.

The two-legged monsters reach the top of the wall, their heads jutting from hunched shoulders. When they look upward, my heart fails me at the sight: their bestial faces are modeled on my father's, though the dark queen has reshaped his handsome features into something out of nightmare. With an effort, I remind myself that this isn't really him, that he died before the queen had a chance to work her cruel will on his flesh. I can only hope I'm right, and that no part of him survives in these vile things I must kill.

I wave a hand before the monsters can spring from their perch, and the poisonrose vines I've planted at the top of the wall wrap around the brutes' thick ankles. It was a poisonrose bite that killed Dominique's mother, turning her body to a shriveled husk, her once-beautiful face to a fleshless skull. But she was human; these creatures are not, and their coarse, scabbed skin is too thick for the delicate teeth of the flowers to prick. I direct the vines to hold onto their captives as long as they can, then whistle for the captain of the guard. While the beasts struggle fiercely at the top of the wall, Aurelia's archers appear at second- and third-story windows of the Cathedral, where they're easily able to pick off the exposed monsters. The ungainly bodies slump against the wall, their legs held by poisonrose vines. It's a fiendish sight, with thick black blood dripping down the wall to mingle with the green of the vines and the pink of the blossoms. Mercifully, in their death-rictus, the monsters' faces lose all resemblance to my father's. I whisper a plea for forgiveness all the same, though from whom I don't know.

A moment later, I'm stunned to see some of these mutations, having avoided Aurelia's volley, break free of the vines and jump or slide to the stone. A pack of fell-cats follows, the agile felines bounding too lightly over the wall for my vines to snare them. Some of the two-footed and four-footed beasts die in their steps as Aurelia's troops rain arrows from above. Others race for the Cathedral and outbuildings where the city's defenders have taken up position. When the dark queen's legions find the doors barred, they grip stone outcroppings with claws or fingers and begin to scale the walls. Many take arrows in the chest or face and thud to the ground, but many more climb relentlessly despite the feathered shafts adorning their backs and shoulders.

The beasts bearing my father's face are somewhat slower to reach the buildings than the fell-cats. Those trailing the main body of attackers are met by a rush from Gideon's troops, who've waited until the brutes ran past their redoubt then cut them off from the rear. The old fire-starter's ragtag army carries weapons ranging from swords and spears to hoes and grappling hooks, but numbers of the monsters fall before their onslaught.

A shiver passes through my skin at the arrival of a new peril.

I turn my bird in time to see a flood of poison arrow frogs hopping over the wall, finding purchase on pavement, then catapulting themselves toward Gideon's troops. In their rear, surging over the bodies of the dead humanoid creatures, an even more sinister threat appears: black serpent-shapes that might have been birthed from the dark queen's hair, their slender bodies and whip-like speed making them impossible for Aurelia's archers to hit. I realize with a shock that these are the mobile parasites that infected Gideon and Dinah; it could be that they're what hexed Rebecca, what's causing the villagers' stupor as well. If they're not stopped, there will be none left to defend the city, even if there were anything left to defend.

With no time to decide, I call on the stratagem I'd hoped never to use.

The stone terrace between the perimeter wall and the Cathedral groans, shifts, and cracks, jagged scars running through the pavement like strokes of lightning. Sharp slabs burst upward, and Delilah's ground forces are thrown in the air when they're not impaled by blades of stone. Before the frogs can regain their feet or the black snakes their momentum, the ground drops out from beneath them, tons of rock echoing in the depths as a cloud of dust fills the air. My sole remaining wyrm has spent much of this week burrowing beneath the city's outer rim, and it's weakened the square to such an extent that a few well-placed strikes with its teeth and tail were enough to bring down the whole. It grieves me to think I've ordered the destruction of one of the city's crowning glories, a marvel I doubt can ever be replaced. But a great number of the dark queen's minions lie buried beneath the wreckage, and nothing that carries itself on belly or legs can cross the gaping chasm that now separates the wall from the main compound.

A short cheer rises from Aurelia's and Gideon's troops after the last rumbles of the cave-in subside. Then it's back to the bloody work of picking off the humanoid brutes and fell-cats that have reached the buildings. Some of the monsters have forced their way through windows and are being fought hand-to-claw by soldiers and civilians, men and women and barely grown children. Though I know I can't risk my own life and thereby deprive us of the Ecosystem's support, my skin burns with so many sensations of pain and terror, I feel as if I'm the one being assaulted by these creatures from the dark queen's wicked imagination. What's worse are the times I feel a stab of pure agony followed by complete silence and insensitivity. That occurs when one of the city's defenders falls. Then another life I was sworn to protect is lost to me, and the healing power that flows through my hands is as useless as my grief.

I scan the mass of soldiers for Isaac's life force, but in the chaos of fighting, I can't pick him out from the rest, can't say whether he's joined the ones I can no longer touch. Reluctantly, I pull myself from my fruitless search and wheel my bird back out over the battlefield. The action in the city is at a stalemate for the moment, and it's up to Aurelia and Gideon to hold their ground. Meanwhile I have to check on the status of the queen's forces, the legions that haven't taken part in the attack. I need to know whether there's any hope for us, or whether my mother's city is truly lost.

I soar over the battlefield, lashed by wind and rain but steadied by the imperturbable bird that bears me. When I reach a point directly above the edge of the trees, an unexpected sight meets my eyes: though the forest remains as impenetrably dark as before, no new creatures emerge to join the assault. I spin to face the city, find that the battle between our army and the queen's monsters rages on, but nothing crawls from the abyss my wyrm has produced. Can it be that Delilah has exhausted her forces? Can it be that she's underestimated our strength, and that if we hold on against her a little longer, we might yet gain the victory?

Thunder rumbles, or so I think. Then I realize it's the sound of wingbeats as the dark queen's beast rises from the darkness a third time. The black reins she held earlier are clutched in her hand. I can't see what's at the other end, though I can tell that they trail behind her into the forest. She pulls on them, and it seems as if the darkness itself rises from the ground, a wave so vast it could cover the entire city. A rush of hot wind slices through the freezing rain, and the earth shudders as if something immeasurably huge tramps across it.

"Your forces have fought well, rabble that they are," she says in a quiet voice. "But their fight has come to an end."

Again, she pulls on the reins, and again, the shadow rises, the earth rocks. There's a note to her words I find hard to place: a note of hesitation or even sadness, as if she regrets what she's about to do. As if, whatever rough beast strains at the end of her web, it's something even she, the dark queen Delilah, is loath to unleash.

"Learn the true meaning of suffering, little queen," she says. "Learn, and despair."

Her hand opens, and the dark reins fall. Instantly, she

wheels her mount and vanishes into the trees, and though I can't read her mind any better than I can the minds of her monsters, the last glimpse I have of her face shows me that the icy mask has vanished, replaced by the wide-eyed look of the girl she used to be. The dark queen wasn't reluctant to act—she was *afraid*. Horror grips me at the thought of what could have made her so.

The darkness launches itself into the air, and at last I see.

I LEARNED OF tyrannosaurs and pterodactyls, mammoths and megalodons, from the books Angelica picked out for me in the library.

The thing that lifts itself from the earth below dwarfs them all.

As it rises, I realize that what I took to be the shadowed edge of the forest *is* its body, a tree-covered mountain that lay camouflaged by darkness and rain. Now it shakes the trees from its back and rears on its hind legs, coming within reach of my position hundreds of feet above the ground. When it spreads the wings that serve in place of front legs, they span the horizon as far as I can see.

Its body is black as night, its skin scaled like a serpent's. Spikes jut from every part of its measureless length, and each tip of its many-forked tail carries a barb twice as long as I am tall. At the end of seven sinuous necks sit as many heads, each more grotesquely shaped than the last, all with jaws that could swallow me and the gryphon at a single bite. When it comes closer, I see that the dark queen's abandoned leashes trail from each of the necks, as if each head obeys a separate will instead of one.

The name of this thing flashes into my mind.

Armegaddon.

A monster that took all of the dark queen's power to

create, and, now that it's been set free, I doubt even her power can control.

Flame blooms around me. I don't know where it came from, unless it issued from the thing of darkness that rises from the earth. My gryphon screams once, a most unnatural sound, and drops from the sky with me clinging to its back. The scent of charred flesh and feathers engulfs me, and I know the bird is dead. My own burns are less serious, but I have no time to heal them. I call out to the last three bloodbirds that circle nearby, and they catch my arms just as the gryphon crashes to earth. It lies motionless, cold rain sizzling against the remnants of fire that lick its body.

The bloodbirds carry me over the city wall as the Armegaddon turns in midair, the wind of its wings toppling trees in the forest. Its mouths split wide, some to send streams of fire across the distance between us, some to thunder a challenge to the city. The members of Aurelia's and Gideon's armies pause as the monster's roar shakes the Cathedral. Even the creatures that obey Delilah's will seem cowed by the sound, her power alone overmastering their impulse to flee. From the large number of black shapes that litter the ground, it's obvious our troops have triumphed, though at great cost to themselves: most of the human bodies piled among the misshapen monsters offer no response when I reach out to them. Tears sting my eyes when I remember something my grandfather told me when I first learned of Miriam's betrothal to Isaac: *She will fight to defend her love. She may die to defend it.* The people of the city have fought, and died, to defend the thing they love. And now, I must tell them that both their love and their losses have been in vain.

"Retreat!" I cry, and they look upward to see their queen

arrive with singed clothing and blackened skin, barely holding onto the talons of three spent bloodbirds. Aurelia appears at a window of the Cathedral, her uniform gashed and blood streaking her arms. For a moment, her face collapses with the dismay everyone around her must feel. But then, using her broadsword to slice cleanly through the humanoid beast she's fighting, she lifts her voice and calls out to her troops.

"Heed the Queen!" she shouts. "Make for the rendezvous! Retreat! Retreat!"

I've no time to see if her orders are obeyed, as the exhausted bloodbirds let me go a few feet from the ground, and I splash down in bloody water. I try to stand, but find myself too weak to get my legs under me. I'm about to try again when an iron hand grips my arm and draws me to my feet.

"Mistress Sarah," Gideon says. His long hair hangs wet and bedraggled, but the black blood that mingles with his beard is not his own. "Are you hurt?"

Under the old firestarter's gaze, my tears flow in earnest. "It's over," I say. "We have to evacuate, or we're all going to die."

"Mistress—"

"Do as I say," I command him. "Carry as many of the wounded as you can. Leave the dead."

I take a step away to repeat my order to his troops, but my legs give out, and I fall into Gideon's arms. He lifts me effortlessly, then turns to face his citizen-soldiers.

"You have heard the Queen," he says, his voice much harsher than usual. "The city is lost."

An ear-splitting roar sounds overhead, and the place where we stand is cast into shadow as the huge shape of the

Armegaddon soars above the Cathedral. Balls of flame streak to earth, exploding on contact. Human and inhuman creatures scream as their flesh is seared from their bones. I try to reach out to the wounded, try to heal their burns and broken bodies, but there are too many of them, too much suffering, too much death. The Ecosystem has fallen silent; every living thing—whether bloodbird, vine, or human companion—has closed its mind and its will to me. The only sounds are those the Armegaddon makes, or causes others to make: the gale of wings, the crackle of flame, the pleas of the dying. Even my great wyrm burrows desperately into subterranean caverns to escape the terror that flies above, and my heart breaks as I call out to it.

Come back, I cry. *Do not abandon me now.*

It responds without words, but with a shame and grief as deep as the earth itself. Then it's gone, and I'm alone.

Something booms overhead, and I look up to see the top of the Cathedral explode as the spiked tails of the Armegaddon rip through stone as easily as paper. Chunks of rock topple to the ground, crushing yet more of my people as they fly for safety. Gideon hunches over me as if his body alone can protect me from tons of falling masonry. There's a sharp cracking sound, and he stumbles and falls, spilling me to the blood-soaked ground. My head strikes stone, and I lie still, facing up into the sky.

The Armegaddon rises above the city, a cloud that swallows all light and rains fiery death. I struggle to move, but consciousness slips from me. The Cathedral splinters like wood beneath an axe, and I watch through darkening eyes as the City of the Queens falls to nothingness around me.

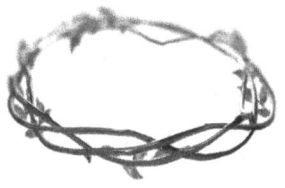

I COME TO with a splitting headache in a room lit by torchlight. A damp, musty smell fills my nostrils; directly above me, thick roots dangle from a ceiling of dirt. I'm lying on something soft, but when I turn my head to take in more of my surroundings, stabbing pain squeezes my eyes shut. I'm definitely concussed, though not so severely, I hope, that I can't call on the Ecosystem to heal the damage. Tentatively, I put out feelers, listen for a response. It's faint, but the voice is there. It begs my forgiveness for fleeing from the Armegaddon, but I shush it, then draw its power into my body to fix the head wound and the minor burns I suffered. My mind sharp and my limbs whole, I sit up to look around.

We're in a cavern beneath Celestina's garden. Our rendezvous point.

I found it the week before the dark queen's arrival. It connects to a tunnel that leads northward out of the city, not, as I'd assumed from the vision of my grandmother and grandfather's nighttime tryst, westerly, toward the village. How Seraphina kept it hidden from her mother, when all I needed to do was probe the garden grounds with my queenly power to discover its position, is beyond my understanding. Well before the queen's army reached the city, I ordered all noncombatants, children and elderly and any too sick or weak to fight, to take the tunnel to freedom. Rebecca, as the only Sensor among us, led the escape party in the company of several of the city's healers. Reluctant as I was to send her on such a mission only a week after her encounter with the dark queen, I was even more reluctant to expose her to the queen's power once again. I communed with her through the Ecosystem before the battle began, and she assured me that all were alive, waiting in the pain tree forest north of the city for my signal to return.

They won't receive that signal. The chamber shakes as the Armegaddon prowls the city above our heads, its body smashing buildings to rubble, its breath burning to cinders what it doesn't smash. I fear that its weight will collapse the underground city too, but for the moment, our shelter holds.

Others are in the cavern with me, wounded citizens lying on mossy pallets like my own while healers, Caleb and Noah and a few others, circulate among them. Soldiers with no training in the healing arts, their only advantage being that they're able to stand on their own feet, scurry around at the healers' orders, offering water and helping bind wounds. When I expand my sensitivity to encompass the room, I detect fractures, burns, and lacerations, but none of the graver injuries I witnessed in the city. My heart lurches when I realize there's no sign of Gideon, and I wonder if his soldiers obeyed my final order and left his dead body above.

Fearing the worst, I beseech the Ecosystem to locate his life-force. The answer comes back more quickly than I had any reason to hope: he's alive, suffering from a concussion and burns worse than mine, and being treated by

Michael in a smaller chamber adjacent to this one. I know I should let my father's apprentice finish his work, but I can't resist taking up the strands of healing in my own hands to restore the faithful firestarter to himself. There's an exclamation from the room where Gideon rests, and Michael appears, his face and blond hair sooty but his eyes filled with relief.

"Queen Sarah," he says. "We were afraid—"

"I'm okay," I say. "Where are the others? This can't be all who survived."

His face falls. "Many died in the city. The captain of the guard ordered the most serious cases—"

"Where are they?"

He gestures toward the exit tunnel. "There are many, Queen Sarah...."

"Take me to them."

He helps me to my feet. At our touch, I feel his own injuries, more painful than he's willing to admit: flesh-burns over a swath of his back, chips of flying stone that he removed, one by one, from where they'd embedded themselves in his calves. I'm quick to heal these wounds, and he smiles in thanks. The deeper pain—friends lost, his city conquered—I can't heal. When we enter the tunnel, I'm gratified to find that the man Michael loves beyond all others, the dark-haired guard Luke, has survived, as has Aurelia. A bloody gash on her cheek will need my attention, but it's nothing compared to the scowl that's settled on her face as she looks out over the bodies that cover the floor of the tunnel.

There are too many of them to count, stretching far away into the darkness. Some have died in the time it took me to recover, but the great majority moan weakly against the agony of charred flesh and crushed bones, missing limbs and bloody dressings that barely cover the damage to their insides. Those who delivered them to this place sit as if in a daze against the walls of the tunnel, scores of strong men and women who seem as helpless as children in the face of such devastation. For myself, I'm staggered by the sheer number of the wounded, the realization that most of them will breathe their last within minutes if I can't save them.

"Queen Sarah?" Michael prompts.

"I'm sorry," I say. "Please leave me. All of you," I say, raising my voice. "I need to be alone."

A flicker of her past suspicion crosses Aurelia's face, but she signals her troops to exit the tunnel. The men and women rise listlessly and follow their captain. Michael is last to go. The expression he shows me as he departs is something I can't read.

When they're all gone, I sink to my knees on the dirt floor, bow my head. I remember the first image I saw of Queen Dominica in the colored windows of the queen's council chamber: a solemn-faced woman with gray eyes, surrounded on all sides by the bodies of the sick and dying. Angelica scoffed at the legend of Dominica healing thousands in a day, and I know now that at least part of the story depicted in the window couldn't have been true, for Dominique was only a girl of seven when she accepted the queen's bargain and began the work of healing. But I hold that image in my mind nonetheless, and as I spread my hands over the first of the wounded who lie before me, I speak to her, implore her to listen.

"Dominique," I say. "Show me how you did it. There's no time to heal them all the way I learned. There must be another way."

The room remains silent, except for the groans of the dying. If she could hear me, I feel as if I know what she would say. *There are limits to what even a queen can do. Are you sure you are ready to give so much of yourself? Do you understand that, once given, the gift can never be returned?*

"I do," I say. "Whatever the cost, I accept it. Show me, I beg of you."

There's still no reply, except for the echo of my own words. But I think I see the gray-eyed woman in the window smile sadly, and behind that smile, I can almost glimpse the girl she was, the girl who dreamed of laughter and love and joy only to lose it all. The brave little girl who risked everything to save the world that had wounded her so.

It starts in my hands, a surge of power unlike the gentle tingling I've grown accustomed to. From there, it spreads until it encompasses my entire body, then radiates outward to fill the tunnel, a field of energy with me as its nodal point. As it grows, I lose all sense of wielding conscious control of this power: it's as if *I* have nothing to do with it, as if I'm merely here to witness its work. I can't say how much time passes—*time has no meaning within the Ecosystem*, Celestina once said to me—nor can I feel the individual wounds that cry out for healing: the gashes that must be bound, the burns that require my balm. All I'm aware of is a keen sense of need, so sharp it would cut me in two if the power that flows through me weren't equal to meeting it. But that power holds, and when it's reached as far as it must, it lets me go. An overwhelming sense of serenity washes over me, and though I know in a dim corner of my mind that I've forfeited many of the things my heart longs to have, I can't hold back the grateful tears that bathe my face.

The men and women who line the tunnel are beginning to stir, rising on legs that have been restored to fullness, running their fingers over healed flesh with murmurs of amazement. Only those who died before I arrived remain silent and unmoving. When the rest see me, they rush to my side, catching me as I fall. Their lips murmur the words *Queen Sarah*, and for the first time, I'm not tempted to tell them it's just Sarah. I lay my hands on their foreheads, feel the health flowing through them, and it's almost too much for me to bear.

When next I see my face in the mirror, I suspect it's Dominica's mournful visage I'll see.

A hand touches my shoulder. I turn to face a woman with dark hair and bright eyes, who smiles at me before pulling me into a hug. Her warmth and solidity tell me I've healed her along with the rest, though I feel as if I've failed her.

"I'm sorry, Leah," I whisper. "I couldn't save Beulah. I tried, but—"

"Hush," she says. "We'll find her. This isn't over."

I pull back to look my friend in the eye. She's crying for her beloved, but she smiles for me. With our arms around each other, we return to the main chamber.

Aurelia glances up as we enter. The wound on her cheek is healed—the power must have spilled out from the tunnel to touch her as well—but the greater change is in her eyes, which widen in wonder at the company that fills the passageway behind me. Leah and I approach her, and my feet seem to float above the floor, while at the same time my heart lies heavy in my breast.

"We're leaving," I say to the captain of the guard. "Right now."

WHATEVER GRACE PERIOD I've earned from Aurelia is over just like that, and we're back to our old ways.

"Leaving?" she says. "When was this decided?"

"The moment Delilah sent that monster against us," I say. "We can't fight it, which means it's time to leave."

"And so it is," she says. "Your people await your order. But you cannot be among them. Nor can the captain of the guard."

"Aurelia," I try to reason with her. "If we stay here, we're dead."

"If we leave, the city dies," she retorts. "I will not abandon her."

We face off for a minute, and much as I admire her loyalty, I can't help thinking how easy it would be to cast a spell of sleep over her and let her be carried bodily from the city. Easy now, hard later. She'd never listen to me after that point. It's with mixed feelings that I tell her what I've had in mind all along.

"I'm not abandoning the city," I say. "I'm going to look for help."

"And I'm going with her," Leah chimes in.

Aurelia frowns at both of us. "What help can there be beyond our walls?"

"You're forgetting that Delilah and I aren't the only

queens left," I say. "There's one more out there, and we need to try to find her."

The frown deepens. "You mean—?"

"Yes," I say. "We need to look for Celestina."

My announcement doesn't change Aurelia's expression all that much. She might be learning to trust *me*, but she most assuredly doesn't trust Celestina, the queen who *did* abandon the city. Her mouth opens to protest, but then she looks around the cavern and clamps her lips shut. Maybe it's the reminder of the masses I just healed, or maybe she's waiting for us to be alone before letting me have a piece of her mind. I'm thankful that Leah won't give her that chance any time soon.

The exodus is quickly organized. Our supplies are minimal—water, torches, medical kits—and our entire population is able to walk on their own. We'll move slowly with so many people having to tramp through such a narrow tunnel, but as long as the roof holds, we should meet up with the earlier evacuees before another day passes. My greatest fear is that the Armegaddon might depart the city to scourge the earth in other places, so I'm anxious to get moving lest we emerge to find Rebecca's camp besieged by a dark cloud that burns with fire. As my last act before leaving, I instruct the roots that carried Leah to this shelter to take care of the dead bodies I left in the tunnel. It's not a fitting burial for those who died defending the city, but we can't risk the pestilence that might result if we leave them unattended.

Aurelia reports to me. "All is in readiness, My Queen."

"Good. Make sure the healers spread themselves out evenly. Tell them to look for signs of fever or weakness. It's possible I missed something back there."

She bows. "Your Majesty."

"And don't let anyone fall behind," I add. "Put Luke or somebody at the rear of the column, and tell him to keep everybody moving."

"Of course, My Queen."

She stands waiting for my order to move out, but for some reason, I can't give it. There's something I've forgotten, I'm sure of it, but I can't think what. I look around nervously, find our troops and supplies in apparent order for the evacuation. Leah smiles encouragingly, squeezes my arm the way she always has. Yet I can't shake the feeling that something's missing, something I never should have let slip my mind....

"Where's Isaac?" I say suddenly.

Leah's eyes widen as if she's awakening from the same dream as me. "He—"

"Was he hurt?" I cut her off. "Did he come down here?" I hear the panic in my voice, but I can't control it, not even when I turn to the captain of the guard. "Aurelia, where is he?"

She shakes her head, obviously at a loss. I'm stunned to realize he's missing, but even more, I'm stunned that I haven't thought of him practically since the battle began, certainly not since I awakened. Was he among those I healed in the tunnel? Or does his body lie with the dead?

"We have to find him," I say. "We have to—"

A booming noise from above shortens my thought. There's a rumble in the cavern floor, a shower of dirt from the ceiling. Desperately, I cast my power through the earth, upward to the queen's garden, out into the city beyond. I can't detect the rubble of fallen buildings or the bodies of the slain, but if I can find some sign of movement, some trace of him....

He's there.

My breath catches in my throat as I spot him limping through the ruined city, ducking behind masses of stone to avoid the predators that roam the streets. He's in pain, not only from his leg but from multiple smaller wounds he suffered during the battle, but he stops only long enough to evade capture, then forces himself on again. His progress is terribly slow, but he's had hours to open up a space between us. Wherever he's going, he's much too far away for me to chase him down, bring him back. Save his life.

"Oh, Isaac," I say, though I know he can't hear me. "Isaac."

The cavern booms again, and the floor quakes. People scream in terror, then turn toward me. Even Leah, strong as she's trying to act for my benefit, looks ready to run. I'm blinded by tears, but I don't need to see people's faces to read their thoughts: have I healed so many, rescued them from the dark queen's grasp, only to let them die? Aurelia steps to my side and places a hand on my arm.

"My Queen," she says. "It is time."

I search for Isaac once more, but he's vanished, whether hidden behind stone or buried beneath the ground I can't tell. My subjects await my word. It takes all my power of will to give it to them.

"Move out," I say. "Leave nothing behind."

I'm obeyed, by all but my own heart.

WE WALK IN silence save for the tramp of our feet on bare earth. Leah tends to me, speaking softly, holding me against her as if I alone am bereaved. With each step, I tell myself the ache will subside. What a fool I am!

It's daybreak when we emerge from the tunnel. We hike through the rain to find Rebecca and the several hundred residents whom she led from the city sheltering in the southernmost edge of the pain tree forest, its pores safely closed at my command. There are tearful reunions, even more tearful realizations that some will never return. Gideon catches Rebecca in his strong arms and hoists her high into the air, which makes her giggle for what must be the first time since her encounter with the dark queen. She's a child closing in on her eighth birthday, but when I look into her solemn eyes, they carry the wisdom and sadness of one on the verge of womanhood. I remember myself at that age, and I wish I could have shielded her from the burdens that hardened me.

Following a morning meal under sopping boughs, I sit with my lieutenants to plan our next move. The majority of the city's populace will camp here, in a place no less safe than any I can think of. Leah, Aurelia, Gideon, Michael, and Luke will travel with me in search of Celestina, whose facility at hiding herself from the eyes of the Ecosystem hasn't ebbed: I've been searching for her since we emerged, and I've come no closer to detecting a trace of her than when I began.

I wish I could recommend to Leah that she not join us, but I fear I wouldn't survive the ensuing argument. Rebecca, however, will have to stay here to perform Sensor duties, while Caleb and Noah, along with the rest of the healer corps, will help her care for the refugees. If Delilah or her creatures find them here, the littlest Sensor will do what can be done. We all know there's little she can do, but we also know that my presence can only delay, not change, the outcome. Aurelia would stay and fight the Armegaddon by herself, but I've convinced her—for now—that the best chance for us, for our city, and for our people is to find the missing queen.

I'm in a rush to leave, but everyone is exhausted, so I let them rest through the afternoon. The frigid rain that fell for the past week tapers to a drizzle then ceases altogether; if the storm was indeed the dark queen's doing, it seems it's served its purpose. While the others sleep, I climb a hill and ask a lone hexlox tree to lift me into its upper branches, where I can look back toward the city. From this distance, I see nothing but a blanket of black cloud that hangs in the air and won't dissipate no matter how hard the winds blow. Beneath that pall of darkness, I envision the queen perched atop a throne of skulls in her brood chamber—the one place her Armegaddon hasn't destroyed—and wielding power over her city of the dead.

The only one who truly lives in that city is the boy I love, the boy I've lost. I search for him, thread my mind through the labyrinthine caverns of a sanctuary in ruins, but I can't find him. I tell myself that's because I can't search through tons of fallen stone, tell myself he can't elude me forever. I tell myself many things, but all the while, there's only one thing that comes true.

With each passing moment, he gets farther and farther away from me.

BOOK TWO
WARD

*Perhaps this is the hidden meaning in the howl
of the wolf, long known among mountains,
but seldom perceived among men.*

—Aldo Leopold,
"Thinking Like a Mountain" (1949)

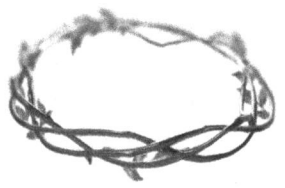

A CRACKLING CAMPFIRE draws the faces of my companions from the dark. We don't need the blaze to ward off the Ecosystem—the forest will remain calm as far as my influence extends—but the night's cold, and we've few blankets to share. Most of the faces look back at me with mingled hope and doubt, but Aurelia won't look at me at all. She glances to the side, her lean countenance worn and weary in the firelight. When she turns to me at last, her eyes simmer with anger.

"You led us from the city to search for Celestina," she says. "And now you inform us that you don't know where to search."

"I led us from the city because we would have died if we'd stayed there," I answer. "I told you that."

"You also told us—"

"That we needed to *look* for Celestina," I cut in. "I made no promises. I merely offered us a chance."

"But if we can't find the former queen…."

"A chance, Aurelia," I say. "Nothing is a certainty."

"The city will die without us," she says. "That is a certainty."

"Give Sarah a break," Leah jumps in. "She's doing the best she can."

I smile at her for her effort, but the reminder that this is the best I can do doesn't lift my spirits much. Nor does it mollify Aurelia, who glares at my friend before stalking away from the fire. This was the conversation I didn't want to have, the conversation I knew I had to have—the one where I was forced to tell everyone in our party that we might be setting out on a wild gnoose chase. I could have told Aurelia that my father was the one who first advised me to search for the missing queen; he was convinced the city was doomed without her. But my father's dead, along with half the city's population, and Aurelia's standing with her back to the rest of us, her rigid posture accentuated by the fire that outlines her figure.

As I watch, she takes a deep breath and lets her shoulders relax. When she returns, her expression has shifted subtly, from anger to resolve.

"What are our hopes of success?" she asks.

"I've been probing the Ecosystem all day," I say. "So far, Celestina hasn't turned up."

"Which means...."

"As I see it, there are three possibilities," I say. "One is that she and Angelica are dead. Dead things drop out of the Ecosystem's hive-mind, and out of mine as well."

The group is silent at this pronouncement.

"It's also possible the two of them have found shelter from the Ecosystem's eyes," I say. "In an ecozone that's not under my purview, like the area around the village. If they're hiding someplace like that, I doubt we'll ever find them."

More silence. Leah's about to offer her input, but I cut her off before she can antagonize Aurelia any further.

"The likeliest possibility is that Celestina is masking herself," I say. "As a queen, she has the power to make the Ecosystem blind to her presence, and there's no reason she couldn't shield Angelica at the same time. If that's what she's doing, then we have to find a way to penetrate the shield."

"And you know how to do that, right?" Leah asks. "As a queen?"

"Actually, no," I say. "But I haven't given up trying."

At these words, the captain of the guard shoots me another dangerous look. I know I have to do something to restore her faith in me, or in our quest, but I honestly can't think what to do. So far as my limited experience goes, if a queen chooses to mask herself from the Ecosystem, there's no power on earth that can strip her mask away.

Having no other ideas, I close my eyes and reach out once more, searching for any sign of the missing queen. I touch the edge of the urthwyrm desert to the northeast, smell the mud of the mangrave swamp at its western border. I attempt to turn my thought westward, back to the village where my adversary arose. All is darkness in that direction: though Delilah now dwells in the city, her web has taken root to stay. I stretch my power to the breaking-point, but there's nothing to find—no mark of Celestina's dainty foot on the earth's surface, no trace of her sweet scent on the breeze. The thought that she might truly be dead, leaving me alone against the dark queen, makes me shrivel into myself, the light of my power winking out like a candle snuffed by a strong wind.

But as the circle of my sensitivity collapses inward, it picks up something I'd missed in the effort to range beyond our present location. I open my eyes to the expectant faces of the group.

"Someone's tracking us," I whisper. "Behind that ridge."

Five heads turn incrementally toward the rocky outcropping that rears above our campsite. "Is it...?" Leah returns my whisper.

"It's not Celestina," I say. "It could be one of Delilah's servants. There's something strange about it, something I can't lock onto."

"We will find out soon," Aurelia says, her hand on the hilt of her sword. Gideon looks ready to join her, though his only weapon is a burning brand from the fire.

"Wait," I say. "I've got it."

A short scream sounds from behind the ledge. Aurelia and Gideon spring to their feet and disappear for a moment, only to return with a squirming bundle held between them. It wouldn't be a fair fight even if the captors were less powerful than those two, for at my command, a cluster of virago creepers has snared the sneak, wrapping tightly around the person's body. Aurelia and Gideon are none too gentle as they deposit the figure at my feet.

That's when I discover that it's a teenage girl, dark-skinned and petite, not to mention wide-eyed with terror. The creepers cover the lower half of her face, so I can't be sure who she is, though the half I can see definitely looks familiar. Her mouth labors beneath the suffocating wrap, but not only for breath; she wants to say something. I oblige by asking one of the creepers to withdraw.

"Don't hurt me!" she gasps the moment she can. It's when I see her whole face that I recognize who she is.

"Lavinia? What are you doing here?"

Angelica's ex-girlfriend looks at me tearfully, but

doesn't speak. Aurelia pulls her sword free and steps to the captive girl's side. "Answer the Queen."

She does, but only with more tears. I instruct the creepers to release her, which they do with some reluctance; they thought they were going to earn a tasty treat for their service. Lavinia tucks her arms tightly against her sides and lowers her head, while her shoulders shake with sobs.

"No one's going to hurt you," I say. "You're just lucky the Ecosystem didn't catch you before we did."

That doesn't help her tears. While she cries, I scan her small, delicate body for injury, but I encounter the same problem as when I first became aware of her presence: something's blocking me, some power that feels uncomfortably familiar but that I can't identify. It's too strong for me to believe it comes from Lavinia alone; she's not a healer, much less a queen. Her obvious distress at being lost in the Ecosystem convinces me that she's merely a common resident of the city, though if that's the case, I can't understand why she'd defy my orders and follow us to this place.

I stoop at her side and lay a hand on her nearly buried head. Physical contact doesn't breach whatever power protects her, but it does reveal that she's freezing cold beneath her tunic, and practically starving on top of that. I gesture to Leah, who drapes a blanket over Lavinia's shoulders.

"Come on," I say. "Let's get you something to eat."

She doesn't resist—much—when Leah helps her to her feet and guides her closer to the fire. She sits without looking at anyone, reaches mutely for the bowl of nuts and greens Michael offers her. When she extends her hand, the firelight catches a bright glint at her wrist, and I see for the first time the source of the power that enfolds her.

It's a silver bracelet shaped like a braided vine, with silver flowers sprinkled along its length. I wear a matching set, though mine are tarnished by the Armegaddon's fire. No trick of the firelight makes the metal seem to twine and tighten about Lavinia's wrist: some art I don't understand gives these implements the power to bind anyone but a queen to the Ecosystem's will. Celestina wore the same style of bracelet herself, designed to look like her beloved silverbloom bush, and she tried to use the ones she'd given me to shackle me in her brood chamber when she fled the city. But whether she was the one who fashioned these magical objects or whether hers were fixed on her arms by some other power—her mother, perhaps—is something I don't know.

It's obvious, though, that the bracelet is causing exquisite agony to the girl who wears it now. When she's not cramming food into her mouth, Lavinia claws at the metal with her other hand, and her wrist is torn and bloody as a result. That's what would have happened to me in Celestina's brood chamber if I hadn't been able to unlock my queenly power: the constricting circlets would have driven me to the point of trying to bite my own hands off. How this torture device found its way onto Lavinia's wrist is beyond me, as is her pursuit of me and the others.

I wait until the famished girl sets aside her empty dish before asking her. "Lavinia. I promise I'm not going to hurt you, but you need to answer me honestly. Okay?"

She looks doubtful, but nods.

"Let's start with the bracelet," I say. "Where did you get it?"

"From … from Angelica," she says. "The Queen gave it to her."

I try not to let my surprise show. "When was this?"

"A few months ago," she says. "Right before Queen Celestina took the throne. And then Angelica gave it to me when we … when we…."

"When you were courting," I say. "She didn't ask you to return it afterward?"

Lavinia flinches at the reminder of their break-up. "She said she didn't want it anymore. She was really angry about something the Queen had done. Angelica told me to keep it, but she made me promise never to put it on."

"But you did."

She starts to scratch again, then twists her hands together miserably. "I was afraid it would get lost when we left the city," she says. "When Angelica disappeared, I thought she was dead. I didn't want to lose this, too."

I know what she means. I miss the Sensor's token I gave to Miriam, the healer's token her alter ego stole from me. Sometimes the littlest things are the hardest to let go. "But now you can't take it off."

"It's stuck," she says, pulling at it with fingers hooked beneath the circlet. "As soon as I put it on, it felt like it was … burning. Like a kettle right off the fire. It's gotten worse since yesterday."

"And that's why you decided to follow us?"

"I didn't want to," she says. "I didn't even know where you'd gone. But somehow, I found my way here."

I sit back to take this in. Aurelia's wearing her customary expression of distrust, and I know what's in her mind: Lavinia's a spy, a tool of the dark queen, a threat to be disposed of. But Aurelia hasn't worn the silver bracelets, doesn't know their power. *I* don't know their full power, for that matter. I reach for Lavinia's hand, but as I draw near, some force repels my fingers—the same, I suspect, that clouded my perception before.

"Lavinia," I say. "Give me your hands."

She tries. The hand without the bracelet, her left, joins mine easily. The right, by contrast, seems frozen, unable to move. When I reach for it once again, it jumps back as if its owner has received a shock. I feel the electric tingle in my own fingers, the hairs rising on my arm in response.

"Hold still," I tell her. "And try to relax."

She obeys me the best she can. Without touching the bracelet, I cup my hands in the air around it, then reach out with my mind to detect its power. What I feel is a field of energy that surrounds the silver charm, its filaments extending from flower to flower to wrap Lavinia's wrist. It's something like the dark queen's web, but I know at once that it doesn't belong to her. I also realize that, against all odds, we've gotten the very break we needed.

"There's a reason Angelica told you not to wear this," I say. "It uses the Ecosystem's power to bind one person to another. It's impossible for anyone except the most advanced healers to break."

Everyone crowds close as if to see the invisible lines of force radiating from the bracelet. "How does it work?" Leah asks.

"The same way insects send signals to each other," I say. "Attraction, danger, that sort of thing. But in this case, it's much stronger than any insect could produce. A queen poured her will into it, and it possesses her power of command."

Michael speaks from behind Leah's shoulder. "Celestina?"

"None other," I say. "When she left the city, she must have been in too much of a hurry to retrieve it, or maybe she didn't think anyone would be able to discover its secrets." Probably, I say to myself, because she assumed that the only other queen in the vicinity—me—was trapped in her brood chamber. "Lavinia wouldn't have put it on if the Queen's power wasn't calling to her, but as it turns out, that's the best thing that could have happened to us."

"It is?" the girl asks.

"Sure enough," I say with a smile. "Celestina's at the other end, and you're going to lead us straight to her."

WHILE THE OTHERS prepare our campsite for sleep, I instruct Lavinia to lie down on the blanket and relax, arms at her sides. Now that I know what I'm dealing with, I'm able to touch the field of power that emanates from the charmed object, though I'm cautious to use only the lightest of pressure as I run my fingers along the strands. If I know Celestina, she's totally forgotten about this gift to Angelica, and the last thing I want to do is remind her. For the same reason, though I could use my power to remove the bracelet, I can't take that risk. Lavinia will have to wear it until we locate the refugee queen, and in the meantime, the most I can do is soothe the burning and heal her wounds.

The exhausted girl drifts in and out of consciousness as the hours wane. During one of these spells of half-sleep, Leah stops by to bring me a cup of water. She leans over my shoulder to watch while I work.

"You're sure this is safe?"

"Pretty sure. I'm only tracing the signal. That shouldn't have any effect on the wearer."

"And your own bracelets," she says. "You couldn't track Celestina that way?"

I shake my head. "With my power over the Ecosystem, the bracelets don't bind me to her anymore. Which means they don't connect me to her, either."

"Hm." She watches in silence for a moment. Lavinia moans softly, and I can see the radiant image of the Queen flickering through the girl's tortured mind.

"Why do you think Celestina gave the bracelet to Angelica in the first place?" Leah asks.

"Out of spite," I say. "But Angelica was smart enough not to put it on."

"What do you mean?"

"You should have heard some of the things Celestina said about her, Leah. She'd have been only too happy to turn Angelica into her slave."

Leah flinches at the word *slave*, and I picture her as she was before the battle, bowing and scraping under the dark queen's power. I'm about to say something in apology when Lavinia stirs and opens her eyes. Tears sparkle in their corners, silver like the queen who calls them out. Leah stands, a hand trailing from my shoulder before she goes.

"I used to think love was the strongest thing that binds us," she says. "Now, I'm not so sure."

With that, she heads to our woodpile to build up the fire. Aurelia joins her, the two of them speaking in low voices—making up for their earlier disagreement, I hope. A stray thought of the boy I left behind in the City of the Queens causes my hands to hesitate before returning to their work.

It's past midnight when I reach the end of the strand. Lavinia is utterly spent by her ordeal, but the pain has grown too great for her to sleep. Seeing her so vulnerable makes my anger swell at the selfish monarch whose bracelet she wears. I remember the burning sensation I felt the first time Celestina touched me, and I realize as never before that from the moment we met, she was using her power to bind me to her. I wonder if, before she left the city, she found a way to trick Angelica into wearing one of her bracelets. How she would have laughed to watch the red-haired healer, humbled by the charm's power, come at her beck and call!

I use the simple technique I learned from Isaac to ease Lavinia into dreamland, then pour my power into her to keep her sedated while the night lasts. She should wake in the morning with her flesh unscarred and her mind, if not completely untroubled, at least free of the wracking pain and fear she's carried this past day.

I rise to find the others wide awake and awaiting my report by the roaring campfire. Aurelia in particular isn't about to let me wiggle out of this, not even for the night. "Well?" she asks.

"I found her," I say. "I couldn't tell whether Angelica is with her, because the binding relates to the Queen alone. But Celestina's out there. Alive."

"Where?" the captain of the guard presses.

"Far away," I admit. "She had well over a week's head start, and with her queenly powers, it's likely she didn't walk. Actually, knowing Celestina, it's certain she didn't walk."

Aurelia exchanges a look with the others. "*Where?*" she repeats.

I sigh, but I have no choice but to answer. "In the mountains north of the urthwyrm desert. I'm not sure why she chose that direction, unless she figured no one would be stupid enough to follow her. It's not the safest place in the world."

While they listen, I expand on my understatement. I've never come within twenty leagues of the mountainous region to the far north, but thanks to tonight's work, I've now visited its dizzying heights twice in my imagination, the first time being when I searched for Miriam the day she went missing in the Ecosystem. What I saw on both of those visits were treacherous peaks sheathed in snow and prowled by lone chimaerae and packs of sleek white terror wolves. What I felt was biting cold, frigid winds, and sudden squalls that blanketed the world in white. Such an ecozone might be survivable by a queen, and possibly by the single servant under her power. But I have grave doubts about leading an entire company of neophytes there, especially with the renegade queen to add to the place's existing dangers.

"I'll go alone," I tell them. "A group our size will only attract Celestina's attention. While I'm gone, you can work on a plan for retaking the city in case I don't return."

Gideon is first to raise his voice in protest, but he's quickly joined by the others, Leah most vocal of them all. Aurelia is the sole exception. For once, the captain of the guard expresses neither approval nor disapproval, her eyes narrowing in a way I can't read. Much as I've grown to dread her objections to my orders, her silence is even worse.

"Aurelia?" I say.

She regards me a moment longer before retreating to the edge of the darkened woods. The others glance between her and me, then busy themselves with the tasks they completed hours before. Left alone, I find my steps drawn to where Aurelia stands, as if she holds power over an invisible bracelet that's fused to my wrist.

"What is it?" I ask her. "What's wrong?"

She won't look at me. I feel the energy bleeding from her skin: a combination of disgust, anger, and—something I don't expect—a deeply personal grief I can't name. I'm about to reach out to her, seek to still the turmoil in her mind, when she speaks.

"The lives of the queens are unknown even to those of us pledged to their service," she says. "From my girlhood to this day, I have seen them as figures of such great power and glory that I could not possibly grasp their thoughts."

"I told you I'm not like that," I say.

She shrugs. "In some ways, perhaps not. But in others, you possess the very qualities of which I speak: power, pride—and arrogance."

"Arrogance?" Now I'm the one who's mad. "I've treated you—I've treated everyone—as equals. I've let you speak your mind, I've asked for your help—"

"No," she interrupts. "You hear our words, but you do not listen to our hearts. You say that you wish to protect us, but you do not hesitate to take from us the most important thing we possess."

"Which is what?" I snap.

"The right to decide our own fate," she says. "And to die, if die we must, fighting for the thing we love."

My anger fizzles, replaced by shame and weariness. "I don't want anyone else to die on my account," I say. "I'm so sick of death."

She turns to face me. Tears I never thought I'd see on her lined cheeks gleam red in the firelight. "You hold great power in your hands, Sarah," she says. "So great, it must harrow you that you do not wield power over death itself."

I swallow down the dreadful emptiness that threatens to overcome me at the thought of my loved ones' deaths: my mother's, my father's, Leah's, Isaac's. I'd rather die myself than be left to face the world without them.

"But the lust for such power is an evil thing," Aurelia says. "It has twisted Delilah's soul, and it will twist yours too, in time. Let it go, My Queen. Care for the living, but do not cling to the dead."

I hang my head while the captain of the guard folds me in her arms. Through our touch, I feel the many whom Aurelia has lost over her long years: her husband, most of her friends in the city, the members of the guard who fell before the Armegaddon—including the soldier she cries for today. Still it is she who comforts me, who strokes my hair as my own mother once did. When I step back from her arms, she gives me a wry smile.

"We will make a queen of you yet," she says in a teasing voice that's my second surprise these last few minutes. "Your friend agrees."

"So you and Leah have been teaming up on me?" I say, trying to fit a joke to my words.

"Only for your own good," she replies in kind.

"I guess I should thank you," I say, and then: "What was your son's name?"

She looks at me in shock, then seems to remember my power as pureskin.

"It was Raphael," she says. "He was beside me in the Cathedral when the fire-monster struck. I left him among the fallen when you gave the order to retreat."

"I'm sorry," I say. "I didn't…."

"No," she says. "You were right to issue that order. He

105

was the only child of my body, but it was time I returned him to the Ecosystem from whence he came."

We embrace one more time, then walk back to join the others.

OUR MOUNTS RUN through the day, seemingly tireless despite the extra burden they bear. I've ridden a warhog once before—briefly, in an attempt to stop it from skewering Isaac and me—but I've never felt the raw power of these armored pigs gobbling the ground under their hooves, the wind of their speed blowing in my face. Thanks to Gideon, each of us is equipped with a hastily constructed saddle and bridle, just enough cloth and rope for us to hang onto. Still, it's a bumpy ride, nothing like the fluid slither of the giant wyrms I've ridden before. When I catch a glimpse of my companions' faces, I'm not sure if they're about to whoop with joy or scream in terror.

But it's the best I could come up with on short notice. The wyrms are many times faster than anything that runs on four feet, but they would never survive the frigid north. Even the warhogs will have to deposit us in the foothills of the mountains, and then we'll proceed on our own.

With our inadequate clothing and time too precious to return to the main camp for more, I've recruited some of the Ecosystem's least creatures to prepare us for that icy trek. The pain tree forest hangs heavy with the nests of slickworms, inch-long larvae that will become huge, bat-winged moths in time. Meanwhile, their primary occupation is to convert the organic matter they nibble nonstop into a tough, stringy substance that's something like cloth. The trees are festooned with their handiwork, and it gives me an idea: rather than killing animals for their fur, might I teach the worms to spin their threads into coats and blankets and wraps for our feet and hands?

I try out my plan the first night of our journey, when we dismount to sleep and to give the pigs time to fill their paunches. On their maiden attempt, the worms make a horrible mess of things: though Leah provides me with a pattern to pass on to them, it's far too complicated for the blind, simple creatures to follow. I remember the meticulously stitched bags my seamstress friend crafted for our initial journey to the City of the Queens, and I cringe when I inspect the slickworms' output, a pile of sack-like blobs with three head-holes and meandering sleeves as likely to strangle as warm us.

I thank the worms nonetheless, and bundle their efforts to dispose of on the next day's ride. Maybe, at that, the blind, simple creature is me.

The next night goes better. The worms, I've learned from yesterday's fiasco, are at their best producing items piecemeal: a patch here, a swath there. I set small gangs to work constructing the individual components, then stay up late with Leah to stitch the pieces together using extra threads supplied by the worms. Lavinia turns out to be a fair hand with our pain-tree needles, or at least fairer than me—which is nice, since she hasn't helped with any of the other chores on this trip. When we're done, we have a pile of off-white garments that should meet our needs: hooded cloaks, fingered gloves, a set of combined leggings-and-boots, and lots of thick, lumpy blankets. We won't win any prizes for beauty, but we'll be warm, and perhaps camouflaged from the eyes of mountain predators. As an extra precaution, Leah and I spend the last few hours of the night sewing together sheets we can use for tents.

Just in time, too: the pain tree forest gives out on the third day of our run, and we enter a treeless area skirting swampland on the west and the urthwyrm desert on the east. We'll meet with no slickworms from here on out.

Even more worrisome, we won't meet with much to eat. The warhogs have no problem gobbling the razor-sharp blades of sawgrass that grow in abundance along the swamp's edge, but such a meal would slice human intestines even if we could digest it. Gideon and I could try our hand at catching snakes and frogs, but the lifelong residents of the City of the Queens have never eaten animals before, and something tells me their stomachs would rebel against the attempt. Berries won't keep us going for long, certainly not when we reach the mountains, where there will be none to gather. I puzzle over this dilemma for the rest of the day, but when the sun falls into the brackish waters to our west, I haven't arrived at a solution.

Aurelia senses my disquiet and approaches me. She's been more than usually attentive to my moods since she shared the story of her son, and she's too good a commander not to have noticed our dwindling food stores herself.

"Does anything edible grow in the desert?" she asks when I tell her the problem.

"Not much," I say. "A few flowers that aren't lethal to humans is all."

"And the wyrms themselves?"

"No go," I say, shaking my head. "Urthwyrms produce a neurotoxin that would have us seizing in minutes. I could try to neutralize it, but we wouldn't know I've failed until we were all dead."

"I see." She gazes into the swamp-murk, which looks like a cloud of blood in the light of the setting sun. "You command the creatures of the Ecosystem in these regions?"

"More or less. But I can't command anything to throw itself on the fire so we can enjoy a nice roast."

"You can't?" she says. "Or you won't?"

"Take your pick."

"I will assume that you won't," she says with a smile. "But surely, you can command living things to share their food with us."

"We can't eat sawgrass."

"No," she says. "But we can eat what the birds bring. I've seen that you are a particular favorite with the feathered tribe."

Her words remind me of my gryphon, dead on the field of battle outside the city gates. But she's right: birds have saved my life more than once since I became queen, and I'm embarrassed I never thought of calling on them in our current crisis.

"That's settled, then," I say. The nearby birds—dreadwings tending their nests in the sawgrass, bloodbirds circling high above the marsh—hear my voice and flock to me, landing on my shoulders and arms. For fun, I ask one to roost on Aurelia's crest. She scowls before walking off to give me privacy with the birds. With her long, gaunt frame, she looks like a picture from one of the children's books I read. Something called a scarecrow, from the days when birds were scared of people and not the other way around.

It's another three days' journey to the mountains, during which time we're liberally supplied by my flying army: fish and small mammals for Gideon and Leah to cook, nuts and berries and edible shrubs for everyone else, including me, to transform into a hearty if unappetizing stew. We know we're drawing close to our destination when the level basin that contains both swamp and desert heaves upward in ripples, then hillocks, then hills, the landscape marching inexorably toward higher ground. There's a dark stripe on the northern horizon that stands starkly against a whitened sky, and as we bound closer over fields dotted with berserkflowers and craggy boulders, the stripe sharpens into a jagged outline like a vast, unruly forest.

But it's rock, not wood, that roots this forest to the earth. Enough life swarms over the mountains to take shape in my mind: dense groves of fear trees, similar in form to pain trees but able to grasp and claw with prehensile branches; roving packs of terror wolves with daggers for teeth and nearly human forepaws; isolated chimaerae fearsome enough to send even the wolves scurrying for cover. Though I've seen this mountain range in my mind's eye, I'm taken aback by its size, its stillness, and perhaps most of all its silence: much as I call out to it, it refuses to answer. If anything, the silence grows deeper the closer we come, until it falls on us as heavily as the shroud of shadow from the mountains' white-capped peaks.

The warhogs have been bucking against their halters since midday: reluctant as they are to abandon me in this forbidding place, they know the time has come. I call a halt and, while the beasts stand patiently, my companions and I unload our water, weapons, and cold weather gear.

Then the pigs are off, tossing their tusks in what might be a farewell or might simply be exuberance. I watch them go, envying their freedom. They look like children as they gambol across the fields of many-colored berserkflowers, which try ineffectually to nip through the pigs' tough, armored hides.

When the black shapes have vanished, I turn to my friends. The faces they show me are nowhere near as joyous as the pigs' maneuvers. Leah and Lavinia are already starting to shiver.

"Suit up," I say. "It'll get cold in a hurry when the sun goes down. We'll pitch camp here and resume our march at daybreak."

"How can it get any colder than it is already?" Leah asks, with mingled wonder and dismay in her voice.

"Just wait," I say. "In the wild, one ecozone abuts another directly, with little transition in between. Right now we're at the juncture of arid desert to the southeast, marshland to the southwest, and freezing mountains less than a league ahead. We're all going to see snow before this is over, and lots of it."

They take this in quietly. The soldiers among us try to keep their teeth from chattering. Everyone else has given up and is shivering away.

"Wouldn't it be best to cover more distance before nightfall?" Luke asks.

"Too risky," I say. "The foothills aren't as bad as the higher elevations, but there are still plenty of ways to die here. We travel by daylight only."

No one argues. Gideon and Aurelia create frameworks out of fallen fear tree branches while Leah and the boys use leftover pieces of slickworm string to lash our crude tents in place. To my surprise, Lavinia gets a fire going and a meal started. While the others serve themselves, I pull Aurelia aside, ostensibly to chart tomorrow's route. There's no need to tell everyone the real reason just yet.

"I'll take first watch," I say. "I'll call for you after two hours, then either Luke or Gideon can spell you."

She nods, her hand straying to the sword at her belt. "What is it you fear?"

I sigh, both grateful and a bit annoyed that she's learned to read me so well. "Terror wolves sometimes come down into the foothills. I'm not confident they'll back off when I tell them to."

She holds up a burning brand. "Do they fear fire?"

"That depends," I say. "Are you planning to shove that down their throat with your bare hands?"

The shock shows on her face. "I wouldn't have thought that necessary."

"Then you don't know much about terror wolves," I say. "Because the thing with them is, they don't always take the hint."

I STAY AWAKE all night, watching for the sheen of gibbous eyes in the fire's glow. Unlike virtually every other creature in the Ecosystem, terror wolves will boldly approach a campfire, knowing there might be a meal to be found. And they won't scamper off unless you give them plenty of incentive.

The night passes without incident, the new day dawning pale and cold. I rouse the others to the breakfast I've prepared. They huddle close to the fire while they slurp down steaming broth. Aurelia conceals beneath gruff responses and a flat expression her displeasure at not being awakened during the night. I'm not about to apologize. I don't need to sleep just now, and I'm not sure I *could* sleep if I were half-dead on my feet. Call me arrogant, but too much depends on this expedition for me to nod off.

After our perfunctory meal, we move out. I send the bloodbirds that delivered today's feast back to Rebecca's camp to report on our progress. With her prior experience Sensing via bloodbird, she should be able to read the information I've left in the creatures' minds. I'm more interested in the birds' return report on the status of things back home. This far north, I can't see the darkness hovering over the city. All I can see is the white veil of a squall coming down from the granite peaks that loom above us.

It hits us as we stumble through the foothills, which grow increasingly steep as we proceed. One second, the day is clear and painfully bright, with white stuff covering the boulders and reflecting the sun. The next, the whiteness washes over us, and we're floundering in a world of shadow and vapor. I've heard of snow—the Conservator of the Sensorship spoke of it as something from earth's distant past—but I've never experienced it, and the shock of cold is nothing compared to the way it erases the companions walking two feet in front of me. I scream a halt against the wind, and when that doesn't work, I do something I vowed I'd never do: I send out ripples of power to command my team to stop. Their ghostly forms freeze, then take drifting steps toward me until I can touch solid bodies and assure myself they're all there.

"We need to ride out the storm!" I shout loud enough for all to hear. "If we keep walking, someone's sure to get lost!"

I can't see their faces, but I feel them nod in agreement. We draw close, sharing warmth. Leah fumbles for my hand, whether to reassure me or to keep from being blown away I don't know. The wind howls and the snow swirls about us, but our slickworm wraps work even better than I hoped, and it's actually a bit toasty in our little knot of bodies.

The storm moves fast, sweeping down the foothills in a matter of minutes. I doubt we'll have such luck when we get higher into the mountains.

"We'd best tie ourselves together," I tell the others when the winds have died down enough for me to speak in a normal voice. "We'll have to move extra slowly, poking the ground in front of us with our staffs." I demonstrate with one of the walking sticks Gideon carved from pain tree branches, the top end shaved sharp to double as a spear. My

115

halting gait puts me in mind of Aaron in his final days, or of Isaac after his encounter with the urthwyrms. "I'll take the lead and keep alert for danger, but I can't sense unstable rock or faults in the ground. If anyone feels the slightest wobble, stop dead and signal the rest."

Heads nod within slickworm hoods. Gideon ties the ropes tight, and we move on.

Our progress is even slower than I anticipated. The ground is treacherous, with lichen-covered rocks sprinkled with snow from the passing storm, which makes them slick to walk on. In the gullies between stones where the sun seldom reaches, snow has gathered to a depth of several inches or even feet. After poking my staff into one such drift and watching the branch disappear to the hilt without touching bottom, I decide we have to avoid these crevices altogether, which means lots of halts and conferences to negotiate a path around them. In my bulky clothing, tiptoeing across the land with no idea what lies beneath, I can imagine how the common villagers felt on our journey to the City of the Queens. The memory of sprinting barefoot over the forest during my Sensor days would make me laugh, if my nerves weren't too edgy and my concentration too focused to do anything but creep another inch forward, then another, then another.

We break for a meal no one feels like eating, then move on. The ascent is much steeper here than before, and everyone labors to climb, using the sharp ends of their staffs like picks to pull themselves upward. I've placed the least fit members of our team—Lavinia and Leah—in the middle of the line, figuring they lack the sensitivity to detect dangers or the dexterity to avoid disaster. But they're a drag on the rest of us, the more so the higher we climb. If it gets much worse, we'll have to discard the walking-sticks and pull ourselves up with the strength of our arms, and that's something I doubt either the frail girl or my doughty but inexperienced friend can do.

The sun plummets behind the foothills much sooner than I expect, bringing cold and another storm that forces us to stop for the night. Looking up at the mountain, I'm frustrated to see how little progress we've made, though I take some comfort in the fact that Celestina's trail remains as bright as the crystals that glisten around us. Lavinia warms her hands by the fire, the bracelet having practically frozen to her wrist. Given all she's been through, I suppose I should be thankful she's still on her feet. But another sleepless night punctuated by howls that might belong to a predator even more deadly than the wind keeps me from being thankful for much at all.

The next day passes like the first, except the terrain becomes even more rugged and our arms and legs grow ever more weary. Our bloodbirds fail to return from checking up on Rebecca's camp—not surprising considering how far away we are, but yet another thing to add to my cares. We're out of the foothills by now and making for the higher elevations, which means much slower going to help each other up rocks and to avoid icy patches disguised as solid ground. The only compensation is that it doesn't snow all day, so we get by without ropes. Everyone, that is, except Leah and Lavinia, who I insist remain anchored to Gideon, oldest and strongest of us all. Leah protests that she can manage without anyone's help, but she quiets when Aurelia throws her a look as frosty and imperious as the mountain itself.

Evening has fallen by the time we deposit our flagging bodies on the spot I've been eyeing all day, a shelf of rock that looks relatively sheltered from snow and wind. While Michael and Luke pitch our tents and prepare our campfire—with zero assistance from Lavinia, whose strength has failed over today's brutal stretch—I confer with Leah, Aurelia, and Gideon about what the morrow may bring.

"Are you still able to detect Celestina?" the captain of the guard asks.

"Clear as day," I answer. "I can't see her—that is, I can't tell you what she's wearing or anything like that—but I can feel her more strongly than ever. She's no more than a day ahead, depending on weather and terrain."

"And can you tell if Angelica is with her?"

"We should assume so," I say. "And we should also assume that her presence might complicate our negotiations. If Celestina took a hostage because she was afraid we'd come after her, I'm not sure what she'll do once she's caught."

Gideon, faithful old Gideon, nods. I can read his feelings like a book, and they consist entirely of determination to stand by Mistress Sarah. Leah does even better, squeezing my hand to communicate her support. I brace myself for Aurelia's response, which I can tell isn't going to be quite as uncomplicated.

"There is something about this that troubles me," she says, and I let go of the breath I've been holding. "You say that Celestina made straight for the mountains after her flight from the city?"

"As far as I can tell."

"And yet here she remains," Aurelia continues. "If her objective was to elude pursuit, why did she not continue on her course, and put the mountains between us? Why linger here, when her own survival must be imperiled by this place?"

I hesitate before answering. It's not only that I don't want to lower myself in Aurelia's esteem. It's that the same question has been gnawing at me.

"I don't know," I admit at last. "There's something unusual about this part of the Ecosystem, something I don't remember feeling the first time I came into contact with it months ago. It seems ... a bit wild. Out of control."

"The dark queen?" Leah asks.

"No," I say. "There's no sign of her, no trace of her web. It feels more like this area isn't ruled by *any* queen, like it's got a mind of its own. I've been calling out to it ever since we left the forest, and it definitely hears me, but it refuses to answer."

"Then you lack the power of command over these regions?" Aurelia asks.

"I didn't say that," I answer. "I just don't know."

I look at the three of them, my first two lieutenants and the battle-scarred woman whose trust I'm still not sure I've fully earned. To my relief, neither Gideon's nor Leah's expression changes. Somewhat to my surprise, no more does Aurelia's. She claps a hand on my shoulder, and I feel both the strength in her grip and the sadness that's settled into her bones at the death of her son.

"Tonight, you sleep," she says. "Gideon and I will share the watch."

"Wait," Leah says. "I'll watch, too."

I smile at her, and exchange a private look with Aurelia.

As long as the captain of the guard keeps one eye on my friend, I suppose I can allow myself a night's rest.

"Thank you," I say, realizing as I say it how exhausted I am from climbing, and even more from worrying. "But wake me up the second you feel anything wrong."

We return to camp and take part in the skimpy meal the boys have prepared. If my bloodbirds ever return, I'll have to remind them that human beings can't survive exclusively on wilderberries. Before bedtime, I instruct Leah, Gideon, and Aurelia in the finer points of detecting terror wolves: look for the eyes, listen for a snuffling sound, sometimes accompanied by a puff of steam from their breath if the moon's visible, which at the moment it's not. They nod and offer assurances, but it's like telling them to keep an eye out for wraiths. Leah's determined to be brave for my sake, but her face tells me that my lesson has done nothing but terrify her.

I fall asleep alone in the tent that's been reserved for me and Leah. Michael and Luke share another—absent Gideon—while Lavinia sleeps without Aurelia's company in the third. My dreams are of ravenous howls right by my ears, yellow eyes as big as a fist flashing open before my face.

Those eyes turn into Aurelia's as I'm shaken awake. The captain of the guard stoops by my side, and I sense her urgency immediately. "What's wrong?"

"Softly," she says. I realize how loud my voice sounds in the silent night. "Another squall moved in while you slept. It—"

"Is everyone all right?"

She breathes quietly before answering. "Michael and Luke are unharmed, as is Gideon. But the girls are gone."

I FLING OPEN the tent flap to a world draped in dazzling white. The snow continues to fall, blowing in silken curtains across the bright light of day, but it must have tapered from the blizzard that dumped several feet on our camp overnight. Three half-seen bodies—Gideon's, Michael's, and Luke's—fight through drifts to join me and the captain of the guard.

"What happened?" I ask everyone and no one.

Gideon hangs his head. "I have failed you, Mistress Sarah."

"Don't worry about that," I say. "Just tell me what happened."

He raises his head, but his expression remains crestfallen. "At the height of the storm, we were unable to see. When the worst of it passed, we found this."

He points to the tent where Lavinia slept. Unlike the other two tents, which stand despite the snowy caps that weigh them down, hers has collapsed into a shapeless mound, half-buried by drifts. My heart leaps at the thought that the girl might be trapped inside, but falls when I realize that Gideon and Aurelia are too conscientious not to have checked for that.

"And Leah?" I ask, dreading the answer.

"Gone," Aurelia confirms. "I was right beside her, but

when the storm lifted...." She shakes her head, the snow turning her red crest to an old woman's white.

"Are there any tracks?" I ask. "Human, or… otherwise?"

Luke is first to answer. "The storm would have erased them. We found no blood, but…."

"Terror wolves don't leave blood," I say. "They drag their prey back to their dens to share with the pack."

I stand still and send out waves of power, commanding the Ecosystem to locate the beasts that stole our two most helpless companions from our midst. I receive no response: whatever's out there, it spurns my summons. If anything, I hear a hollow, barking laugh, as if the perpetrators are howling their defiance in my ears.

"Break camp," I tell the others. "And hurry. I can't feel Lavinia anymore. She must have lost her bracelet."

Gideon's a bronze blur against the whitened world as he leads the efforts. Within minutes, we're packed and ready to go.

We flounder through waist-high drifts, careless of what lies beneath. Gideon and Aurelia use their chests and walking-sticks to forge a path, while Michael, Luke, and I follow like clawshoe rabbit kits hurrying after their dam. The blizzard picks up in intensity as we exit the shelf of rock and strike out into an open stretch that runs between towering crags. I call out to my bloodbirds, hoping they might be close enough by now to swoop down and carry us over the snow, but I receive no more response from them than from the mountains. Across the valley, great sheets of white are loosened by the storm and cascade down the peaks. Though the snow looks as harmless as powder from this distance, there might be tons of it thundering from high in the air. We'll never be able to go that way, and if the wolves were foolish enough to pursue the route through the mountain pass, they're buried beneath the avalanche with their victims.

"Follow me!" I scream against the wind. "Toward the forest!"

"The fear trees!" Michael responds, and I realize how small my own voice must sound. His is a thin cry in the face of the gale.

"I'll hold them back!" I shout. "It's the only way!"

I veer away from the pass and try to cut across the valley toward a stand of fear trees rooted to a somewhat gentler slope. If not for Gideon and Aurelia, I wouldn't get far: the snow is up to my throat, and each step is a battle against a nearly solid wall. The indefatigable duo somehow force a trail with their arms and staffs, giving me a chance to focus on the trunks that loom closer with each punishing step. As the trees' thoughts take shape in my mind, my heart sinks like a fiery brand in the snow, sputtering briefly before being snuffed out.

The trees are hungry, and they care nothing for the word of a queen. Their branches, which look like enormous clawed hands sheathed in an armor of dark green quills, spread wide to clutch us the moment we come within reach.

"Gideon!" I shout. "Can you make fire in this wind?"

He turns to look at me with his one remaining eye. His white beard, snow-thickened, is double its already impressive size. "I will try, Mistress!"

Aurelia and Luke hammer a bowl-shaped declivity around the five of us, in which Gideon crouches while we shield him from the storm. Carefully, almost reverently, he removes his equipment from his supply bag: flint, tinder, pain tree branches roped together with slickworm thread, a flask of some tarry substance with which he bathes the end of each bundle. He strikes the flint repeatedly, producing a spark each time, but each time losing it to the wind that whips around the bowl. We pull closer, try to block the gale with our bodies, but the flame won't catch. I'm about to tell Gideon to stop trying—we're wasting time, and I'll lose all sense of direction if the storm reshapes the hills much longer—when, with a cry of pain, the old man holds up his tar-blackened palm, from which a flame dances. He touches it to one of the bundles of wood, and the torch springs to life, just in time for him to pass it to Aurelia and plunge his hand into the surrounding snow.

"Gideon!" I admonish, and he looks up guiltily, like a little boy caught playing with firesticks by his mother. I reach for his hand, coax him to withdraw it from the snow. It's badly burned, but I draw enough power from the earth deep beneath our feet to heal it. I've seen Gideon perform many feats of valor, but I never expected him to sacrifice his own hand to bring us the gift of flame.

"Don't ever do that again!" I say to him, and his abashed look deepens. "But thank you," I add. "For everything."

He straightens, though he doesn't smile. I guess he can forgive himself now for his lack of vigilance at the campsite.

I turn to the others. "Michael, Luke, take a torch. Hold it in front of you where the trees can see it. And be prepared to use it if they get close."

"Can these trees move?" Michael asks.

"Their branches can," I say, indicating the coiled limbs within throwing distance from where we stand. "They strike like birds of prey, but they might be scared off by the fire."

With Aurelia using her staff to shove snow aside and the rest of us holding our torches at arm's length, we fight through the drifts to the border of the forest.

The branches shrink back, sensing the heat and smelling the oily stink of the burning brands. There's a slim strip of ankle-deep snow between the trees and the valley, and we hug that margin, keeping our distance from the branches to our left and the deeper snow to our right. I search the minds of the trees, find them furious at our ploy. They've seen no fire except that which is produced by the occasional lightning strike, and they didn't know humans were clever enough to make it. For that matter, they've seen few humans. Only us, and a woman in a white cloak whose power was just enough to hold them at bay....

"Watch out!"

It's Michael who shouts, right before an enormous branch descends from on high to knock the torch from his partner's hands. Sweeping sideways, the branch throws Michael toward the valley, and he vanishes in a sea of white. Gideon, torch in one hand and spear in the other, is fending off a flurry of branches that have taken their leader's hint and are trying to douse our fire. One of the limbs closes around the old man's body, risking burns in its attempt to crush the life out of him. Gideon howls in fury as it lifts him from the ground, but his arms are pinned by the branch's claws, and he can't fight back. Aurelia ducks beneath branches to sink her sword into the tree's trunk, and a shudder passes through it. But then another tree catches her arms, and my two lieutenants dangle helplessly above the snow in a grip like iron. The tendons in Aurelia's neck stand out as she wrestles to free her sword, only to have one of the branches pluck it from her hand and hold its edge against her throat.

Rage courses through me, so hot the snow melts in a pool around my feet. I send out one final command to the trees.

Heed me, I tell them. *Release your prey, or die where you stand.*

The fear trees aren't intimidated. Their inhuman voices taunt me as their claws close fast on the struggling forms of my friends.

A burst of power erupts from me, catching the trees by surprise. Against their will, I command them to wrap their own limbs around their trunks and squeeze, which causes their clawed branch-ends to gouge through thorny bark into tender pith. The branches that hold Aurelia and Gideon rip apart, dropping their victims while pitchy sap explodes from the shredded wood. The wounded trees stagger, try to retreat—but they're not ambulatory, and they can't pull free from the rock deep beneath the snow.

Not until I free them myself, compelling their roots to relinquish their grip on the ground.

With nothing to hold their ungainly weight, the trees pitch forward and topple down the slope into the deeper snow of the valley. There, they'll quickly drown, or die a lingering death of starvation. Their frenzied shrieks fill my mind, but I'm done with them. The trees deeper in the grove don't stand in my way as I dig through the snow to find my fallen lieutenants.

They break the surface, bruised and gasping but alive, covered with sticky sap from the trees. Luke struggles up the slope with his partner in his arms. Michael's pale skin has turned blue, his white cloak a shocking red. Luke lays him on the ice-melt at my feet, then steps back, his face a single plea. Pulling strength from the snow-shrouded earth, I close the wound in Michael's side, restore the steady beat of his heart. I can't stop Luke from throwing his arms around him the second Michael's eyes open. Healing the others of their relatively minor cuts and contusions is but a moment's work. The dying trees stranded on the slope below us whimper for relief now that they've seen my power to heal as well as harm, but I have more pressing concerns.

Where did they go? I ask the trees that remain standing. *Show me now.*

The trees brood in sullen silence until Aurelia and Gideon scramble in the snow for their weapons, which they brandish with grim faces. Then the trees raise their branches high, opening a lane through the grove. When I stoop to the ground, I see the faint impression of humanoid tracks in the snow, and to either side, a furrow where a body was dragged. A shimmer that's not snow leads me to Lavinia's bracelet, which is flecked with her blood, bright red in the cold. The instant I touch the circlet, I feel that its warmth has departed, leaving nothing but frozen metal.

"They came this way," I tell the others. "Celestina was warned about us. She released the bracelet's hold on

Lavinia, but she wasn't content to let it fall off on its own. She had the wolves chew it from her wrist."

"Then these beasts obey the Queen?" Michael asks.

"Not exactly," I say. "There's a compact between them of some kind, something I've never felt before. The same with the trees. It's not the power of command, but...."

"But it is power nonetheless," Aurelia says softly, and gestures with her head deeper into the trees.

I stand to look where she indicates. The grove has gone quiet, even the wind dying down in the shelter of the woods. White shapes, their color the same as the snow, sit on their haunches, forming a loose circle around us. Their snouts are blunt, giving their faces a human aspect. They make no sound, but where sunlight beats a path through the shade, puffs of white vapor mark their steady breathing. In the deeper shadows of the fear trees, other shapes flit ghostlike as they prowl on silent, restless paws.

One of the creatures lifts its head and lets out a long howl, and the terror wolves close in upon us.

THEY DON'T ATTACK. If they did, I'd fight them, but given how much energy I've expended on the trees, I'd surely lose.

There are scores of them, possibly hundreds. They slip in and out of the dappled shadows beneath the trees, their coats so perfectly matched with their surroundings that every time I think I've got the count of them, two or more shapes separate from the whiteness to confuse my eyes once again. Even more strangely, I can't seem to tally them through my connection to the Ecosystem: I can feel their presence as well as see their bodies, but I can't pin their numbers down. It's as if they truly are ghosts, their white pelts floating above the snow with no more substance than their silvery breaths.

The wolf that signaled the others approaches me, padding forward on paws elongated to resemble curled fingers. This one is bigger than the rest, and its face is even more human than theirs, with a high forehead and icy-bright blue eyes. It comes so close to me, its snout almost touches my cloak. I speak to it calmly, hoping my plea may cajole what my power can't command.

We're travelers, I tell it. *In search of two we lost, another who came before them. Will you lead us to where they are?*

The alpha wolf snuffles and jerks back, snarling softly. Its mind is a blank to me, a sheet of ice. I might as well be talking to the wind or the snowfall, for all my words can alter the course its thoughts have set.

The alpha emits a series of short, coughing barks, and four additional wolves slink forward to join it. They crouch before their leader as it continues to deliver itself in grunts and panting breaths I can't help thinking of as speech. When it finishes, the others respond with sounds of their own, high-pitched whines unlike their leader's guttural talk. The brief conference ended, the four wolves sidle up to my companions, their flattened noses snuffling the scent of human. Then each wolf grips the hem of a cloak in its teeth, while the leader grips mine. It tugs, and though I feel the power in its sleek body, I'm convinced it has no intention of dragging me away as its pack did Lavinia and my friend.

"They want us to come with them," I tell my companions. "I think we'd better obey."

"Do you understand their language?" Michael asks.

"Not a word," I say. "But I understand their teeth."

I could swear the leader chuckles deep in its throat as it lets go of my cloak and turns to trot into the forest.

We follow. The other wolves release their captives as well, but they remain as close as ever human guards did as they pace by my companions' side. The alpha wolf lets me walk without an escort, unless I count the shadowy forms that flash behind the trees, their footfalls as quiet as snowflakes. After the initial conversation, there's not a sound from the leader or its pack. Even their panting breath is hushed, as if they're wary of letting slip any secret of these mountain haunts. I keep my thoughts to myself too, for I sense that the wolves don't want the sound of my voice to interrupt the stillness. Compared to the wolves, however, my companions and I make enough noise blundering through the snow that I know for a certainty the creatures have tracked us all this time.

We pass through the soft carpet of white that's accumulated beneath the trees, then strike higher, stonier ground where boulders lie exposed to the sky. In the brightness of the open range, the wolves' pelts flash against the snow with blinding intensity, making it impossible for me to distinguish their numbers. I've decided by now, though, that this is no ordinary pack. I know little of terror wolves, but I do know that within the Ecosystem, the size of a predatory grouping never rivals that of their prey. These mountains host herds of migratory carrionbou in the tens of thousands, which means the wolf packs that pursue them are sure to be orders of magnitude smaller. What den could contain numbers like this, what law could prevent deadly rivalries from springing up on a daily basis among contenders for the top spot? Whatever the explanation, I'm witnessing something that was never meant to be: a gathering of wolves that might represent the entire population of the mountains, brought together by a power and a purpose I can't fathom.

It seems hours that the wolves bound—while we slip and stumble—over ice-coated rocks, the ascent steepening as we go. From time to time, the alpha looks over its shoulder, but it approaches us no more, and its deputies make no effort to assist us. The snowfall tapers then dies. The daylight brightens intolerably, and I have to squint against the multiple, overlapping layers of white: snow, ice, wolf, sky. At our current elevation, our cloaks and hoods have lost the power to shield us from the cold; my cheeks burn, while my fingertips tingle in a way that has nothing to do with the Ecosystem. My legs grow weary from churning endlessly uphill. I realize we've had nothing to eat since last night, and I doubt any bird can reach us here to deliver the day's meal. That there might not *be* a day's meal—or, to put it differently, that *we* might be that meal—hasn't escaped my mind. Terror wolves are particular about sharing their catch with the entire pack. If even greater numbers lie ahead, the five of us will do little more than whet their appetite.

And yet, something tells me we're not taking this trip merely to end up in a wolf's belly. Everything about these creatures is unaccountable, and their reason for shepherding us across the mountains must be no less so.

At long last, when I feel on the verge of dropping at the wolves' feet and begging them to act their species and finish the job, we top a steep rise and look out over a vast glacial plain. Squinting against the snowpack, I make out a sheer cliff face glowering across the white expanse, and I realize that's where the wolves intend to lead us. For the first time since we started this journey, the leader vocalizes again, emitting a succession of barks and yips that sound as if it's excited, like a weary traveler within sight of home. The other wolves respond in kind, setting off such a racket I have to hold my half-frozen hands over my ears. If the beasts bounded before, they positively dance across the snow plain now, making great leaps and sudden stops, twirling in the snow, tangling with each other and carelessly nipping their fellows' flanks and necks. The only wolves that don't join in the general melee are the four guards, which stare at us with yellow eyes and nudge the backs of our knees with their noses. When we step onto the hard crust of snow, they trot directly behind us, as if they fear that in the open we might try our speed against theirs.

The walking is easier on the frozen plain, though we have to take care to avoid crevasses that appear unexpectedly as blue cracks of unknown depth against the white. I suspect—but I'm not brave enough to test my theory—that the wolves following on our heels would catch our cloaks if we should take a misstep. The unvarying brightness of the snow makes it hard for me to judge the distance to the cliff, but as we approach the soaring wall of stone, I perceive a darker vertical against the uniform gray. What at first appears no more than a scratch-mark gradually widens until I'm able to make out a defile that splits the cliff in two from base to sky. Though the pack ahead of us appears to be running at random, the alpha aims straight for this opening, and I'm certain that once it enters, the magnetic attraction of their leader will pull the others into line. Sure enough, the moment the alpha's form disappears into the defile, the rest of the wolves leave off their frolics and race to catch up, churning snow until they stream into the pass like a river of white froth following its appointed course.

My companions and I are last to enter, the guard-wolves showing no impatience to hurry us along. Inside the defile, my snow-blinded eyes can't make out the forms of the wolves ahead, but I can hear them, the echoes of their barks and growls seeming to multiply the already enormous pack tenfold. I crane my neck to search for daylight, but I catch only glimpses of sky against protruding rocks and the traces of vegetation—fear trees mostly—that cling to the sides of the ravine. This would be a perfect place for a chimaera attack: solitary hunters that nest on the highest crags, they'd find easy pickings in this narrow, inescapable gorge. Yet the wolves seem unperturbed, making enough noise to attract a flock of chimaerae, if chimaerae flocked. My sense of the peculiarity of this group deepens. Their numbers, their communication, their boldness are unlike anything I've seen. Anything, that is, that doesn't hunt with knife and fire and build villages of stone.

Light floods my eyes as we emerge from the tunnel. When I recover from the glare, I'm half-convinced I'm seeing things, for we've entered an enormous bowl of rock ringed by ledges that look as if they might have been carved by human hands. Terror wolves occupy these platforms in numbers that take my breath away. There must be thousands of them, ranging in age from the pups that wrestle with their litter-mates amidst piles of fear tree branches to the seniors, their pelts dulled to a mangy gray, that lounge unblinking on the lower levels. In this multitude, it takes me a long time to find the alpha, even longer to believe that such a congregation could be ruled by a single wolf. Finally, though, my eyes fall on the one whose face I recognize from the forest. It sits on its haunches directly across the bowl from where I stand, on a projecting ridge shaped uncannily like a throne. Even from this distance, its intelligent eyes probe mine, as if it's seeking, like me, to plumb the other's thoughts.

What are you? I ask it. *What have you become?*

As if in answer, it lifts its head and releases a howl

unlike any I've heard thus far: a long, ululating note, with an ever-changing pitch and timbre that should be far too complex for a wolf's teeth and tongue to produce. Gnoosebumps spread across my arms as I realize that it's actually *speaking*, or attempting to, mimicking sounds it's heard before, sounds it's been taught. They're not comprehensible to me through the thick layers of wolf-tongue, but there's no doubt it's trying to communicate, to make its mind known in an articulate way the Ecosystem has never attempted with me.

But it's not, after all, with me that it speaks. Another figure steps forward from the shadows at the rear of the throne-rock, taking its place at the alpha wolf's side. This figure is garbed in fur as white as the wolf's, but it stands facing me on two legs, not four.

"Sarah granddaughter of Seraphina," the figure says, and the voice is instantly recognizable, though its words seem inhuman after the wolf-talk. "Was the throne of the city not sufficient distraction for you, that you must harry me here?"

SHE THROWS BACK the fur-trimmed hood that shadows her face. Her almost-black skin leaps out against the white; her hair, all trace of silver gone, is black as well, tumbling down her shoulders in loose curls. Though she's so small the sitting wolf's head reaches the height of her chest, she commands my attention as she did the first time I met her in her candlelit throne room.

"Your Majesty," I say. "I wasn't expecting quite so elaborate a welcome."

Celestina's face clouds, and I have the feeling she's close to stamping her petite foot. When she speaks, though, her voice carries the calm, haughty cadence she perfected in her short time as queen.

"As you know, I have renounced the title of *Majesty*," she says. "I have found sanctuary among my consorts here, and when they told me of your coming, I was eager to receive you in a manner befitting the city's new queen."

She inclines her head slightly, and there's movement on the ledge behind her. Two wolves come forward from the shadows, tugging something with their teeth that resists mightily with each step. In the end, though, the captives are no match for the wolves, who drag the slick-worm-bundled forms of Leah and Lavinia to the front of the platform. My friend puts on a show of bravado, but Lavinia makes no effort to disguise her terror. The wrist that bore Celestina's bracelet is wrapped in a blood-soaked strip of fur, though thankfully, the wolves have merely gnawed her flesh rather than taking the whole hand off.

"I little thought this impudent fool would dare show her face here," Celestina says coldly, while Lavinia cringes beneath her stare. "Yet even she, I'm afraid, is not so foolish as you."

I say nothing. Even if she weren't surrounded by a numberless host of terror wolves, I'm determined not to rise to her bait.

"Did you honestly dream that you could enter my domain without attracting my notice?" Celestina goes on. "Did you imagine you could search for me using my own tool, and yet shield yourself from my eyes? I thought I had instructed you better than that, granddaughter of Seraphina. Or if not me, has the Ecosystem not taught you the folly of your ways? Has bitter experience not shown you that to wield power is to expose yourself to ruin, and that those alone who relinquish all claims are truly free?"

"You're the only one who sounds bitter," I say. "And it looks to me as if you're still throwing your power around pretty generously."

This time, she does stamp her foot. "Not so!" she says. "I have forged a compact with these beasts, it is true, but one that requires no service except that which they can easily render. I have released them from the queen's meddlesome demands, and in so doing, I have freed myself."

The alpha wolf looks up at these words as if it understands. Celestina reaches down to stroke its pelt, and I feel the spark that passes between them. When its gleaming eyes turn back to me, the mystery of this place troubles me no longer.

"So you've shared your power with the pack," I say. "You've given their leader the queen's power of command. In exchange for what? Free lodging in the mountains? Protection from pursuit?"

For once, Celestina is the one with nothing to say. I can tell she was enjoying her stratagem, and she's peeved that I've seen through it so quickly.

"You're playing with fire, Your Majesty," I tell her. "You think you've freed the wolves, but you've done just the opposite. You've remade them in your own image, and that's not going to end well."

She pouts, but finds her voice. "Better for them to live as we do than to live as slaves to a queen's arbitrary power."

"No!" I say, so loudly the wolves raise their heads in alarm. "You don't get it. You never got it. The queen's power gives her a *responsibility*: to care for her creatures, to heal them when they're suffering. Not to compel them, much less to twist them into reflections of her own mind. And certainly not to run away like a child because she's too scared to grant to others what she demands for herself."

Celestina's spitting mad now, but so am I. The reproving look Leah throws across the bowl says in so many words: *Do you really expect her to come back to the city if you keep insulting her?* I'm too angry to care, and if anyone thinks I'm going to abase myself before a spoiled brat like Celestina, they're barking up the wrong sickenmore.

"You know that there's another queen," I tell her. "A dark queen, given body by the spirit of Delilah. She's responsible for the black web, the corruption of the Ecosystem. My father lost his life in her lair, and brave citizens lost theirs when she attacked the city. If you'd stayed and helped us fight, it might have been different."

The proud chin drops. "I have heard rumors of this," she murmurs almost too softly for me to hear.

"Then *do* something about it," I say. "Stop hiding from who you are, and start serving your subjects as a queen ought."

Celestina turns from me, raising her hood to cover her face and hair. Her hand trails across the scruff of the alpha wolf, which looks up at her and whines in the first sign of frailty I've seen from the beast. The silver nail polish Celestina favored in the City of the Queens is gone, and her wrist is bare of the bracelets she wore during her short reign.

"Take your company with you," she says in a hollow voice. "And return to this place no more."

At the wave of her arm, the wolves nudge the skittish Lavinia and my fiery friend down the stone ramp that leads to the floor of the grotto. Celestina gathers her furs about her, and her white cloak winks out as she vanishes into the darkness behind the throne. Aurelia curses under her breath and spits on the ground after the Queen's departed figure. The rest of my companions beseech me with their eyes, but I have nothing more to say. I step away from the four guard wolves and nod at Leah, who takes Lavinia's hand and hurries across the bowl to join us. Together, we head for the exit.

"Wait!"

The voice echoes sharp and clear across the grotto. I turn to see a tall figure standing beside the alpha, her long red hair falling upon a fur-lined robe like the Queen's. I reach out across the gap and breathe with relief when I find that Angelica is unharmed.

"Is it true?" she calls out to me. "What you said about the city and … and about Gabriel?"

"I wouldn't have come all this way just to lie," I say.

"Celestina!" she speaks in an angry tone, and the Queen reappears as if she's been conjured from thin winter air. "You promised me," Angelica says. "You said the city would be safe."

Remarkably, Celestina has no retort. Even more remarkably, she shrinks away when the red-haired healer strides across the platform and grips her shoulders. With the long sleeves of her robe, I can't tell if Angelica wears one of the silver bracelets.

"I'm going back," she says tensely. "I never should have left in the first place."

"My dear," Celestina says, and I'm surprised to hear no trace of the condescension she normally lavishes on that term. "What hope can a mere healer offer against the dark queen of old?"

"They'll need all the healers they can get," Angelica answers. "And soldiers. Won't you?" she asks, turning her face toward me.

"We need everyone we can find," I say. "Everyone who's not afraid to die fighting for what they love."

Angelica's shoulders sag. Then she draws herself up to her full height, towering over the girlish figure of the Queen. Celestina tilts her head to look into Angelica's eyes, and the moment seems to freeze as solid as the icy landscape.

"My Queen," Angelica says in a soft voice. "Will you let me go?"

Celestina chews her lip, opens her mouth to answer, but she never makes a sound. A swift shadow passes over the grotto, and the wolves erupt in a chorus of frantic yips and howls. The alpha throws back its head and issues a fierce bark of command, but it's unable to restore order as the pack breaks in a hundred different directions at once.

I look up as the leaping shadow blocks the light of the sun.

THE CHIMAERA LANDS above the highest ledge of the bowl, its foot-long claws holding it to the nearly vertical rock face. A full-grown terror wolf yelps like a pup as the great beast scoops it up in its maw and downs its prey at a single gulp. With a roar, the chimaera launches itself into the air, sailing above the heads of the terrified pack.

Chimaerae can't actually fly, but their jumping ability is incredible. The monster lands on the opposite wall, where it repeats its performance with another wolf.

By this time, most of the wolves have deserted the ledges and tumbled to the floor of the grotto. The chimaera follows, pushing off the rock wall and landing with an earth-shaking thud among the squealing pack. With each clawed front foot, it lifts a wolf to its mouth and rears its head back, the wolves vanishing down its throat without a trace of blood. It shakes its shoulders and glares around the bowl of rock, green eyes glittering like a serpent's.

Everything in the Ecosystem has its place and its purpose, but the chimaera is hideous to my sight, an assemblage of claws and scales and fur so poorly matched each of its limbs might belong to a separate creature. Only when it's bounding after its prey does its body seem to fit together, becoming fluid and swift and almost beautiful.

And utterly deadly.

Two more wolves disappear down the beast's seemingly

bottomless gullet. The rest are streaming toward the only exit, thousands of white-furred predators turned into a tide of field rats in their desperation to escape. The alpha is impossible to pick out in the flood of snowy pelts, but even if it were issuing commands at the top of its lungs, its followers would be too terror-stricken to heed its voice. The first of the pack are about to throw themselves into the defile that leads to safety when another shadow falls from the sky and lands as a solid form in front of the exit, blocking the wolves' path.

"Impossible," I breathe.

The second chimaera's roar sends the wolves scurrying back into the grotto. There, panic makes them wild, and they attempt a charge at the first monster, seeking to overwhelm it with their numbers. It snaps at the closest wolves then springs free, its mighty leap carrying it above the wolves to the now empty throne-rock. From that pinnacle, it bellows what I think is a challenge until I see the dark shapes that rise above the rock wall in answer.

It's a pack of chimaerae—two, five, ten, twenty—each of them scaling the wall at a different point until the entire bowl is ringed with monsters hanging from the rock like obscene bats. Though the pattern of the creatures' bodies is roughly the same, with an oversize head and front shoulders, nearly skeletal midsection, and powerful haunches, each misbegotten beast is shaped differently enough that it might be an original creation, an offspring without sires. In the chimaera pack, the mutagenic spree that gave birth to the Ecosystem reaches its logical culmination, with each chimaera practically a species unto itself.

143

But that's why there *are* no chimaera packs. Why there never have been. Not, that is, until now.

The apparent alpha of this pack—the one that attacked first—emits a roar as mangled as everything else about it, filling the air with the calls of fifty different creatures at once. The other beasts respond by leaping to the floor of the canyon, no two chimaerae landing in the same spot. Though I can't track all their movements from my position at the center of the milling terror wolves, my connection to the Ecosystem tells me what shouldn't be: it's a coordinated attack, more perfect by far than the maneuvers of the true pack hunters who've become the chimaerae's prey. The monsters have divided the bowl into quadrants, each quadrant further subdivided into a five-pointed configuration with a chimaera at each point. There's no chance for the wolves to escape: though they're thousands against twenty, they'll be torn or swallowed by the marauders, down to the last wolf.

And to the last of us, too.

"Celestina!" I cry out, though I can't see the former queen amidst the melee of wolves. "How could you share your power with *them*?"

I hear nothing through the babble of wolf and chimaera snarls, until a faint voice floats above the din. "This was none of my doing! My allies should have been strong enough to—"

A thunderous roar drowns out her protest as the chimaerae launch their attack.

Wolves scatter to escape the monsters' claws, but not before many white shapes are sent flying into the air to land with snapped backs and bloodied pelts. Others flow over their attackers in numbers so great the chimaerae are transformed into balls of roiling white fur. Yet far from bringing the monsters down, the covering of wolves slowly thins as underlying claws and teeth rake and devour them. Some wolves try to dart past the sole chimaera that guards the exit, but it's as if they're galloping directly down the creature's throat as it shovels them into its jaws. The alpha is the only chimaera not to join the assault; it roosts comfortably on its stolen throne, green eyes alertly flicking across the battlefield. I try to read its mind, but fail. Still I know that it's giving orders to its legions on the ground, directing them to close in on the dwindling pack and the puny cluster of humans at its core.

"Gideon!" I call out to the old firestarter, who's close at hand, fending off cowering wolves with his staff. "Light your staff on fire! The sharp end! Quickly!"

The old man doesn't waste time debating, but instantly reaches for his flints. With the enclosed grotto cutting off the wind, it's a mere moment before the top of his staff bursts into flame, and he hands it to me. I close my eyes and send out a single word of command.

Come!

Then I can do nothing but wait as the chimaerae force the wolves toward us in an ever-shrinking noose. The first thought I've picked up from the monsters' leader enters my mind, an anticipatory gurgle at the prospect of tasting softer meat than wolf-flesh.

"Sarah!" Leah cries, and I follow her pointing finger to the top of the bowl.

The dark shape that rises behind the chimaera leader and drops to the canyon floor isn't a new member of its pack. It's a bird with solid black body and flashing white head, one of the few winged creatures that inhabit the mountain heights. When I called out to it, I had little hope it would respond any better than the other beings in these parts. Luckily for me, its roost is so high, at the very peak of the rocky crags, its mind seems to rise above the spell that Celestina has unwittingly cast over the far northern regions. It lands beside me, its keen golden eyes and hooked beak giving it an expression of steely calm that's exactly what I need amidst the chaos that surrounds me.

I have come, My Queen, it says, or that's what I hear. Then it spreads its wings and, with me gripping its talons in one hand, takes flight.

The bald evil isn't strong enough to carry me far, which makes it fortunate that my flight is so short. It drops me on the ledge beside the chimaera leader's throne, and as the beast turns its attention to the newest morsel that's landed near its jaws, the bird dives at the monster's face, battering it with powerful wings. The chimaera thunders its rage, opening its mouth wide enough to swallow five terror wolves at once. That's when I grip the burning staff like a spear and drive it through the roof of the monster's maw.

The chimaera shrieks, an unearthly sound like a multitude of throats wailing in torment. The fire of the still-burning stake dances before its eyes, which burn with a green flame of their own. In its terror at the fire, the creature rakes its own face with claws able to sink into solid rock. Failing to dislodge the torch that way, it leaps blindly from the ledge, but succeeds only in smashing its head against the far side of the bowl. It falls awkwardly to the ground, where a troop of wolves swarms over it, unfazed by the fire and determined to even the odds. The alpha wolf, I see from its larger-than-normal size and intelligent face, is the one that leads the charge. It's helped by the bald evil, which streaks toward the downed chimaera and uses its beak to tear the monster's eyes from its head, whereupon the beast's forked tongue lolls from its mouth and its body lies still.

The other chimaerae pause for a moment, rocking back and forth on their front legs like ghastly bears in doubt whether to charge or retreat. Then, leaderless, they revert to form, some of them flinging themselves up the steep rock walls to escape the pack hunters, others swiping randomly and ineffectually at the smaller creatures that bedevil them. The alpha wolf stands astride the body of the dead chimaera, howling instructions to its pack, and the remaining wolves assemble themselves into strike teams, which circle the bewildered monsters and attack from all sides. Wolves fall dead before chimaerae claws, but now that the pack's tactical advantage has been restored, chimaerae succumb too. Soon there are only three of the monsters left, two of which are struggling to scale the walls to free themselves from the maddened wolves.

I signal to my courier, and as it flashes beneath me, I leap to catch its talons and ride its dive to the canyon floor.

Aurelia meets me when I alight. Her blade steams in the cold with the greenish blood of the chimaerae she's slain. Michael and Luke stand nearby, scratch-marks on their arms from wolves that tried to scramble over them in the mad rush for the exit, but with no more serious wounds. Gideon approaches me, hefting a burning fear tree branch with which he protected Lavinia. I hunt for Leah, and find her just as she pulls the gore-covered staff from the chimaera leader's muzzle. Her eyes burn as brightly as the staff did, but she shoots me a grin when she sees me looking.

"My Queen," Aurelia says. "Now is the time to flee this place."

"The bird can't carry us all," I say. "And the exit's still guarded."

It's true. The second chimaera to appear is the only one left in the bowl, and though it's no longer commanded by the leader, its instinct is to fight to the death now that it stands alone. It crouches with its huge, misshapen body backed against the tunnel mouth, great numbers of wolves lying bloody and motionless at its feet. I search for my bald evil, but find that it's consulted its own interest after the chimaera leader's death, and now appears as a tiny black speck against the whitened sky.

"Stay close to me," I say to the others. "We'll take it together."

I've no sooner given the order than a flash of red appears from nowhere, snatching the sharpened staff from Leah's hands. So armed, Angelica advances on the lone chimaera, which narrows its eyes and raises the bristles on its back. Faced with this single assailant, the monster seems not only relieved but delighted, as it opens its mouth in a near-smile to drip burning venom on the snow.

"Angelica!" I call. "Get out of there!"

"Be ready to take the others!" she shouts back, her eyes never leaving the beast that blocks her way. "And the Queen!"

"Angelica!" another voice shouts, and I see it's Celestina, who's come up behind us. Her eyes widen as the red-haired healer takes a long stride toward the beast, swinging the spear like a club. The chimaera shies, then rears on its hind legs to bat at the dancing tip. Angelica feints again with her weapon, but her foot slips on a patch of ice, and she falls with the spear trapped beneath her.

Before I realize what she's doing, Celestina has left my side and flown to Angelica's. The chimaera instantly lunges at this smaller prey, its claws outstretched and its mouth gaping to swallow the girlish figure. I send out a desperate command, but the beast brushes it aside as it descends on its victim.

At the last moment, Angelica throws herself in front of the Queen, and the chimaera's claws tear through her chest, emerging from her back covered in blood.

"Angel!" Celestina screams, with an anguish in her voice I never thought I'd hear.

The chimaera savagely yanks its claws from Angelica's body, dropping her to the ground. Before it can reach for Celestina, she seizes the spear from Angelica's limp hand and drives it through the monster's eye, and with a high-pitched shriek nothing like a chimaera's roar, it slumps to the reddened snow.

We rush to Angelica's side. The Queen is kneeling in her blood, which pours from four terrible wounds that penetrate her from front to back. Angelica's face has gone as white as the snow, and when I touch her cheek, it's just as cold. I twist her long red hair around my fingers, pull her robe down over her shoulders to reveal the full extent of the damage. As I do, my eyes fall on a mark above her shoulder blade, just where her freckled skin slopes upward to her graceful neck.

A silver bloom, inked with such skill the red drops of her blood seem to glisten on the petals like dew.

CELESTINA SOBS INTO her hands, which are drenched in Angelica's blood.

"My love," she wails. "My love!"

Angelica makes no response. Her breath is a whisper, her pulse almost gone.

"Save her!" Celestina implores me, clutching my cloak with bloody hands. Her eyes are red from crying; seeing them this close, I'm struck that the silver sheen they used to possess has vanished, leaving them flat and gray. "Heal her! I know you know how. I taught you myself."

My hands tremble as they flutter over Angelica's body. I healed countless people in the tunnel, some of them almost as gravely wounded as the girl who lies before me. I expelled the dark queen's power from the body of my best friend without even knowing she was nearby. Why, then, do I find this single life beyond my reach? I'm like a novice again, fumbling and tangling the threads I seek to mend. With every second I fail, more of her blood spills onto the snowy ground, fanning around her in the same bright red color as her hair.

It's useless. I can do nothing. I feel the power within me, know it's as strong as ever, but it can't touch this newest victim.

"A willing sacrifice," I say to myself. Then, to Celestina:

"Your Majesty. You have to heal her. You're the only one who can do it."

"I cannot!" Celestina cries. "I have renounced my power. Oh, my Angel! I have killed you!"

She lowers her head, kisses Angelica's frosty lips. But though she tries to breathe warmth into the ravaged body, there's too little left to respond to her urgent pleas.

Something nudges past me, a soft, wet shape. I look down to see the alpha wolf press its nose against Angelica's motionless side. It glances up at the sobbing Queen, its eyes gleaming with what I might almost believe are tears. Then it nuzzles under Celestina's arm, and at first she pulls away, her cries intensifying. But the wolf persists, and at last, she removes her hands from her face to study the creature.

Their eyes lock, the ice-blue eyes of the wolf and the gray eyes of the Queen. I feel the understanding that passes between them. The wolf bows its head and lets Celestina take its face gently in her blood-stained hands. Their eyes close, and their breath steams in the frigid air. When the wolf lifts its head and opens its eyes, I see that the spark of humanity has left them. The creature stands, shakes its pelt, and trots off to join its pack as they race through the tunnel into the snow-covered range.

Celestina opens her eyes next, and they flash with the silver luminescence I remember so well. Her tears have dried on her bloodied cheeks. Laying her fingers lightly on the silverbloom tattoo at Angelica's shoulder, she speaks in a tender whisper.

"Come to me, my love," she says. "It is not your

time yet. Come to me now, that I may take you in my arms again."

I hold my breath, waiting, barely daring to hope. Time lengthens and freezes in the way I've known it to do when a queen bids the Ecosystem to answer her call. It seems as if the whole world is locked in a single snow crystal, slowly spinning through space.

Then, all at once, Angelica stirs, a vaporous breath trailing from her mouth. Color blooms in her cheeks, spreads down her neck until it's not only her blood that stands out brightly against the snow. Her eyes open, green as a meadow. The Queen's tears are no more joyous than mine as Angelica's lips shape themselves into a broad, dazzling smile.

WE TRUDGE ACROSS the snow fields, Angelica reclining on the sledge Gideon constructed from the remains of the wolf pups' nest. Her cheeks, peeking out from the extra slickworm cloaks we've piled around her, are rosy with life and cold. Celestina walks beside the sledge, holding her hand. The Queen beams with light and brims with laughter such as I've never known from her.

She talks. The normally gossipy Angelica remains silent, a placid smile on her lips while Celestina gabs.

"We were playmates as children," she says. "In the early days, before I was cloistered by my mother to train as queen. From that point on, we saw each other seldom, but every chance I got, I would slip away to seek her out. My love, my life, my Angel."

She leans over to kiss Angelica, and I'm amazed that the once reserved Queen seems to keep no secrets anymore. I guess, now that the fell-cat's out of the bog, she sees no reason to pretend.

"In my thirteenth year, when my monthly time came, my mother explained to me the mysteries of childbirth," Celestina talks on. "She impressed upon me that, as queen, it would be my duty to take a lover to bed, and so perpetuate Delphina's line. I bridled against this fate, but what could I do? My mother grew weaker by the day, and the throne drew ever nearer: my promise, my prison."

"You're laying it on a bit thick, aren't you?" Angelica says with a smile.

Celestina playfully taps her cheek. "This was how I felt at that time," she says. "I saw the walls closing in upon me, with no means of escape. The boys my mother chose as likely mates for me found no favor in my sight. I could see only you, my love," she says softly, and this time, Angelica's emerald eyes grow misty.

"But the day came at last," Celestina continues. "My mother's health failed, and no miracle could restore her. On her deathbed, she made me swear a vow to carry on her name once she was gone. I was crowned the city's queen, and torn from my love forever. From that day forward, I could look on her no more, but must content myself with gazing at the silver blossoms that adorned my garden. Cold comfort they were to me, when my arms longed for her living touch."

"You might have told me that at the time," Angelica says, sounding as if they've had this argument many times since they came to the mountains. "Instead of leaving me with that stupid bracelet and making me think you'd forgotten me."

"Never could I forget," the Queen says. "But neither could I allow myself to remember. The charm-band was an invention of my grief, a thoughtless longing for what I could never have. And so I sought to harden my heart against you, rather than let it wither away for want of its one true desire."

Once again, she bends down to give Angelica a deep, lingering kiss. I turn away to let them have what little privacy the open sledge affords. My thoughts return to the cruel words I heard the two of them speak about each other in the days before they fled the city: Angelica's taunts and slurs, the Queen's disdain. I thought they hated each other's guts. I guess I have a lot to learn about love.

I look to the rear of our train, where Lavinia walks. The girl has her head turned to the side, either not hearing or ignoring the happy couple's now much softer words. My heart goes out to her. From the start, I thought it odd that one so lively as Angelica would court such a timid creature, but it dawns on me that the likely reason was Lavinia's chance resemblance to the true object of Angelica's affection.

And me? I remember Angelica's kiss in the library, only the second kiss I've had in my life. I remember the sadness that passed from her to me when our lips met, a sadness I attributed at the time to her breakup with Lavinia. But I also remember the bright blur I perceived in her thought, something she hid from me, something that hurt too much to show. Had I been able to make out its shape then, I know now that what I would have seen was the silver blossom she bore on her skin in memory of her beloved, the same flower that Celestina brought to life in her secret garden.

Having finished with their kiss—and having lavished a few extra, unnecessary minutes on tidying and plumping Angelica's blankets—the Queen resumes her narrative as if not a moment has passed.

"And so you see that I departed the city for love, not fear," she says. "In the wild, far from the haunts of men, I dreamed that I and my Angel might live out our lives as we pleased, not as it pleased others to have them lived. I had felt a slave all my days—a slave to habit, to fashion, to law—and I longed to be free to love at last."

"That's all well and good," I say. "But there's more to life than love. There's caring for others. Doing what's right. Sacrifice, no matter how much it hurts."

She studies me silently, her head cocked to the side. I can't tell whether she's abashed or amused. Then she lets go of Angelica's hand and places her palm against my cheek, and her warmth floods me like a ray of the sun falling on chilled stone.

"I am sorry, my dear," she says solemnly. "For the wrongs I have done you, as well as the wrongs done to you that were none of my making. It is my wish that you live to know such love as I have known, such love as you will suffer anything not to lose."

I turn away, while my heart twists at the thought of the boy I left behind in the city. The boy I would love, if he didn't love another. The boy whose heart I may still need to break, and whose beloved I may still need to slay.

But I say none of this to Celestina, nor to any other. I watch Leah walking with her head held high and a forced smile on her wind-burned cheeks, though pain radiates from her at the uncertain fate of her own true love. And I listen to the murmured endearments the Queen pours into Angelica's ear, her words too soft and the wind too strong for me to make out anything more than the impassioned throb of her voice.

NEVER HAVING CLIMBED up a mountain before, there's no way I could have known it would take even longer to climb back down. Some of that has to do with Angelica—she swears she's strong enough to walk, but Celestina won't hear of it—but most of it has to do with sheer exhaustion, hunger, and cold. While there's no shortage of snow to melt for drinking water, bald evils, I discover, regard themselves too highly to scavenge food for human beings. We have a bit to eat thanks to the roots and nuts Celestina stashed in the wolves' grotto, but Angelica needs those delicacies the most, leaving the rest of us to nibble the bitter herbs in Michael's pouch. By the time we reach our base camp in the foothills, we've all lost weight, and a full seven days have passed since we were last here.

Everyone collapses. That includes Aurelia and—I'd never have believed it if I didn't see it with my own eyes—Gideon. The old man has shown superhuman fortitude for as long as I've known him, and the mountains were no exception: he's the one who took extra turns hauling Angelica's sledge, gathering wood for the fire, shedding layers of slickworm clothing to keep our patient warm. Now he lies on his side, his beard thawed of mountain ice, his mouth gaping and his breath, I worry, carrying a bit of a liquid rattle. I check his health from where I sit, and there's no immediate cause for alarm, but I'm going to have to watch him. Which mostly means I'm going to have to be stricter with his regimen and not allow him to take on the burdens of two or three.

We spend the night huddled around the campfire, too tuckered to do anything more than stare vacantly into the flames before falling fast asleep. In the morning, I wake to the sound of metal clashing, which frightens me until I discover that Leah has risen early and talked Aurelia into giving her lessons in sword-fighting. From the warmth of my bed, I watch my friend's clumsy thrusts and parries, all the while trying to look as if I'm not watching. In an hour's time, Leah has thrown back her hood despite the chill and stands much less awkwardly, feet planted and blade singing as it slices the air. When the lesson's done and she bounces over to show me the short sword her instructor has given her, her face and eyes have recovered their usual shine.

"My old sewing mistress used to tell me that the pin is mightier than the sword," she says. "But I think I'll take the sword any day."

She slides the blade into its scabbard with a satisfying snap, then bustles off to help the others ready our camp for departure. For the first time, I wonder what Leah used to think of me before we became friends, when I was just the latest Sensor to join the mysterious clan of warriors from which the village commoners were barred.

While Gideon slumbers on—I admit I cast a small sleep spell on him to ensure he stays put—I welcome my flock of bloodbirds, who've been waiting in the foot-hills for our arrival. They bring food, but no news from Rebecca. I access their memories, only to find something that disturbs me deeply: though they made contact with her in the pain tree forest, she couldn't or wouldn't communicate with them. So many things have refused to speak to me on this trip, perhaps I shouldn't be surprised—but I never expected Rebecca to shut her mind to me. I deposit the details of our journey in the birds' brains and dispatch them ahead of us, but my urgency to return grows deeper than ever before.

Our warhog squadron shows up by midmorning, and, with Angelica cradled in a sling designed by the fully restored Gideon, we're off again. Despite my haste, we're forced to move more slowly than before, and it's another interminable trek before the beasts deliver us to the place where our journey began. Leah practices her new talent whenever we stop, the clash of her blade against Aurelia's forming the music to which I fall asleep each night. Meantime Celestina entertains her beloved with queenly tricks: coaxing flowers to change shapes and colors, orchestrating blurjays to sound out Angelica's name. I'm encouraged by the Queen's vivacity, even more so by the return of her powers. She's had a lifetime of training, as opposed to the mere week I spent under her tutelage. Together, perhaps we can defeat the darkness that covers the land to the south.

We roll into camp late on the eighth day since we left the mountains. At our arrival, a great cheer goes up from the multitude, who know nothing of Celestina's treachery and who welcome their departed queen back with a warmth that makes her eyes glow. If I'm at all resentful of the attention she receives, it's more than balanced by my relief at seeing everyone alive and undisturbed by Delilah's army. While Celestina and Angelica tell the tale of their elopement, greatly embellished for the ears of the simple folk who've never been permitted to peep into the private lives of the queens, I take my best friend and two chief deputies to stretch our stiff legs and search for Rebecca.

We find her alone on a hilltop, her hand resting against the same hexlox tree from which I tried to scout the city before we headed north. Standing by herself, with no adult nearby to shrink her to child-size, she strikes me as taller than she was three weeks ago, her legs as gangly as a killdeer's. She doesn't budge at the sound of our approach, and I can tell that she's Sensing, deep in her trance-state while she sends out fingers of will to the surrounding woods. When she turns to us at last, I'm struck by the gravity of her face. Then a smile restores her to girlhood, as do the skip and leap she takes into Gideon's arms.

He squeezes her in a hug that makes me wince in memory of the spinal injury she suffered only months ago. I let her smother the old man in kisses and listen to her enthuse over the berserkflower necklace he's braided for her before I pull her aside for a private conference.

"I was worried about you," I say. "You didn't answer my birds."

"I've been practicing new skills," she says by way of answer. "I haven't had time for anything else."

The mystery of her remoteness is cleared up, though it raises another mystery. "You've been Sensing all this time?"

"More or less...."

"For three solid weeks? Without taking a break?"

"Well," she says, "not the *whole* time. But most days and nights...."

"You haven't been sleeping?"

"Not much," she admits. "But come look."

Together, we climb the hexlox tree. For someone who's on minimal sleep, Rebecca moves with surprising focus. She points at the sky, where the clouds that poured cold rain on the city have given way to sunshine.

"It hasn't rained since the day you left," she says. "But there's a mist over the city, if you look close."

I squint, and I see what she means: a dark miasma that gathers in the open plain where the city must lie, too low to be clouds. "The Armegaddon?" I guess.

"I haven't seen it the whole time you were gone," she says. "Not even its fire. But there's more."

She waves her hands as if to gather the evening air, and my nose twitches when I pick up the scent of rot. I hesitate to tell her what it is she's smelling.

"It's not bodies," she says, as if she's read my mind. "Not from this far away. It's *that*," and she points at the mist again. "The queen is making changes to her web. Mutating it, or ... or something."

"But why?" I ask. "Why would she do that when she's got control of the city? Unless," the thought strikes me like a blow to the stomach, "she's planning an attack on the rest of the Ecosystem."

Rebecca considers this. "It could be," she says. "But it feels more like she's troubled, like there's something she wants in the city that she didn't get. I keep trying to figure out what it is, but...."

"It's hard to Sense behind her web," I say.

"I know that," she says crossly. "But after all I've learned...." She bites her lip, blows out a hard breath. "I keep thinking I'm going to be able to do it. And then, every time I feel like I'm getting close, I lose my way."

I study her face, the shadows of the hexlox leaves patterning a brow that's drawn tight in concentration. It's obvious to me that her power has blossomed in my absence, which must mean I was the one unconsciously holding her back. I wish I could shield her from the dangers that lie ahead. I so want her to be a child, if only for a while longer.

"I'm sorry, Rebecca," I say. "I know I've asked a lot from you."

"It's okay," she answers. "I'm not that little anymore. I'm eight now."

I look at her, horrified. "I missed your birthday?"

"We didn't really celebrate it," she says. "But I knew."

We climb down from the tree, where we're met by Gideon, Aurelia, Leah, and a newly arrived Celestina. Rebecca gawks at the Queen, which does nothing to shrink Celestina's already swollen ego. A less welcome addition to our party is the elderly housekeeper, who drags her body up the hillside several minutes behind the sovereign she used to serve. If I thought she'd be happy to have Celestina back to primp and preen, her perpetually grouchy face suggests otherwise. Without a word to any of us, she approaches Rebecca with a dark cloak in her outstretched hands.

"Mistress," she says reprovingly. "You'll catch a chill."

It's not chilly at all, but Rebecca doesn't object as the old woman bundles her in the wrap, nor when she grips the child's hand in her gnarled claw. Gideon looks on in puzzlement as Rebecca retreats down the hill with her escort, taking small steps to match the tottering housekeeper's pace. I hear Rebecca saying something in a hushed tone, her words broken from time to time by the woman's grunts, before both of their voices fade away. When they're gone, I glance at Gideon, who throws me a pleading look.

"Go," I tell him. "Make sure those two don't get into any trouble."

He skedaddles down the hill, acting more like a spurned playmate than a man of better than seventy years.

As the four of us walk back to camp, I repeat my conversation with Rebecca, which has made me even more anxious to discover what's happening in the city, not only with Delilah and her web but with the one I left behind. I say nothing about that last part, but Aurelia appraises me knowingly.

"You believe the girl, then?" she asks. "That the dark queen's designs have changed?"

"I believe we'll never know until we enter the city."

"And yet there is great risk in such a course," Aurelia persists. "We might consider sending scouts first, to determine—"

"No," I cut her off. "I'm not sending anyone else in there to face whatever Delilah's got waiting for them. We go ourselves, or no one goes at all."

Aurelia falls silent. What I don't tell her is that I'm as nervous about this journey as she is. I tremble when I recall the Armegaddon's flames wrapping around me, its body smashing the Cathedral like a child's house of sticks.

"We must think this through," Celestina muses, tapping her lip with a finger that still looks naked to me without its silver polish. "Have you consulted the Ecosystem on this matter?"

"I've pretty much given up on that," I say. "It wouldn't talk to Rebecca, and it won't talk to me."

"I will assume that has nothing to do with any ... inelegance on your part," Celestina says, smiling loftily. "And yet, might not its silence tell us more than words could say?"

The question takes me back to the first lesson I had with her, when I was a mere beginner every bit as much in awe of her appearance and abilities as Rebecca seems to be now. Just like then, I'm convinced she knows the answer. Only this time, under the probing power of her gaze, I think I know it, too.

"The Ecosystem can't tell us what the dark queen's up to for the same reason it can't reveal what happened eighty years ago," I say. "What became of Delilah, or why the Sensorship relinquished control of the village to the Wardens. The web blocks anyone or anything from the outside. Which also means...."

"That this is not the first time the dark queen's web has dwelt upon this earth," Celestina completes my thought. "That it was born in the days when the village was founded, and that it was involved in the very doom to which it now keeps us blind."

I stare into the Queen's calm eyes. The late-day sun should warm me, but I feel as cold as ever I did on the mountaintop. An image dances through my mind, an image of black hair waving as if with a life of its own: the dark queen's hair, or Miriam's following her return to the village. Somehow, in the days before her wedding, the strands of her hair developed the ability to detect the dead—or at least, the dying. Could that be the connection? Could something have happened to her that made her susceptible to the dark power that had lain in wait all along? I'm trying to trace this thought to its end when Celestina speaks.

"The answers to these questions might once have been sought in the village," she says. "There they lay, buried and forgotten, for eighty long years. But they reside in the village no longer. You are right, Sarah granddaughter of Seraphina," she shocks me by adding. "We must enter the City of the Queens at morning's first light, and there learn the truth."

THE MORNING'S FIRST light isn't much to speak of, the clouds returning to blanket the sky as we start our march to the city. If I were to allow myself to be credulous, I'd swear that's a sign that Delilah knows I'm back.

We walk beneath dripping branches, the foul smell I detected the day before seeming to be drawn out by the rain. Our company is small: me, Leah, Aurelia, Gideon, Celestina, and Angelica, and her only because neither she nor the Queen could bear to let the other out of her sight. Luke and Michael begged to join us, but I ordered them to remain behind to help Rebecca defend the camp. I know that's a futile gesture if our mission fails, but it would be equally futile to send troops against the dark queen. Our force is meant to slip into the city unnoticed, not to battle an army or an armored monster.

We've walked for much of the morning, taking frequent breaks for Angelica to rest and Celestina to fuss over her—which, truth be told, Angelica doesn't seem to mind one bit—when Aurelia holds up a hand to stop us. I've been scanning the forest the entire time, as has Celestina when she's not preoccupied with her duties as caretaker, and neither of us has felt anything amiss. But with Rebecca's strange, fractured tale fresh in my mind, I'm brought instantly alert when the captain of the guard gestures for us to gather around her.

"See," she says simply.

I do, but just barely. Threaded among the moss and leaf litter are delicate fibers of the dark queen's web, looking more like individual hairs shed by some forest creature than the monstrous parasite that smothered the western forest just weeks ago. When I close my eyes and send my power rippling toward the organism, I feel something I don't expect: it's not taking root, not growing at all. Rather, it appears to be shrinking, as if these few particles are all that remain of what was once a more robust growth. Hesitantly, I reach out to touch one of the strands, but no sooner does my finger make contact with it than it crumbles to dust, sending up a fine spray that stinks briefly before the wind blows it away.

Celestina bends by my side. "What do you make of this?" she asks.

"I don't know," I say. "But stay on guard."

"Indeed," she says, drawing herself erect with a regal air. "I would not have thought to exercise sound judgment, if not for my liege's direction."

I glare at her retreating back, as does Aurelia. The captain of the guard has accepted Celestina into our company, but only as a necessary evil. I don't think she'll ever forgive the former queen for abandoning the city.

We press on. In no time, we find a patch of ground sprinkled with something that looks like dark green moss from a distance. On closer inspection, we discern the presence of the web once more: black tendrils glistening with droplets of rain and emitting the rotten stench I remember from my nearly fatal encounter with the mature parasite in Dinah's bedroom. And yet, unlike that time, these tendrils don't move, and when I nudge them with a toe, they break into pieces, leaving only the fine sprinkling of threadlike fibers we saw before.

"What in the...?" Leah mutters, looking at me for explanation.

I have none to give. "Maybe this is part of its life cycle, and it's reseeding itself to grow again. Or maybe it needs more rain than it's getting, or more...."

"More what?" Angelica asks.

"Bodies," I say. "We've seen how it takes root in human flesh—the villagers', and especially Miriam's. With what happened to the city, maybe there's nothing left for it to ... to feed on."

The instant I say that, I wish I hadn't. Leah turns away, though not before I see the look of nausea on her face. Even Celestina seems unable to offer a retort. I might not be much of a queen, but I guess I still have my way with people.

And so it goes, Delilah's black vines appearing in scattered patches as we press closer to the secret entrance I'm hoping remains clear of infestation. The rotten smell intensifies with each league we cover, and I begin to feel as if the air itself might be laden with the mist I glimpsed last evening. As a precaution, I order everyone to cover their faces with leftover pieces of slickworm weave. Celestina eyes me with arched brows, and I suspect she's not the only one who doubts how effective a strip of cloth will be in preventing the parasite from taking root inside our bodies.

"My Queen," Aurelia says, and both Celestina and I turn our heads. "The entrance approaches."

"I know," I mutter irritably, though the truth is, I'm

too distracted by my own thoughts to notice the tingle in my skin that tells me we've arrived.

We step through the last of the trees to find the hidden entrance to the queen's garden swathed in black vines, but not entirely blocked by them. Something about the lazy way the strands hang from the arched opening draws my attention, and I reach out a hand before Leah or Aurelia can issue a warning.

My fingers close on one of the vines. It feels chalky and limp, not at all like the coiled, fibrous tissue I've felt before. I break off a handful and pulverize it into ashy dust in my fist, then, against my better judgment, bring it close to my face and inhale the scent of rot, so strong it nearly makes me gag. I brush my hand clean and watch the residue sift to the ground. I'm about to enter the tunnel when Aurelia holds out an arm, her blade gripped tightly in her fist.

"Are you certain this is not a trap?" she asks.

"I'm not certain about anything," I say. "But there's only one way to find out."

"That seems poor strategy," she mutters.

"I heard that," I say, before ducking beneath the vines and setting foot inside the tunnel.

I can't see much in the semidarkness until Gideon lights one of his ever-present torches, and the walls spring into view. I'm unsurprised to find the queen's web hanging from the low ceiling and crawling down the walls to the dirt floor. Yet like the strands that drape the entryway, these interior ones are motionless, seemingly dormant; they don't shrink from Gideon's torch, though I know from past experience that fire can destroy them. Rebecca's words from last night echo in my ears, and I wonder if the dark queen's intent is to lure us into her citadel, where her latest experiment with her web lies. For a moment I'm torn, itching to discover what awaits us but dreading it all the same.

I can't risk it. Not for me, less so for the others—especially the weakened Angelica and my steadfast friend, whose drawn blade will avail little against the queen's power. There's risk in my next course of action too: if Delilah hasn't detected us yet, what I'm about to do will announce our presence as clearly as if I hitched another gryphon ride into the city. But I see no alternative.

I close my eyes and reach out to the Ecosystem, the part of it that lies deep enough beneath the dark queen's city to heed my voice. Behind me, I feel Celestina gazing on in wonder; she's seen me fight chimaerae, but she never guessed I can command a creature even she had no luck mastering. I permit myself a small smile of satisfaction before turning to the object of my quest.

Once more, I call for you, I say. *Once more, I have need of your strength.*

I feel the vibrations in the ground immediately. They're coming from deep down, as deep as this creature can burrow to hide itself from the dark queen's mind. As it draws closer, my companions feel the tremors too, and Aurelia shouts in alarm, perhaps thinking it's the awakening of the Armegaddon that shakes the ground beneath our feet. The black web responds at last, but it's torpid and frail, turning to powder as it tries to pull itself loose from the walls. The air fills with ashy residue, so much that our masks can't prevent us from breathing it in. I have no doubt the dark queen, fingering the strands of her dying web as she sits on her throne of skulls, knows what beast I call to my aid. But there's nothing to be done about that, and so I call out again, in words meant for her ears alone.

You want me, Delilah? You'll have to catch me first.

The wyrm's head explodes through the tunnel floor, pulverizing the strands that were too confused or sluggish to attempt a retreat. I reach out to pluck clods of desiccated web from the creature's teeth, then pat its slimy flank. Wyrm-thoughts roll from the bundle of nerves that substitutes for its brain: apologies for its failure during the battle, joy that I've returned, promises that it won't desert me again. And something else: an excitement I've never felt in a wyrm's slow, steady mental processes, which have to travel the entire thirty-foot length of its body to take shape. It's itching to show me something, but it's being uncharacteristically coy about it. It wants this to be a surprise.

I give the wyrm one more pat then turn to my companions. "Saddle up," I say. "There's plenty of room."

They edge close to me, warier of the wyrm than of the feebly twitching remains of the web. Gideon is the first to lay a hand on the straps that circle the beast: master of saddle design himself, he must be comforted to see that this mighty creature is willing to bear human riders. Of all my companions, it's Celestina who seems most hesitant to approach the wyrm, as if she fears it might seek revenge for what she and her mother did to its fellows. Angelica, by contrast, clambers into the saddle without assistance, her eyes shining in the darkness. She's joined by Leah, who hops nimbly aboard for the second wyrm-ride of her life. I hope this one ends a lot better than the first.

Once everyone's secured, I take my position at the front of the many-seated saddle, just behind the wyrm's snout. At the touch of my hand, the creature shoots from the tunnel into the forest, then reverses itself to rocket down the underground passage it just dug. Gideon's torch is extinguished by the wyrm's speed, and we're plunged into the dark.

Celestina's scream accompanies Angelica's, though the latter's is a scream of excitement, not terror. The wyrm doesn't slow as it reaches the bottom of its tunnel and levels off to trace a path deep beneath the secret exit; if anything, its speed increases now that there's less risk of its passengers falling off. Though I can see nothing, I take comfort in the fact that, this deep down, all I can smell is clean, rich soil, not the horrid stench of the dark queen's web. My power tells me what my eyes can't: the wyrm's tunnel is empty of the black vines, which makes me question again what happened to Delilah's wyrm-army. In the village, the burrowing creatures dug a maze of underground corridors through which her web was free to flow, yet here, it seems as if the web has been confined to the surface. I wonder if that's why our wyrm is so excited, if it's merely thankful not to have to defend its home against Delilah's minions.

We must have reached a point beneath Celestina's garden—one level deeper than the corridor where I healed the survivors of the dark queen's war—when the wyrm slows and comes to a rocking halt. We dismount, Celestina needing Angelica's support for a change. Though the place we've stopped is dark, I see light up ahead, the warm glow of fire spilling from a side tunnel. With the wyrm slithering beside us, we approach the source of the light and peer through the opening, only to draw a collective breath in shock.

There are people down here, at least thirty of them crammed into a cavern no larger than my bedroom in the Cathedral. Where they came from I can't imagine, until I realize they're survivors of the late war, residents of the city who neither died during the Armegaddon attack nor found their way to the cavern beneath the queen's garden to evacuate with the rest of us. A few are former villagers who've outlasted everything the Ecosystem and then the dark queen could throw at them: the destruction of their home, the ambush by the poison arrow frogs, the assault by Delilah's forces. Several others wear the uniform of the city guard, and one—a teenage girl I've heard Michael address by the name of Flora—is an apprentice member of the healer corps. Their faces are filthy, their clothes tattered almost beyond the bounds of modesty; they're bruised and bandaged, several walking with the help of crutches and two unable to walk at all. But they're here, undefeated, alive. Somehow, they rose from the wreckage of the city and found a hiding place right beneath the dark queen's nose.

If my wyrm had vocal cords, it would be purring with delight. I pat its flank and assure it that this is, indeed, the best surprise it could have showed me.

But it hasn't showed me all. There's a stirring at the back of the cavern, and a voice is raised in a whoop of delight. One figure detaches itself from the crowd and limps forward until he's standing right before me. His face and hair are smudged like the rest—by a coating of mud that must have been slathered on by hand, I see now that he's close—and his beard has grown much fuller in the days since I last saw him. But his grin breaks through all the layers of disguise at the sight of me.

"Couldn't stay away, could you?" Isaac says with a laugh. "Welcome to the underground, Queen Sarah."

BOOK THREE
SEARED

The earth is a fine cradle. We are
all bound to sleep there.

—Michael Perry,
"The Big Nap" (2005)

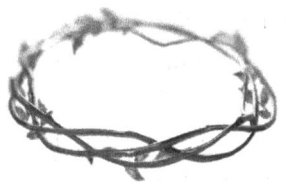

I DON'T KNOW whether to be elated or furious. Being me, I settle for furious.

"You could have been killed!" I yell at Isaac in a manner most unseemly for a queen returning to liberate her conquered city. "And you didn't even have the decency to tell me where you'd gone!"

He grins sheepishly. "I'm pretty hard to kill. As you've probably noticed."

"That's not the point!" I rage. "I ordered everyone to retreat. Do you think you're some kind of exception?"

"I think it's time you stopped trying to save me from myself," he says. "Weren't the mangraves and the urth-wyrms enough for you?"

I can't believe he'd joke at a time like this. I wish I could wipe the smirk off his mud-covered face, but I'm afraid of what my hands might do if I tried.

"Anyway, I'm here now," he says. "And I've been scouting what's left of the city for the past three weeks without so much as a thank you, so the least you can do is listen to what I've found out."

"I don't see why I should thank—"

"Patience, My Queen," Aurelia cuts me off. "There will be time to punish the transgressor later."

Is it just my imagination, or is she making fun of me?

Judging from everyone else's smiles, including Leah's and Celestina's, they're in on the joke, too.

I rein in my temper while Isaac gestures for us to sit. We do, but he leans against the wall, his leg too stiff for him to find a comfortable position on the ground. A few of his companions, including Flora and a teen from the village named Jacob, drift over to join us, so I'm forced to make introductions of Celestina and the rest. Angelica seems bemused to meet Isaac at last, after all she's heard about him. She must wonder how this muddy raga-muffin could have been built up into the prince of my lovelorn tales.

But the more he talks, the more she leans forward to listen. The others are equally attentive. I seem to be the only one incapable of appreciating the wonders he describes.

"I've been pretty much everywhere in the city since you left," Isaac begins. "It's dangerous out there, of course, but if you know what you're doing, you can get by. Especially at night. So far, I've scoured the ruins of the Cathedral, the library, the public grounds, the queen's compound...."

"The brood chamber?" I ask.

"How in the Ecosystem would I get in there?"

"Never mind."

He shoots me a strange look. Beneath all the mud, his features are animated as they haven't been for months, and his eyes glow. "Anyway, the queen's compound is pretty much the only thing still standing. The residence, the council chamber. I haven't been able to get into her throne room or garden, but I'm working on it."

"Why would you want to do that?" I demand, anger rising again.

"The obvious reason," he answers. "Inside information."

I glare at him, but he seems unfazed as he continues.

"The queen's forces are spread out over the city, but they're a pretty pathetic army of occupation, if that's what they're supposed to be," he says. "Most of the animals are gone, the cats and things. Just about the only soldiers she has left are the people she took captive in the village, all of them walking around with empty eyes and halters around their necks. Some of them might not even be alive anymore." His face falls, and he adds: "Like Daniel. He's on his feet, but his body's breaking down. I actually think he's been dead since the attack in the gathering hall."

I know how much Daniel meant to him, but I doubt he'd find much comfort in my condolences. Leah jumps in before I can offer any. "What about Beulah?" she asks.

"She's not out in the streets like the others," Isaac answers. "The queen seems to keep her close by."

I picture Beulah as I saw her last, immobilized on the lawn by grabgrass, the dark queen's leash around her neck. If what Isaac says is true, the queen must still have some use for her, if only as bait. I touch my friend's hand, but my attempt at calming her does nothing to soften the fire in her eyes.

"Anyway," Isaac says after a pause. "The point is, it's pretty much a dead zone out there, which has made it easier for me to dig through the rubble and find survivors. Sometimes I take Flora with me, to set broken bones and stuff. The queen's slaves don't seem interested in the living, if they're aware of us at all."

"What happened to the rest of her army?" I ask.

He shrugs. "Hard to say. The thing with all the heads is

too huge to hide, but I haven't seen it for weeks. It used to circle over the city, then one day it was just gone. Some of the other monsters I've found dead. Or, in a few cases, I'm the one who made them dead. The black weed burns fast, though the stench it sends up is enough to choke a jackalass."

I bite my tongue on the obvious rejoinder. "So the creatures you've burned were infected by the black web?"

"Something like that," he says. "You're the expert around here. If I were guessing, I'd say there was nothing left of their bodies *but* the web, like it had eaten them away from the inside."

"And Miriam doesn't care that you've been going around burning her creatures?"

"*Miriam* isn't the one I've got a quarrel with," he says. "Only the dark queen."

"Isaac," I say, "You do realize that Miriam is like the others, don't you? If it's true that the web consumes its host—"

"Don't say it," he warns. "Don't you dare say it."

Silence reigns save for the crackling of the torches. The others shift in their seats, and Leah moves closer to me. Isaac holds my gaze for a long time before pressing a hand against his forehead.

"Just let me finish," he says. "The point is, the things she created are giving up the ghosthawk. The vine doesn't last forever. It grows like mad, but then it withers and flat-out dies, just melts into the ground or flakes off into the air like it wasn't there to begin with. I don't know about the forest, but here in the city, it's pretty much run its course."

"That could change," I say. "If she finds your hideout, she'll have a whole new crop of bodies to feed it with."

"She won't find us," Isaac says defiantly. "The mud throws her web off. It can't detect our body temperature or tell that we're living organisms or something. I've walked right past piles of the stuff on my search-and-rescue runs, and the vines haven't even bothered to raise their heads to see if I might be something good to eat."

Which is fortunate, I think, since he certainly wouldn't be able to outrun them. Even now, he's wobbling on his one good leg, his body emanating waves of fatigue so powerful they're close to overwhelming the feverish energy that's sustained him this long. If he keeps up this pace, he'll burn out like one of the dark queen's creatures.

"You've done an amazing service to the city," I say, while my mind screams at me: *patronizing shrew-cat!* "From now on, we don't go anywhere without mud or fire. Gideon, can you get some additional torches going?"

The old man leaps to his feet, but his movement seems to rouse Isaac from his semi-stupor. "I'm running this show," he says. "And I know how to make fire just fine."

"Nor do I intend to daub myself with … *mud,*" Celestina chimes in, her dainty nose wrinkling.

"The dark queen knows we've returned," I say to Isaac. "She might not be able to detect *your* people, but she'll trace *us* right to your doorstep. I'm sorry. We didn't mean to blow your cover, but we have no choice but to move out."

He opens his mouth to object, but the words never leave his throat. A booming noise much louder than that which my wyrm made shakes the cavern, throwing Isaac against the wall and causing chunks of dirt to shower from the ceiling. I reach out through the realms of the soil, fearing the Armegaddon has returned. To my even greater shock, I discover that what's headed our way is a fleet of seven urthwyrms, far fewer than prowled the caverns beneath the ruins of the village but enough to destroy every one of us like a pack of cornered molusks. They're moving slowly—for wyrms—as they chew through rock and dirt, but they'll be on us in minutes. We've even less time than I imagined. Isaac must believe me.

"We have to go *now*!" I shout at him. "Tell your people to leave everything and follow me if they want to live."

Isaac stares at me, dazed and disoriented. He's chosen the very worst moment to succumb to exhaustion. The other stowaways turn to him, but he's incapable of giving orders. I'm about to grab him with both hands and cart him from the room when Flora lifts her voice above the rumbling in the walls and floor.

"Listen to the Queen!" she says, and the others snap to attention, all but Isaac. She turns to me. "What of the injured? Some of their wounds are too grievous for my skill."

"I'll take care of that," I say, but I haven't begun when I feel Celestina's power flow outward in warm pulses to touch each member of Isaac's team. Crutches are thrown aside, bandages discarded; the non-walkers among the bunch stand on their own feet again. Celestina throws me a smug smile as we leave the cavern. Much as she didn't want to be queen, she's not about to let an upstart like me warhog all the glory.

Our wyrm leads us back to the main tunnel, then darts down a side alley and signals me to follow. The others charge after us, with Gideon and a few others holding torches aloft to light our way. To my utter surprise, Isaac runs along with the main body of fugitives, taking long, loping strides like his old self. When I look closely at him, I see that's he's no longer favoring his injured leg, no longer holding his left arm rigidly against his side. Celestina must have done something to mend the wounds I've been powerless to touch. Her ability to heal his suffering baffles me, but there's no time to dwell on it before the dark queen's wyrms arrive.

Now that it's free of the main thoroughfare, our wyrm pursues a course through tight tunnels that undulate up and down in the manner of its movements. No trouble whatsoever for the mighty creature that leads us, but the steepest of the trails forces us to slow down to help the newly healed. The wyrm's agitation increases with each delay. I touch its side and feel the source of its anxiety: though it tried to keep us as far as possible from pursuit, the enemy wyrms have taken a route perpendicular to ours, aiming to cut us off in mid-tunnel. Our wyrm lingers over a deep drop that would be perfect if there were fewer than twenty of us to pile aboard its back. I apologize to it for our human frailty, but I'm insistent: we can't go that way. It shakes its head back and forth indecisively before wheeling to try another road that seems clear of danger.

Yet somehow, its senses—and mine—are deceived. I feel the telltale rumbling in the tunnel the wyrm has chosen, and three heads burst through the wall in front of us, their necks extending across the open space like massive black bars. The floor quivers, and I realize that the other four wyrms have dived deep to hollow out the ground we stand on. My wyrm lunges forward to snap at the three that block our path, but I hold it back with a sharp command. Nothing can be accomplished that way but its death.

I'm gathering myself to attempt an attack on the

enemy wyrms when Isaac snatches a torch from Gideon and jumps forward, lifting the blazing brand like a club. Celestina takes her place by his side, her arms held high and her cry joining his. The next moment, a compact shape flies past me, and I'm left grasping at air.

"Leah!"

There's a flash of light that confuses my eyes amid the darkness and the bodies of wyrms and human beings alike. The tunnel shakes violently, and something shrieks in my ear, or possibly only in my mind.

When next I can make out the scene, I discover that the exposed necks of the three wyrms are burning fiercely, emitting thick black smoke that stinks of the dark queen's web. I can't understand why they don't pull their heads inside the earthen walls to snuff out the fire—until I realize that Celestina is holding them there, using the control her bloodline wields over these wyrms to overcome the dark queen's power. I reach out with my own strength to assist her, and together, we tighten the noose, the wyrms' unearthly wails rising to a pitch only the two of us can hear.

Leah and Isaac hack at the wyrms' bodies with their weapons, joined by Aurelia and Gideon and then by a flood of the cave-dwellers, who batter the creatures with rocks. Under the combined onslaught, the flesh of the enemy wyrms finally bursts, raining in fiery ashes to the tunnel floor. What little is left of them shudders, but they've lost the power to regenerate and will soon be absorbed by the soil.

The four wyrms beneath us have witnessed their brethren's end, and they seek to turn tail and flee back the way they came. Celestina and I hold them in defiance of the dark queen's will, while Gideon and Isaac attack the ground with the butt of their torches and Aurelia and Leah second them with their swords. It's not until our wyrm plunges its head beneath the tunnel floor and bites through each of its foes' throats that they stop squirming and lie motionless. When our wyrm erupts back into the tunnel, the trench it leaves shows us the remains of its adversaries, their heads raggedly separated from their bodies like eelfish on the cutting-block.

"The power of the dark queen fails!" Aurelia shouts. "We must destroy the beast that serves her!"

Judging from the cheer that goes up from Isaac's battalion, not to mention the fearsome expression on my best friend's face as she raises her sword above her head, I'd say all are in agreement.

I glance at the sooty ruins of the three wyrms we destroyed, then turn my attention to the four shriveled monstrosities that lie in the upturned dirt at our feet. They've been dead only minutes, yet they appear mummified, their skin gray and puckered, their many rows of sharp teeth hanging loose from sagging gums. I stomp on the closest one, but it's as if there's no substance to its body at all: my foot bursts through what should have been rubbery flesh, and the wyrm crumbles like ashes on a fire long dead. I rest a hand on Leah's arm, gently lowering her sword until it hangs at her side.

"There's no need to destroy the Armegaddon," I say. "These are its remains."

EVERYONE STARES AT the dead wyrms. It's hard to say whose mouths gape wider, the monsters' or my friends'.

"Impossible," Aurelia speaks for the group at last. "The fire-monster rivaled the size of the city itself."

"But it started out as a wyrm," I say. "Or a lot of wyrms, actually. Delilah must have planted the parasite in their bodies to create something that big. It fed off them and grew until it became the Armegaddon. But it's been dying like everything else. These seven were all that were left of it."

Aurelia's face remains unconvinced. "And its fiery breath?"

"Some spell of hers, maybe," I suggest. "I don't pretend to know her secrets. All I know is that the fire is the reason something that huge consumed itself so quickly. It was burning itself up with every breath it expelled."

"But *why*?" she asks. "Why take the city if she knew she would lose it?"

"Maybe she didn't know," I say. "Maybe she underestimated how much it would drain her power to create the Armegaddon. She gambled everything to win the war, and now she's holding onto the city by the skin of her teeth."

The captain of the guard kicks at the ashes that carpet the tunnel floor. It takes her a while to accept my conclusions, but when she does, she looks up with a fire of her own in her eyes.

"We must strike now!" she says. "Before she is able to replenish her power. We must make her pay for the lives she has taken."

I need no queenly power to know which of those lives weighs heaviest on her heart. Leah steps forward to stand beside the captain of the guard, her face spattered with sweat and ashes but her resolve glowing as brightly as her teacher's. I try a smile for both of them, though my own heart feels heavier than it ever has.

"There's one last thing that needs to be done," I say. "A queen's power lies in her brood chamber, and that's where Delilah will barricade herself now that she knows it's two against one. If we don't take the chamber back from her, there's always a chance she'll be able to regain her strength."

"Where is it?" Leah asks.

"Down here," I say. "The wyrm can take me there."

Aurelia's in the act of sheathing her sword, but she looks up at my words. "You go alone?"

"I have to," I say. "I'm the one who started this war—or my bloodline did, anyway. Celestina can lead you against the dark queen if I don't make it. Her and Isaac."

I turn my eyes to him, but he won't look at me. His thoughts are shrouded, as if the mud cloaks his mind as surely as it hides his face. Before I can say a word, he spins and stomps down the tunnel, and I have to run to catch up with him.

"Isaac!" I call out. "Wait!"

He doesn't. He's moving fast now that Celestina has healed him, and though his long legs are jerky from disuse, they're infused with purpose. I reach out to grip his arm, but he wheels to face me and catches my hand in his.

"I don't want to fight, Sarah," he says. "Not anymore."

"Isaac," I say, keeping my voice low. "You know she has to die."

"I…." His face struggles, and tears draw muddy trails down his cheeks. "I can save her," he says. "You just have to give me time."

"I have none to give."

"Please," he says. "Mimi's been with me since before I can remember. From the time I was little, when I thought about what my life would be, she was always a part of it. I can't give up on her. I'm the only one who knows her well enough to try to bring her back."

I gaze at his face. Muddy and tear-stained as it is, it's the face I've loved since I learned to love, the face that taught me what love is. And yet, as I look into his grieving eyes, I know at last why he can never be mine. I think I knew it all along. He'll risk everything for one last chance to see her, even if that means no more than dying in her arms.

"Okay," I say. "How much time do you need?"

His face relaxes. He even smiles, lifting a corner of his lip in the way that used to set my heart aflutter. "Not long. But you'll have to let your wyrm take me there."

"Of course," I say, and try a joke to ease the bitterness in my heart. "If you fall off, I'm going to call another cicatrix swarm to come and carry you back."

Miracle of miracles, he laughs. "Just as long as they don't try to peel off my scalp." Then he sobers, and his eyes hold mine. "Thank you. For understanding."

"No thanks are necessary," I say, and hate myself for how cold it sounds. But I do understand. I understand more than he knows.

This is what I gave up when I assumed Dominica's mantle. This is why she never married, never joined herself with another. Like the boy I love, she'd already pledged herself for life.

I signal to the wyrm, which comes slithering down the tunnel at my beckoning. Isaac places a hand lightly on its flank, his eyes growing wide as he feels the power pulsing beneath its skin. He seems reluctant to go, and I sense it's not only because of what lies ahead. "At least I'm saying goodbye this time," he says, smiling weakly.

My tears are on my lips, my tongue. I feel as if they'll never stop. My throat tightens as I ask him, "Will I see you again?"

"I hope so," he says. "When this—all of this—is over. But I don't know when that'll be."

"Maybe never," I whisper.

"Maybe not," he says.

I shouldn't do this, but I throw myself into his arms, feel them wrap around me with all his laborer's strength. At our touch, his whole life opens before me, and she's there in every memory, every dream. I pull away and give him one last smile.

"Goodbye, Isaac," I say through tears. I stand on tiptoes to kiss his forehead. "May the Ecosystem hold you in its arms always."

He touches my cheek and smiles. Without a word, he swings himself onto the wyrm's back. It shoots down the tunnel into darkness and is gone.

WITH THE WYRM'S departure, we're forced to make our way to the surface on our own. The creature's spoor lies heavy throughout the tunnels, so it's not hard to find the way forward. It's only hard not to look back.

The tunnels converge on the gulch my wyrm created the day of the battle. In the depths of this pit, Gideon's torches show us the remains of the creatures that were swallowed that day: snaky shadows that must have been the ambulatory parasites, along with the flattened carcasses of fell-cats, warhog hybrids, and spitting frogs. I'm no longer worried about breathing the miasma of the web, but Celestina holds a lacy handkerchief over her face to dispel the stink.

We pick our way to the surface, moving slowly to assist the less able members of our company. In this task, as always, Gideon does the pandalion's share. I'm encouraged to see Angelica negotiating the maze of stone with something close to her normal strength and agility. It's she who helps the less athletic Celestina over the rough spots, she who smiles indulgently at the former queen's gripes and exaggerated yelps. Watching this oddly matched couple in action, I can sense the love that passes between them, even if I can't grasp what attracted them to each other in the first place.

We emerge into a day darkened by clouds, though the

rain has died to a weepy drizzle. The shell of the Cathedral lies before us, and though I saw with my own eyes the monster that brought it down, it's hard to believe such a monument could ever have fallen. Pointlessly, I search the piles of stone and splintered wood for the arched window that belonged to my bedroom. Here in the city center, the decay of the dark queen's web is even more advanced than Isaac described: the rain, far from spawning more growth, has melted the strands into a black sludge, thick as mud and dripping from the stone. In the streets, rivulets ooze with bubbles that emit a noisome stench when they pop. Seeing all this death confirms my belief that Delilah exhausted her power on the fire-beast. Given enough time, I foresee the whole web dissolving into a river of darkness and washing away as if it had never been.

But I can't wait for that to happen. I've mentally allotted Isaac an hour to complete his mission. If he's not back by then, I'll have to carry out my plan without him.

"What is our approach?" Aurelia asks.

"The queen's residence," I say. "There's a surface-level entrance to the brood chamber there."

We advance cautiously toward the queen's compound. With every step, we find more evidence of the destruction of Delilah's army: oily veins trickle between pavestones, black masses that have long since lost whatever shape they once held quiver feebly with the mere illusion of life. The city's pond is coated with black slime that drifts like masses of diseased algae. From time to time, we see the distant outline of a fell-cat or another of the queen's animal allies, but it's obvious they're no longer under her control. Most of them flee when they see us; the more aggressive ones glare balefully, but they always turn tail when Celestina and I flash a warning surge of power. Viewing their starved shapes slinking through the wreckage, I wonder if this is what it was like when the Ecosystem first rose, when there were still some people with the strength of will to resist, some creatures that had yet to unlearn their fear of us as they would in time.

We clamber atop the vestiges of the guards' barracks, and I see what's become of the city's residents now.

Human figures appear below us, former villagers who wander aimlessly with blackened eyes and slack faces. There are only a handful of them, nothing like the numbers Delilah sent against the city. Something must have changed since Isaac's last scouting trip, because the vines no longer encircle their necks—more proof, I take it, of the queen's failing power. My heart leaps at the thought that I might be able to save them as I did Gideon when he was infected by Delilah's web. Yet when we scramble down the rubble to approach a man who looks something like the Sensor named Judah, we discover that there's nothing left of him to save: like Dinah in her advanced state, black tendrils sprout from his mouth and empty eye sockets, as if the parasite has consumed him wholly from within. It's an act of mercy for Gideon to set flame to the thing that wears his body. Flesh and bone burn quickly and leave neither stink nor residue, as if it were only his shadow that remained.

I glance around at the other phantoms who continue their listless walk. Some fall and don't rise; others seem to be flaking to nothingness even as we watch. The shrunken corpse of a woman lies with arm extended and the shard of a stone knife in her hand, but if this was once Esther, the Chief Sensor's black hair has turned as white as snow. Another shade walks within hand's reach of us, the bloody furs that drape his shoulders making me think he might have been Daniel, though the round belly and fleshy face of our longtime Chief Warden have dwindled to sacks barely more substantial than the ashy vines that trail from his shoulders. I'm afraid to touch him, afraid he might crumble to dust before my eyes. I watch until he drifts behind a pile of rock that used to belong to the library, and I recall his speech at Miriam and Isaac's wedding about recovering *edinnu*. Where did he learn of such a thing? How did he know the old stories, the old languages? And, once he's gone, what will be left of the lore he alone held?

"I didn't see Beulah," Leah whispers to me. "Do you think that means she's…?"

I don't know whether she's asking if her beloved is alive or dead, so all I do is squeeze her hand. In response, her grip tightens on her sword. Though I can't help thinking what a poor weapon that is against the dark queen, it steadies me to know that she hasn't given Beulah up for lost.

The sharp spire of the council house rises out of the mist ahead of us. It stands at the near edge of the queen's compound, with the royal residence hidden across the stone courtyard. The colored windows that line the right-hand side of the council house have been shattered, effacing the images of former queens that were depicted there. In the case of the window that was once Leonida's, a new image has been erected, or maybe *grown* is a better word: black strands cling to the window-frame, resolving into the portrait of a tall woman with long, streaming hair. The living tapestry is so realistic its black eyes seem to follow us, its hair to float eerily like the actual Delilah's. Here, at least, the dark queen's web remains submissive to her will. All the more so, I imagine, in the brood chamber to which Isaac has flown.

"Queen Sarah," Flora whispers. "The beasts—"

"I see them," I mutter back.

I should have figured that a web-spinner like Delilah would be drawn to others of her like, but I'm shocked when we round the corner of the council house to find ten or more arachnards nesting in its tower. No creation of the dark queen's, these eight-legged reptiles are one of the Ecosystem's many mutations that make their homes in the canopy of the western forest. Ordinarily, they're solitary, the females so territorial they'll consume hatchlings that are too slow to scamper away. Yet Delilah's power has corrupted them, not only by bringing such an unnatural colony together but by transforming their normally milky-white webs into black strands indistinguishable in color and consistency from hers. The thick webbing blankets the tower, spilling down the front wall of the council house to cover the double doors and stairs. Though I can't see the queen's residence from this distance, I've no doubt that other monsters nest there as well, casting their webs over the grounds and garden. It's fortunate we didn't try to take the secret passage back into the city, for we'd have been snared and stung with the creatures' paralyzing poison, then left to hang until they were ready to drain us dry.

"Horrid ornaments," Celestina announces, as if

she's commenting on a set of draperies she doesn't favor. "Loathsome, scandalous, *sick*. And on the queen's grounds!"

She holds up a hand, and I feel the power emanating from her in an attempt to sweep the arachnards from their nesting-places. The wave passes over the colony, stirring the strands of their webs as if with a light breeze, but all it does is wake the torpid creatures whose hooked claws rest on the webs' tripwires.

Wake them, and make them angry.

Clusters of reptilian eyes flash open, yellow against the rotten purplish hue of their scaled skin. Muscular legs flex like eight-fingered hands opening and closing. Arachnards aren't fast, but they don't need to be, especially when there are so many of them. Hefting their abdomens, they spew sticky spools of black web that catch on the pavestones, then use these ropes to swing or scuttle to the ground. I turn before they can surround us, only to find that they already have: other nests must have lain hidden in the rubble we passed through, and the residents of those nests have emerged to close the circle. We're a sizable body now that we have Isaac's reinforcements, but only a few of us hold weapons, and the majority have no experience in their use. The fear that shows in the faces of Flora and her fellows as the creatures close in tells me they've survived this long only by hiding, not by fighting.

Gideon and Aurelia are the first to act. The captain of the guard lunges at the closest foe, her sword coming down hard on one of its legs. But arachnard scales are as tough as metal, and the blade glances off with a ringing sound. The creature she attacked spits black webbing into the air, a high spout that would snare her if Gideon didn't shove her aside. The old firestarter's arm is caught by the edge of the descending web, but he brings his torch down and burns through the line before the monster can reel him toward its waiting arms. The frustrated beast makes a clumsy leap for him, but he sidesteps easily and shoves his torch into its multiple eyes. The arachnard emits a scream like shattering glass and staggers back blindly, stumbling over stone and flipping onto its back. Leah finishes it off by impaling its soft underbelly with her sword, which emerges dripping with purple blood. She gives her teacher a quick nod before raising the sword to seek other prey.

The remaining arachnards respond as one, casting an orchestrated net above our heads too broad to escape. Before it can descend on us, I call power from deep within the earth to singe the web to cinders. But it's not enough: some of the strands settle on the people farthest from me, and the arachnards pounce as their victims stagger beneath the heavy coils. One man—I never learned his name—goes rigid as an arachnard's stinger pierces his back; he falls to the pavestones while the creature bundles him in thick spirals of webbing. Other members of our group are snared but not yet downed. Leah and Aurelia fight through the web with their swords, Gideon with fire. I struggle to reach the victims in time, but the arachnards are closing fast.

With a cry I expect from a warrior, not a refined daughter of queens, Celestina hurls filaments of the Ecosystem's power at the monsters advancing on their prey. Though her web can't be seen as theirs can, a half dozen of the creatures find their legs bound together as if by powerful cords, and their ungainly bodies topple without a struggle.

It's their own muscles she's paralyzed, but to the eye, it appears as if the arachnards have been felled by a giant's boot. While they lie helpless on the courtyard stone, Celestina advances on them, silver eyes afire.

"I take no pleasure in killing," she says. "Yet never will I permit filth such as you to defile *my* home."

She waves her hands, and the arachnards release a hissing whimper, their bodies collapsing like deflated bladders. I don't really want to know what the Queen did to them, but the putrid smell that fills the air assures me they're dead.

Leah, Gideon, and Aurelia are busy fending off the remaining creatures, with the few members of Isaac's company who know something of arms backing them up. For all their efforts, several members of our group lie tangled on the ground, while one of the creatures has made a leap for the council house wall, a wrapped shape held in two forelegs. I call out to the bloodbirds that have begun to circle high overhead, and they dive to our aid, sharp beaks and claws pecking at the monsters' eyes while the arachnards flail ineffectually with their legs. While the creatures are distracted in this way, the soldiers among us are able to drive blades and torches into the arachnards' flabby guts to finish what the birds have started. Unsightly carcasses litter the ground, and atop each one, a coating of blood-red birds thickens. Soon, I no longer need to call my allies from the skies; they descend on their own, drawn by the spreading pools of arachnard blood and the flurry of activity over the bloated corpses.

"Well struck!" Celestina cries out to Leah, who's sliced an arachnard down the middle and stands with her face coated in purple slime. "Who dares say that the spirit of the queens lives not among the villagers?"

She twirls a hand over her head as if it holds a lariat, then flings the invisible threads at a lone arachnard that's scampering up the rubble to escape. The monster stumbles as its own legs rebel against it and carry it squealing toward the former queen, who watches it struggle for a moment before calling on Angelica to skewer it with a length of splintered wood. When Celestina's eyes light with silver flame and she kisses her partner over the gory body, I get the feeling she's not so squeamish about killing anymore.

The last monster falls before Flora, who's picked up a spear from one of her fallen comrades and shown that she's as fast a learner as Leah or the Queen. I glance over the field of battle and count three of our number slain, with two others having been carried away by fleeing arachnards. Of our core group, all are alive, only Gideon suffering a bad scratch across his stomach that, luckily, reveals no sign of poison. I close the wound quickly, then reach out to locate the prisoners.

I find them not in the arachnards' nests but in the queen's garden, immobilized by poison and wrapped with sloppy threads, though their captors are nowhere to be seen. All around them, I witness what's become of Celestina's lovingly cultivated retreat: the silverbloom bushes lie uprooted and dead, the lanes and flowerbeds are smothered in heaps of black webbing, and the high hedge is nothing but a charred perimeter, burned within an inch of the ground. If the assault on the council house was enough to bring out Celestina's bloodlust, I tremble to think how she'll react when she sees what the dark queen has done to her pride and joy.

I'm on the verge of breaking the news to her—gently, ever so gently—when Gideon's eyes roll upward and he drops to the ground.

I hurry to his side, scan his body to determine what could have struck my strongest ally down. When I find the injury, I can't believe I missed it before: one of the arachnards' stingers protrudes from his back, just above the kidneys. The only thing I can think is that I was too focused on the flesh wound to notice the deeper, more fatal cut. Yet when I call on my power to cleanse his envenomed blood, I discover something more seriously amiss: the Ecosystem doesn't stir. Just minutes ago, it sent me the birds I asked for; just seconds ago, it showed me the captives, the nests, the ruined garden. Now, much as I beseech it, it's fallen deaf, as if we've returned to the dark queen's lair and there's nothing to hear my pleas except the hive that mocks me.

"Celestina," I say urgently. "Can you reach the Ecosystem?"

She smiles as if in anticipation of another sally, but confusion quickly overtakes her face. Her brow knots, her eyes squeeze tight, then fly open. Their silver light, I see to my dismay, has died.

"The earth will not heed my voice," she says. "What can this mean?"

"I don't know," I say. "But help me! He's growing cold."

Together, while Gideon's face drains to a sickly gray and his body curls like a claw, Celestina and I bombard the Ecosystem with queries, supplications, commands. It rebuffs them all. Aurelia kneels by the old firestarter's side, trying to rouse him with voice and touch. Flora reaches for the healer's pouch at her belt, only to find the patient's lips sealed against her medicines. Panic makes my hands clumsy, but even if all my skills were intact, the only power that might save him is beyond my reach.

Finally, I stop trying. I'm shaking with the effort, sweating despite the chill drops of rain that fall on my face and hands. I touch the Queen's arm, and she flinches as if from an arachnard's sting.

"It's no use," I say, unable to control the tremor in my voice. "Delilah is blocking us."

Celestina looks stricken. "How can this be?"

"It must be why she put the arachnards here," I say. "Somehow, when we used our power against them, she cut it off."

"I will not believe such a thing," she says fiercely. "There is no force on earth that can rob a queen of her power."

"Delilah's not of this earth," I say. "Just look."

She follows my gaze. Across the courtyard, black vines spill toward us like rushing waters, lacking only their deafening sound. Some of Isaac's companions try to run, but they're stopped by a second tide of blackness that pours from the council house tower onto the pavement. Before anyone can retreat, we're ankle-deep in squirming vines. Gideon's body is completely submerged for a moment, then it rears up from the inky pool, a thick tendril coiling around him like a charmeleon's tongue. The rest of us are glued to the web as if it's one of the tar pits where, I read in a book Angelica picked out for me, the bones of long-extinct animals have been found. Except instead of us sinking into the web, its level continues to rise: to our knees, our waist, our chest. We're a tiny island in an ocean of blackness, about to be overwhelmed.

But then, when it's reached our throats, the web comes to a halt. A human figure appears at the far end of the courtyard and advances toward us, walking on the surface of the vines as if on the crest of waves. As it draws near, I see that it's the body of Daniel, whose decaying flesh is held together only by the black webbing that swaddles him like bandages. When his mouth opens, a vine forked like a serpent's tongue emerges to lick the air, and the dark queen's voice hisses from her servant's throat.

"Spawn of Leonida, your doom is upon you," the queen taunts me. "And yet, I might prove merciful to your vassals. If they pledge their lives to me, I will let them live as my servants, safe within my arms till the end of time."

"Never!" Aurelia roars. Her hand emerges from the morass, but the web flicks out and takes the sword from her as easily as it might steal a toy from a crying child. Celestina's response is more succinct. She spits at the figure, which answers her defiance with a croaking laugh.

"With you, daughter of Estella, I have nothing more to do," the dark queen gibes. "The line of Delphina was stillborn from the start. But with you, seed of Leonida"— and Daniel's eyes shift to mine, though they're nothing but sightless holes in his withered face—"I have a quarrel that is yet to be settled."

The tongue shoots out and catches me by the throat, cutting off any reply I might have made. I'm torn free of the web, which lets go with a sucking sound that reminds me of the collapse of my village months ago. The vine tightens so painfully around my neck, I'm convinced the queen intends to kill me now—but then it retracts, pulling me into Daniel's arms. His flesh feels soft and rotten, but his grip is unbreakable. When he throws back his head to emit a laugh that stinks of the grave, I see poison arrow frogs crawling within the toothless cavity of his mouth.

"Follow me," Delilah's voice jeers, "and learn the fate of a betrayer of her own blood."

Daniel's body bows mockingly to Celestina, who can only snarl her rage. Then, with me struggling weakly in the dead man's grasp and Leah crying out to no avail, the dark queen's servant strides across the waves to the brood chamber, where my enemy waits.

I'VE WALKED THE queen's path many times before, but never with such a guide. The stench of decay from Daniel's body overpowers my senses as we enter the residence and descend the staircase, where the aroma of moist earth is drowned by the rot of the queen's web. The black parasite is everywhere: clinging to the walls, tumbling down the stairs, snaking along the tunnel floor. I reproach myself for believing Delilah's power to be in decline, curse myself for allowing Isaac to confront her alone. Aurelia was right after all: the death of the web elsewhere in the city was only a lure. While everything else wasted away, the dark queen marshaled her strength in this one place for her final victory.

At long last, the end of the tunnel draws near. I know this only by counting Daniel's paces, for I'm unable to see the crystalline plates of the Ecosystem's first queen, *Apis dominica*, through the black web of her descendant. The hanging strands of that web nearly smother me as Delilah's servant fights his way through. I'd bat the vines away if my hands were free, call the Ecosystem to my aid if its ears weren't shut. The best I can manage is to snap at the web with my teeth, but that does little more than excite it into a frenzy of pawing and probing my flesh.

Daniel stops before the six-sided door to the brood chamber. He lets me go, but his arms are instantly replaced by hundreds of tendrils that emerge from the opening to spin their web around me. As they pull me into the dark queen's lair, I take a last look at Daniel, only to find that he's vanished in the thicket of black vines. I wonder if the web will finish consuming him now that his job is done. I wonder, too, why Delilah chose him for this ultimate torment when so many other creatures might have served her just as well.

The black vines draw me languidly into the brood chamber, as if there's no hurry now that my journey has reached its end. Once I'm inside, they release their hold on me and knit themselves into a solid wall that covers the only way out. Having shown me that there's no escape, the vines nudge me in the back until I turn to face the presence that brought me here.

She's not where I expect her to be. In the dim light of the chamber, I see that there's no throne of skulls as there was in her den beneath the village; there's only the web, which surrounds me on all sides, giving me just enough room to stand. I detect movement overhead, and my eyes travel upward to find the queen hanging directly above me, innumerable strands of hair radiating outward from her cold, frozen face. There's no body to be seen, no trace of the tall woman she was or the frail girl she would become. It's as if she's been absorbed into the web, Miriam's body merging fully with the parasite that possesses it. Only one detail remains of Delilah's past: the carved token that hangs from a single strand of the web, its form that of a coiled serpent and its color an opalescent pink even the darkness can't mask.

"Seed of Leonida," the queen speaks, her mouth

a black hole against brown skin. "You have come here to die?"

The inflection is definitely that of a question, but the words carry a great weariness, almost a sadness, that makes me pause.

"I've come to strike a bargain," I say when I find my voice. "For the city, and the lives of my friends."

The thin lips form a smile that reveals sharp canines. The web draws back from her face, and I see that other figures hang beside her. First to emerge is my wyrm, mighty no longer, its shrunken body twisted savagely as if it's still undergoing its death agonies. Beulah is next, her hair braided with the web, her slim wrists and ankles held by tight loops. My legs tremble as I prepare myself for the queen's final victim, but when he appears, I sink to my knees with a moan.

He dangles from the web, arms outstretched, head fallen on his breast. He's breathing, but shallowly, and with each intake of breath, he shudders in pain. I soon see why: a raised scar runs across the length of his stomach, as if he's been sliced by a blade and the wound has healed badly. His shaggy hair hides his features, yet I can feel the anguish that consumes him, and I know that no matter how great his body's suffering, the knowledge that his beloved did this to him is greater still.

My eyes find the queen's face. If not for the gleaming fangs, it might be the face of Miriam, the young, simple girl I failed so many times. Perhaps, if anything remains of her heart, she sorrows along with me for the boy we both loved. But when she speaks, it's with the voice of the dark queen, cold and remorseless.

"You share a fondness for bloodbirds with your great-grandmother Leonida," she says. "I, too, have birds in my service. They come when I call."

The web around her face shivers, and something flaps within it. As the object solidifies, I realize the strands are forming into a shape, black-feathered and with a huge, ungainly head. It bursts free of the web and flies the short distance to roost on Isaac's shoulder, where I see that it's one of the monster crows we call raveners, except with a broad, toothed mouth instead of a beak. To my horror, it dips this grotesque maw to Isaac's scar and bites, tearing away flesh and muscle. His body jerks helplessly as blood gushes from the reopened wound. The bird is about to gorge itself again when the web descends and absorbs its body, the mouth emitting a raucous cry before it vanishes into the blackness.

I gaze at Isaac. The wound has closed, the scar knitting itself over his skin in a mere second. His body shakes feebly, and a moan like that of a tortured child issues from his cracked lips.

"So it will proceed," the queen's voice fills the brood chamber. "His suffering will be endless, and yours equally so: to watch that which you love the most beset again and again with no hope of remedy, not even of death."

My legs quiver as badly as they did after I was attacked in the lair of the urthwyrms, but I climb to my feet. I waste no time calling upon the Ecosystem, for I know my pleas will go unanswered. Instead, I reach out to the power that used to suffuse this room, and hope that its light hasn't been wholly extinguished.

Dominique, I implore silently. *Hear me now. Give me strength.*

"Enough," I say to the queen. "It's obvious what you really want. Release your hostages, and do with me what you will."

The queen's black eyes gleam with vicious pleasure. The web retreats, dropping Isaac and Beulah to the floor. They lie with no motion save their breath, yet that's enough to make me believe Delilah will honor this final bargain.

"A willing sacrifice," the dark queen speaks, but in a softer voice, with a quality of wistfulness I can scarcely conceive coming from her bloodless lips. "You are mine now, seed of Leonida. At last, I take back what was stolen from me."

The web descends to draw me in. I'm lifted from the floor, brought close to the queen's face. I shut my eyes as her mouth opens, but not before I see the emptiness inside, a bottomless chasm framed by teeth as sharp as a fell-cat's. They snap closed on my throat with such pain it seems my body has been bitten in two, and I slide down into a black pit with no end.

Then a flame blooms in the darkness, and the life of Delilah, the lost queen, unfolds before my eyes.

My child is born today.

Laban and I name him Aaron in memory of my husband's father, and welcome him with observances befitting a son of the royal house of Dominica. My aunts Delphina and Queen Demetria attend the ceremony, with the Queen herself and her daughter Leonida presiding. They lay hands on his forehead, and bless him on the day of his birth.

We do not expect him to live to see another birthday.

To all appearances he was born healthy, a strong boy with a lusty cry. But in the days following the ceremony he grows sickly, his skin hot to the touch, his chest laboring to draw breath. His cry turns to a thin wail. When he wakes me, my heart tears at the sound. I offer him my breast, but he is weak and chokes on my milk. What nourishment he takes will not be enough to sustain him for many days.

Aunt Demetria examines him. She finds nothing, or nothing she can heal. It was the same not six months ago, when she attended to my dying mother, her own younger sister. Then as now, she can offer nothing but platitudes in place of healing.

Sometimes, the Ecosystem gives only to take away. Its mind is not always for us to understand.

Laban grieves, but he is resigned to the Queen's word. Meanwhile my son shrivels, and I grow desperate.

I resort to my cousin Leonida. As children we were playmates, and as we grew, there was little we did not share. Though I see her seldom now that she has begun her queenly training, I trust that she will sympathize with me as her mother cannot. She is two years younger than me and has no child; a husband she will never know, for she will become queen after Aunt Demetria is gone. And yet, she must remember the dreams we traded when we were children, must see that I will do anything to save my son.

She receives me in her chambers. Her golden hair flows over a dress of bloodbird-red. Her blue eyes gaze at me with compassion. I curtsy deeply, and she steps down from her seat to raise me from the floor, her pale hands linked with my brown.

My sweet cousin. Why do you kneel before me?

The tears come. I cannot stop them from flowing. *It is Aaron. My son is dying.*

She holds me, strokes my hair, speaks softly in my ear. *I will do what can be done,* she assures me.

For the first time in weeks, my steps are light as I race back to my chambers. I hold my babe in my arms, and whisper to him that all will be well.

Leonida comes as promised. She examines him thoroughly, spending hours deep in communion with the Ecosystem, seeking the source of his sickness and its cure. When at last she opens her eyes, the smile I remember from our childhood spreads across her face, and I burst into tears once more.

He will live a long and healthy life, my cousin tells me. *In time, he will become a leader of many. You will see.*

I fall to my knees and kiss her hands, thanking her over

and over. When I turn to the cradle where my babe sleeps, I convince myself that already his breathing has calmed, the peaceful look of infancy returning to his dear face.

When I wake the next morning, his flesh burns like fire.

I try to rouse him, but his eyes will not open. His breath comes in fits. I bundle him and fly to Leonida's chamber, but her guards insist that she cannot receive me. I plead with them, show them the form of my son, but they are unyielding. I am tempted to rush at their crossed spears, force my way past or die in the attempt, but just then, the door opens and Leonida herself appears.

She dismisses the guards. I hold Aaron out to her. She touches him delicately, then looks at me with tears brimming in her eyes.

It should have worked, she says. *It should have healed him.*

She casts her eyes about the corridor as if seeking an answer. Then she leans close and whispers in my ear.

My mother the Queen would not approve of my telling you this. But there is a man in the city, a man of great power. Some say it is greater than that of the queens themselves.

A man? Why have I not heard of him?

Few have. His ways are secret, and my mother tells me he is not to be trusted. But it may be that he possesses knowledge we lack. Knowledge that can heal your babe.

At these words, I clutch the burning body of my son to my heart. *What is his name?*

Malachi, she whispers. *He dwells by the eastern woods. Tell no one that I spoke to you of him.*

With a frightened look, she leaves me, sweeping down the hallway in her blood-red dress.

When the echo of her steps is gone, I rise, holding Aaron close. The guards pay me no heed as I leave the Queen's residence. I cross the courtyard with fevered steps, my destination firm in my mind. My cousin has given me hope—hope that where the queens have failed me, one man may yet save my child.

And so I make my way across the city to the home of Master Malachi.

His house sits on the other side of the city, at the farthest remove possible from the Queen's residence. I must pass the cemetery where my mother is buried to get there; I clutch Aaron to me as if my body alone can shield him from sharing her fate. The sound of my baby's ragged breath gives wings to my feet as I rush to throw myself upon the healer's mercy.

When I draw nigh his home, I hear a new sound rising above Aaron's gasps. It's the sound of a human voice raised in a soft chant, the words of which I've never heard:

House of Earth, House of Stone

Grant me vision

Hear my call

He sits cross-legged on a reed mat before the doorway. Accustomed as I am to the dwelling-places of queens, I am struck by how modest his home is, a lowly hovel of stone. The man who occupies this hut is its perfect match: his body, no taller than a boy's, is clothed in a humble suit of loose brown twill. And yet, though his face is that of a young man—younger than Laban, younger than myself—his beard is long, and when he opens his eyes at the sound of my step, he seems unruffled to find me before him. Rather, he gazes at me with a penetration and wisdom I have seen in no other.

My Lady. To what do I owe this pleasure?

My son, I blurt, holding him out without ceremony. *He is dying. You must save him.*

He frowns. *Queen Demetria…?*

She has attempted to heal him. As has her daughter. Both have failed.

Ah, he says, nodding gravely. *I see.*

He rises from his mat and leads me into his home. It is even plainer inside than out: a single room for eating and sleeping, with a stone fireplace at one end. In place of table, chairs, and bed, there are only the reed mats. He takes Aaron from my trembling hands, lays him gently upon one of these cushions, and bends over him, touching his naked body with long, slim fingers. Next he removes a set of devices from a bag that hangs at his side: a hollow tube, a length of what appears to be string, a small circlet of glass. I stand by anxiously, ready to sweep my baby into my arms at the first sign of danger. Malachi places a finger in Aaron's tiny mouth and peers inside with the tube, rests the string on his frail chest with the other end in his own ear, views his eyes through the glass. All the while, Aaron struggles for breath. At last, Malachi returns his instruments to his bag and glances up at me from where he kneels on the floor.

This child has been poisoned, he says.

Poisoned? Of all the words I might have expected the man to say, this must surely be the last. *By whom?*

By whom, indeed? Who possesses the power to counter the processes of life?

The healers? But why…?

He shakes his head. *Not the healers. They lack skill in poisons of such potency, nor have they had the opportunity to administer the dose. But there is another who might have done it, another whose art exceeds theirs.*

My heart freezes as the import of his words sinks in. *The Queen? She is of my own blood. Surely she could not be so—*

Treacherous? He smiles, but there is no humor in it. *And yet, here the boy lies, laid low by a poison so subtle it would have escaped my detection had you delayed your journey even an hour longer.*

Can you save him? I plead.

I can try, he answers.

He rises, leaving Aaron where he lies. From various places in the small room, he collects a motley assemblage of objects: a bowl, a cloth, a flask, a bunch of sticks. The last he places in little wooden stands and sets in a ring around my son, then lights them with a coal from his fire. Threads of smoke rise from the tips, filling the room with a sweet smell. He pours water from the flask into the bowl, then opens another pouch at his side and removes a bundle of green leaves whose scent is even more pungent than that of the burning sticks. He crumbles these leaves in his fingers and lets the bits fall into the water, then mixes the brew with a ladle. The water froths as the leaves dissolve, and the wholesome smell intensifies. Malachi turns to me, his placid eyes revealing a hint of anxiety.

The smoke will open his airway. And the witch hazel elixir will neutralize the poison. But he is small, and frail, and I cannot guarantee how his body will react to the treatment. My Lady, do you wish me to proceed?

I hesitate but a moment before answering. *You must. If he dies, I acquit you of all wrongdoing.*

He nods, though his eyes, I think, grow sad. Placing

the bowl beside my struggling babe, he spreads his arms and chants in a low voice:

House of Earth, House of Stone

Hear my words

Lend me strength

He takes up the cloth, dips a corner in the potion to wet it, then lets a drop fall on Aaron's lips. He repeats the procedure, one drop at a time, while I wait in an agony of doubt. Aaron's chest continues to struggle, and wild thoughts race through my mind: that it is Malachi, not the Queen, who has poisoned my son, that the smoke that fills the room is an essence of evil, the potion he feeds my child a carrier of plague. The queens are wise in the ways of the Ecosystem; how could this little man know what they do not? Malachi places the tips of his fingers on Aaron's chest, and I find that I can tolerate no more. I reach for my babe to scoop him into my arms, but the healer fends me off with a hand.

Wait. His eyes burn into me. *Have faith, and be comforted.*

The next moment, Aaron's mouth opens and emits a weak cry.

I fall to the floor beside him as my babe opens his eyes and stares up at me. Where my tears bathe his face, I see that his color has returned; when I bundle him and bring him close, I feel that his fever has abated. I hold him to me and rock him gently, while the words of relief tumble from my lips.

Thank you. Oh, thank you, thank you, thank you.

Malachi retreats from the room when Aaron's cry turns

to one of hunger. I place my babe at my breast, and look into his eyes while he sucks. I feel strength flowing back into him, and I no longer know or care whether it is Malachi's potion or my milk that has restored him to me.

When he's had his fill, when he sleeps in my arms with peaceful breath and a face glowing with color, I sit with Malachi and ask him to reveal all he knows. He is reticent at first, speaking in the most general of terms; perhaps he fears that, with my lineage, I will betray him to the Queen. But in time he opens up, his eyes glowing with excitement as he tells me of the knowledge he has discovered from books hidden deep in the library. The way of the queens, he tells me, is but one of many paths to healing: if Dominica's heirs can speak to the Ecosystem through their very blood, others can speak to it through medicinal herbs, through song and story, through processes of mind and hand that were known for thousands of years but nearly lost during the upheaval of the Ecosystem and the ensuing reign of the queens. He removes a cord that hangs around his neck to show me the token that was once used to signify the work of these elder healers: a serpent coiled around a wooden staff, carved of a pink stone so finely wrought the creature seems to wriggle in the firelight. When I ask him if he means that the queens have conspired to suppress this knowledge, he grows wary again, saying only that he had not heard of these things until he stumbled upon the lore-books himself. When I ask if I might learn what he knows, his sleepy eyes sharpen.

You are a daughter of queens. Why should you seek a path other than theirs?

I explain to him that I have never trained in the way of the queens—that the succession is fixed, passing from

Dominica to Demetria and then to Leonida. Once my cousin ascends the throne, I might be trained in a limited way should she so decree, to serve as a member of her healers' corps. But she will give birth to her own daughter in time—true queens always bear girl-children—and this child will sit on the throne after her mother is gone.

While I speak, the look in his eyes brightens, and he nods.

Your aunt the Queen is more jealous of her power than I had guessed. I cannot know for certain why she has targeted your son. But I fear for your family should you give birth to a girl-child.

Dread might overcome me at these words, but I master it. For myself, and for my son.

Then teach me. Give me the strength to fight her.

He hesitates. He has given me so much already, I know it is unfair of me to ask him for more. And he is such a little man, a healer and a recluse, no warrior to meddle in the affairs of queens. What he has done thus far might be counted as treason; what I ask of him will surely lead us both to the gallows, should we be found out. When our eyes meet across the sleeping body of my son, the understanding that passes between us crackles with all that we stand to lose.

None may know of this, he says. *Until we deem the time right.*

I place my hand on his. He does not pull away.

It will be our secret, I say.

A NEW WORLD opens before me. I share it with Malachi and no other.

I wake early and take my morning meal, then walk the length of the city with Aaron in a sling across my chest. Now that our son's health is recovered, Laban has resumed his work on the Queen's council, and he does not question how I spend my days. I make sure to return to our home before evening falls. At first, I grow wary as I approach Malachi's hut, glancing this way and that lest unwelcome eyes—those of my babe's poisoner, perchance—should discover me. But I soon learn that no one comes here, so far from the city's center, where only this strange hermit lives. Uneasiness yields to excitement, and with each passing day, my desire to learn what only Malachi can teach me grows stronger.

He begins with the simplest of subjects, reviewing with me as he might a child the names of the parts of the body, the functions of the senses, the work of the various systems and organs. I hold my tongue and smile politely. When Aaron grows hungry, I retreat to a spot behind Malachi's home, an extensive herb garden where he has prepared a mat for me to sit. In time, as we delve more deeply into the man's storehouse of knowledge, such breaks become hindrances, and I nurse openly before my teacher, with only a cloth for modesty. Malachi says nothing untoward during these interludes, meeting my gaze and continuing his lesson over the sound of my son's sucking and burping, but I begin to suspect that his knowledge of the private lives of men and women is purely academic.

In all other respects, however, he is years beyond me. Having established a baseline of knowledge, he moves rapidly to more abstruse topics: the flow of energy that animates the body, the union of mind and matter, the intimate connection between our individual selves and the greater life of the wilderness. On sunny days, he strolls with me in his garden, explaining the names and properties of all that grows there; on days of rain, he sits with me in his home and opens thick, musty books full of terms I've never heard, diagrams I've never seen. Some of these tomes are in languages I can't read, but Malachi can, having taught himself many of the tongues that were spoken in the world before the Ecosystem came. He translates for me, and I thrill at the sound of his words, though I don't understand their import:

House of Earth, House of Stone

Open before me

Make us one

I ask him what it means. He smiles shyly, then does his best to explain.

The world consists of that which lives and that which does not. We are creatures of earth, and yet we live our lives within citadels of stone, seeking to shield ourselves from that which lives. And so, alone among living things, we are only half-alive. When I speak these words, I remove the barriers that deceive us, the barriers that confine us. I beseech the power of all living things to enter our houses of stone, that we may dwell in the world fully and be healed.

I shake my head in confusion. *But....*

You will understand in time, he says.

To shift the conversation to something more within my comprehension, he shows me the instruments he has designed for probing the body and tapping its living energies, including those with which he diagnosed Aaron's malady. I study each one in turn, handling it, attempting to make it operate as designed. Under his hands, these simple tools reveal much, but in mine, they might as well be a child's playthings. When I look at him in embarrassment at my clumsy efforts, he explains that he has trained himself to channel the information that streams at all times from living beings; his instruments merely amplify what his body collects. Until I learn to do the same, the world around me will remain mute as stone.

It is not the microscope that opens the mind, he says of the queer glass circlets that magnify vision to varying degrees, *but the mind that opens the microscope.*

I return home each day breathless, my thoughts buzzing. Luckily the maids have prepared dinner for Laban's return, for I have care for only two things: my babe, and my secret studies. Often I find myself staring blankly across the table at my husband, realizing he has asked me a question but having no idea what it was.

Motherhood, he sighs, trying to laugh. *I had heard of its effect on a woman's head, but I little suspected it would be like this.*

I smile in return, then resort to the chamber I share with my babe. I lie awake while Aaron breathes softly in the crib beside my bed, and I cannot believe his dreams could be any sweeter than mine.

The days pass. Aaron learns to roll over, then to sit, then to crawl—which might be an impediment to my lessons, but Malachi only laughs when my babe finds his way into the healer's bag of instruments. *He is as curious as his mother,* he says, but he does take the precaution of storing his medicines out of reach. When Aaron learns to stand, the herbs and powders move to a higher shelf; when he begins to walk and then run, Malachi concedes defeat and locks everything away in a chest marked with his healer's symbol. Our lessons become something other than they were, alternating between instruction and playtime: for Malachi grows fond of my boy and delights to hold him on his knee, telling him stories and letting him handle the seemingly endless supply of implements the healer removes from his locked trunk. By the time my son reaches the age of four, he has become a wonder to my eyes: taller than most his age, quick of mind and tongue, and with none of the awkwardness of childhood. While Malachi and I talk, he runs in the garden visible through the healer's lone window, and he is so swift and agile, he seems not to stir a single stalk or leaf.

The boy might become a healer himself, Malachi says with pride in his voice. *Like his mother.*

I smile back. For I, too, have grown.

I can't say when it began, when the many pieces of the puzzle my teacher laid out before me started to come together. I can only say that shapes emerged first, then groupings, then constellations, so that now my mind seems to zoom between the stars as Aaron's feet dart along the garden path. I lay hands on my son's chest at night and feel not only his steady heartbeat but the lines of hidden force that infuse and bind him; I reach out to one of Malachi's many herbs and simples—witch hazel, goldenseal, aloe—and feel its life-giving properties coursing through my own body. His microscopes and other instruments I master at last, giving me unfettered access to the invisible world; his diagrams of healing procedures I envision translated into practice, and I lack only a body to perform them on. By Aaron's sixth birthday, when after our private celebration I ask Malachi what today's lesson will be, my teacher shakes his head.

There will be no more lessons, he says sadly.

No more? But why? What have I done wrong?

It is not that. You have surpassed me, My Lady. There is nothing I can offer you now that would not hold you back.

I look at his mournful, youthful face—for he is still the child-man he was six years ago, only his beard having grown longer in that time—and I know that he is right. I need no microscope to detect the blood that flows beneath his skin, no laying-on of hands to feel the energies that stream through his body. It is as if the whole of his life lies naked before me, as if my own body is an instrument far finer than any he has designed. I look out the room's window to the garden where my child plays, and I see something even more unwonted: golden filaments seem to hang in the air like sunbeams, and I know that if I reach out to touch them, they will stir at my call and answer to my command.

What has happened to me? I ask.

He bows his head. I note one other thing that has changed in six years' time: a bald spot has appeared at the crown of his head and begun to make inroads toward his forehead.

You are a daughter of queens. In your blood lies power over

225

the Ecosystem itself. I have helped you to tap that power, and now it has bloomed. I was your master once, but you are my mistress now.

At the sound of these words, the dream in which I've lived for the past six years comes crashing to an end, and I wake to a night far darker than any I've known since the sickness of my child. I rise, stumbling to the door and running to where Aaron plays. He comes to me as soon as he sees me, and when I lean down to pick him up, he places a stunflower bloom behind my ear. Its life washes over me in an overwhelming surge, and I fall to my knees, holding onto my child as if he is my only anchor against a raging storm.

I feel a hand on my arm. It is the first time in six long years that Malachi has touched me, and at his touch, I see everything there is to see about him, even what I should not see.

My Lady. This was the risk we took. But is it not also the boon you sought?

You didn't tell me. You didn't tell me this would happen.

I have never trained a daughter of queens. I could not know what would happen, much as I might hope and dream.

I look up at his face. The sun pours down upon us, crowning his head in gold. My child has skipped away to chase huntingbirds. I place my hand in Malachi's, and he raises me to my feet.

What must I do? I ask.

There are others, he says, and he cannot disguise the eagerness in his voice. *Others who would learn what we have to teach. The time has come to call them to us.*

THEY COME TO us without our having to call. Young and old, men and women, they find their way to Malachi's door, seeking wisdom. Here their lessons begin—at Malachi's hands, but mostly at my own.

He covers the most basic of principles, those that every healer must know. But once our students have learned his lessons, I do not waste time on in-between steps. I move directly to teaching them what I can now do without conscious thought: reach out to the Ecosystem, open myself to let its golden threads flow through my body, and channel that power to achieve the work of healing. I do not know what urgency drives me so; I only feel as if time is growing short, as if the lines of aging on my mentor's crown are accelerating beyond my control. Perhaps it is my own boy's rapid growth that makes time seem to shrink, weeks and even months compressing into a single day. Each evening, when I pick him up at the home of the common folk who care for him, I am struck by the new Aaron who charges down the path into my arms. And so I drive our healers' corps harder than ever Malachi drove his first pupil, and when in the course of the lessons my eyes meet his, I see in him the same resolve that inspires me.

Within twelve months' time, our students have approached the point it took me six years to reach. They lack only one power I possess: though they can summon the Ecosystem to aid in the work of healing, they cannot command it, cannot pull the threads of life in whatever direction they will. Malachi and I spend hours pondering this impasse, debating how to surmount it; both of us grow careless in our desperation to crack the riddle, and there are times when I return home to find candles burning in the windows and my husband long abed. In the end, my teacher is forced to conclude that the power of command is reserved to women of queenly blood, and no amount of instruction can draw it from those outside of Dominica's line. Yet our pupils are keenly attuned to the life of the wild, their hands adept at funneling its energies into the healer's task. It is as if their five senses have been enhanced by our lessons—either that or surpassed by a single sense greater than them all. And so we name them Sensors.

In the second year of our teaching, word goes out to the city that Queen Demetria has died. I attend the funeral as a member of the royal family, though my heart grows hard when I pass by the flower-draped casket and remember my own child's sickness. Leonida is crowned after the customary week of mourning, and I attend the coronation as well, standing at my husband's side with my son holding my hand as he goggles at the new Queen in the crimson gown she favors. At her, or perhaps at her daughter, a golden-haired four-year-old whom my cousin has named Seraphina.

After the ceremony, Leonida pulls me aside. We have been so involved in our separate worlds these past seven years—she with her queenly training, I at my secret studies—we have seen each other only on occasions of state;

we haven't spoken at all since that day outside her bedroom when she set me, all unknowing, on the course that would change my life. I never thanked her then. I wonder if, now she is queen, she has become my enemy like her mother before her.

But I detect nothing in her manner to support such a thought. Her words are soft as she draws me to her bosom.

My sweet cousin, she says, with tears sparkling in her deep blue eyes. *Now that I have a child of my own, I would ask a favor of you, as one mother to her kin.*

Of course, Your Majesty, I say, though I fear the stiffness of my voice betrays me.

My daughter lacks a companion, she continues without hesitation. *Someone of her own blood to watch over her while I am engaged in my duties as queen. Your son seems to have a way with her already.*

She points, and I laugh at the sight of Aaron on all fours, the doll-like child clinging to his back as he shuffles about the throne room floor.

Please, Leonida says, and her tears flow once more. *For the love we shared as children, and the sake of our city.*

I watch the two of them at play, Seraphina's skin as pale as ivory and my son's as dark as teak, and I am reminded of the days Leonida and I used to romp together, childishly unaware of the evils the world holds.

I will talk to … Laban, I say, whereupon my cousin throws her arms about me and thanks me with tears shining upon her cheeks.

That night, I visit Malachi in his home. I have long since ceased making a show of keeping regular hours, and Laban has long since ceased complaining about it.

Do you fear for your son's safety? Malachi asks.

No. She would not be so bold. And yet, there is something about this I do not trust.

He broods before answering.

I would not put your son at risk, he says at last. *All the same, this arrangement might work to our advantage.*

How so?

Leonida is young. She has not shown herself hostile to our order.

She does not know of it.

Let us give her time. Time to prove what manner of ruler she may be. With your son a regular visitor in her household, you will have opportunities to talk to her, opportunities to study her. If she has truly chosen a path unlike her mother's, then the time will have come for us to emerge from the shadows and announce our presence. But if she should prove false....

What, then?

He hesitates, his eyes drifting to his locked chest before returning to mine. *Then we must be prepared to fight.*

Fight? When we are so few?

He smiles somberly. *We are not so few as you think. I have taken the measure of the city, and I know that there are many among the common folk who would rally to our side, were we to call on them.*

I realize what never occurred to me until now: that when I return to my son after each day's training sessions, Malachi does not spend his evenings in seclusion as he did before. *And what would you have us tell them?*

I would tell them that we fight for justice. That we fight to unite our city, riven as it now is—to restore to all the healing power that has been taken from us, and so to build a world of everlasting peace. Are these not ends worth fighting for?

I'm startled to hear such words flow from the normally mild-mannered healer's mouth. His eyes glow with passion, and I see as if for the first time that this is who he truly is, the man who not only saved my child but who would seek to save us all, even if the power of the queens were ranged against him. Only now, he is not the lone hermit he was on that first day; now he too has a queen by his side, one whom he trusts to fight with him until the end. I know at that moment from whence our urgency this past year arose, and I know as well that we have come too far to turn back.

So be it, I say, and seal our compact by placing my hand in his.

We return to our work among our Sensors' corps. Now that we are decided, I find that all anxiety, all uncertainty have fled; I am strong as never before, a daughter of queens in truth, not merely in name. My power flourishes in proportion to my will, and I find that the others are steeled by my resolve, their own capacities increasing in concert with mine. Malachi marvels to observe me training the corps; his eyes shine, his voice rings out loud and clear, and he is transformed as only a clear and honest purpose can transform a man. Each day, when I depart after the training to retrieve Aaron from the Queen's residence, I find my son transformed as well, growing ever taller, stronger, more handsome and wise. I smother him with kisses, but he waves me off in front of Seraphina, whose blue eyes glow with laughter to see her playmate's discomfiture. At home, I no longer tuck him into bed, but watch with a mother's mingled sorrow and pride at the man he is becoming.

And so I am shocked when, on the eve of his tenth birthday, I arrive at the Queen's residence to find my boy sobbing on the stoop before the front door.

Everything falls from me at the sight of him: my queenly power, my dreams for the city's future. I am a new mother once more, and he is the tiny babe who lay struggling for breath in my arms.

My child, I say, falling to my knees before him. *Why do you weep so?*

He chokes out a breath, sniffles, says something unintelligible. I stroke his hair, dab his tears with my fingers. After a time, his breathing settles, and I am able to make out his words.

Sera told ... told me she can't play with me anymore. She says her mother won't ... won't let me. Because I'm ... bad.

Bad? Have you done anything to offend your cousin?

He shakes his head vigorously. *Sera asked me to draw the pink snake, and when she showed it to her mother, Cousin Leo said I was ... born bad. She said ... she said....*

His words trail off into tears once more, and I never hear the rest. Nor do I need to.

I catch him in my arms as if he is my baby indeed, and run with him to the home of the common folk who watched him while I was deep in training. Why I do not return with him to his own home, his own father, I cannot say; but some voice warns me against it. When I have told my child's caregivers a tale of half-truths and kissed his sweet cheek a thousand times—yet still not enough—I fly to Malachi's home, where I find him sitting before the doorway, his head bowed.

We are betrayed, I say to him breathlessly. *Leonida has laid a trap all along, and now she is coming for us.*

He raises his head. His eyes hold a sadness I have never seen in the ten years we have worked and dreamed together.

I know, he says. *She has taken the others already. It will only be a matter of time.*

You must flee! Make your way to the forest, hide within the Ecosystem. Save yourself.

And you, My Lady?

I will remain. To warn the people, and to confront my cousin, as one queen to another.

He shakes his head. *I cannot let you face such a fate alone. And if you should stay and I go, what joy could remain to me then?*

The tears creep down his cheeks into his beard. I kneel before him, and take his hands, and draw him to his feet. We enter his home, and in the last light of the dying day, we are joined as never before. It has been years since I've shared my husband's bed, and yet I know that the man-child I hold in my arms has never lain with a woman, never once set aside the ascetic's vow he took on the day he determined to plumb the Ecosystem's secrets. But tonight, that vow is broken, and we give ourselves freely to a secret even deeper than that which the Ecosystem holds.

After, he circles me in his arms, kisses my hair. *I have deceived you,* he says.

You have not.

I have. On the day you first came to my door. Though I could not have anticipated your coming, when you appeared, I knew that this was a chance I could not let pass by. He gazes at me, tears shining in the moonlight. *I am sorry. I have led you to your death.*

No. You have given me a life.

Your son's.

My own, I say, and kiss him tenderly. *It is more than I could ever have asked of you.*

We lie together throughout the night. For the first time in years, I feel the need to surrender to the comfort of a man's arms, to hear the steady sound of his heartbeat beneath my cheek. In times past, I recall lying with my husband, feeling warm and secure as we clung to each other, whispering, laughing. Now my heart hammers at every noise, and I ache for someone to shelter me from the terror that's coming.

But late that night, when they do come for us, they don't make a single sound.

I HAVE DWELT so long in darkness, my eyes have lost the power to see light.

Or so it seems to me when the scratch of a flint sounds in my place of confinement, and a shapeless red blob appears before me. I squint, try to make out its contours, but it remains a blur, floating out of reach of my chained hands. Then it speaks, and though I can see no mouth form the words, I know the voice at once.

My sweet cousin. To think that you have been brought to such a place.

I swallow, try to answer. My parched throat scratches at my words. *Where is Aaron?*

He is safe. His father cares for him, while armed guards watch that none may molest your home.

And Malachi?

Her laughter pains my ears. *The hermit inquired after you when I visited him. He asked me to give you this.*

The red blur before me moves, and I discern her outstretched hand. A pink shape flashes against her pale flesh.

His healer's charm, Leonida says. *The very mark of his treachery. And now it is yours to wear.*

A string slips around my neck. She is so close I smell the sweet scent of her breath even in the foul stench of my cell. I would strangle her if my hands were free, but I can do nothing save accept Malachi's final gift.

What will become of us? I ask.

Leonida rises and moves away from me. The cell cannot be larger than two paces across, yet I'm unable to make out anything but the blood-shape of her dress, as if it's her daemon and not her physical being that visits me here.

You will be tried for treason against the throne, along with all who aided you. Tried, and exiled from the City of the Queens.

We have done nothing.

That is not the tale the people will hear.

Again, the red shape drifts across the cell, coming to rest before a barred window that shows nothing but darkness beyond. Leonida's words come to me softly, as if I am losing the power to hear as well. Or as if she fears that, even in this dungeon deep beneath the queen's grounds, someone else might be listening.

When first you got with child, she says, *I knew you were a danger to me. Though my mother assured me that you carried a son, still my mind was uneasy. I asked myself, what of another? A girl-child, seed of my cousin, to challenge my own child's rule? I set my thought to this riddle, and it dawned on me that I might turn threat to advantage, adversary to ally.*

I am no adversary. I am of your own blood.

And for that reason, dangerous if not controlled. But how to make the common people perceive the danger? How to show them that, when I cast you from the city, it was to protect them, not to preserve my lineage?

She's silent, as if waiting for me to answer. But the shape of her scheming has become visible to me where her body will not, and when next she speaks, nothing in her words surprises me.

It was I who poisoned your child. Oh, I did not adminis-ter the draught myself. Yet I saw to it that the one who did so should never dare name me as his director, lest he hang on the gallows for his crime.

Laban, I think. The shriek of grief that escapes my soul might be loud enough to kill him, if he has not died of his own grief already. *The Queen*, I say. *Your mother. How is it that she could not perceive what Malachi could?*

My mother grew old. For years, I had felt her powers weaken. Yet I had one final test to administer before I could be sure. When your mother sickened and mine was powerless to heal her, I knew that she could not detect in your son what she had failed to detect in her own sister.

Her sister? Then you poisoned my mother, too?

I did what must be done. And all has come to pass as I designed.

My flesh chills at the presence of this monster who would murder her own kin for lust of the throne. *Then you knew? That Malachi would discover the cause of my child's sickness, and its cure?*

I knew. And, once I had driven you into his arms, I had only to allow fate to play out its course. To let you join your-self with this deluded man and his conspirators, to make real the prospect of revolution in a city that lives daily in fear of the Ecosystem at its door. The unhallowed alliance of Delilah, possessed of queenly powers but not of queenly prospects, with the man who would install her on the throne! Who among the city's residents would not quail at the thought of such an insurgency; who would not think the present queen justified in rooting out the rebels? Who would not rally around the throne of Leonida, that she might heal this great rupture and reign for a hundred years?

She laughs, the sound of her malice echoing loudly in the enclosed room.

You forget one thing, I say. *If there is to be a trial, the accused must speak. And I will tell such a tale as will cast all your lies into doubt.*

Her laughter ceases. The red shape moves closer to me again, so close I can make out her piercing blue eyes through the shroud of blood.

Some might believe you, she says. *But not most. I have extracted confessions enough from your disciples to seal your doom. And yet, I will take one additional precaution to ensure your silence.*

A cold blade is laid upon my cheek. I stiffen, but find the strength to answer. *So you will kill me after all?*

I have told you that I need you alive. As a warning to any who would challenge my rule, and an ever-present threat before my subjects' eyes. But I will order the queen's guard to cut the tongue from your mouth, and tell the people it was done that you might speak no conjurer's spell against them.

I struggle wildly with my chains, and manage to rise to my knees before the Queen jumps out of reach. Yet in the end, it is useless: my bonds hold fast, and no power that I learned from Malachi can remove them. Exhausted, I collapse to the floor, my arms shackled in place above my drooping head. The token at my throat cuts into my flesh, as if to remind me of the acts for which I am to be punished.

What will become of Aaron? I ask. *What will become of my son?*

He will be exiled with his mother. But I promise you, none will lay a hand upon him before that time.

So great is my relief, I almost thank her. Instead, I raise my head to face her, and though I can't see through the red veil, my lips form the shape of a curse. I speak so softly, it is as if I plant the very words in her cancerous soul.

May your own child live to suffer what mine has suffered. And may the memory of your wickedness be a viper in your bosom, however long you may reign.

She does not answer, but I hear the sharp intake of her breath. The words of a queen carry power, even when she is laid low. A moment later, her cold lips press against my cheek, and what little light there is in the room is utterly extinguished.

Farewell, sweet cousin, she says. *I am told the pain is brief.*

What she has been told is a lie. The pain is without end, and there is none to comfort me.

IN THE VILLAGE, I learn to speak with my hands.

It is in such fashion that I communicate with my son, my neighbors, those who used to be my devotees. My discourse is rough and infrequent, but it suffices. There is only one to whom I will not speak, cannot speak. He knows the reason why, and his face grieves every time we pass in the lanes and he sees the token I wear at my throat.

I remember little of my trial. I lay in a daze, moaning with what was left of my tongue while jeering faces passed before me, their harsh words a roar of sound. The fog lifted briefly on our trek to the village, when I felt my son's hand gripping mine. I looked down at him and was startled to see that though his body was that of a boy, his face was that of a man. His father, I later learned, died in the city on the day of the trial, and was found gripping the flask that contained the last few drops of Leonida's poison.

How we found this place, how my cousin knew of its existence, I cannot say. Perhaps it was a city in its own time, though overcome by the Ecosystem many years ago. With her power over the forest, she guaranteed us safe passage to its border, but it was ours to defend from that point on. No more than seventy of us, Sensors and the common folk who succored us in the city, against the wild.

In the first days and weeks of our residence here, Malachi directs the Sensors and commoners as they burn away vegetation from the stone courtyard, refashion the shapes of tumbled houses, begin work on the foundation of the large hall he intends to be a place of gathering and devotion. I scorn their efforts, though my son joins in the work. I expect at any time to be swallowed by forest, and I cannot say to Aaron or any other that such a fate would not be welcome.

Months have gone by before I am enough myself to realize that my woman's blood has not visited me once since we arrived.

Against my will, I approach Malachi. He has set up housekeeping on the western edge of the village, preferring even now to maintain solitude from his people. His herb garden grows again, thanks to the seeds he was able to spirit away from the city; his reed mats have been rewoven, his healer's tools rebuilt. The only difference is that now his home is no more humble than any other's.

My Lady, he says in wonder when I appear at his door. *I am … so happy to see you.*

Must talk, I sign to him. *Important.*

He invites me into his home, but I stand on the cobbles outside his door with arms folded across my chest. At last, I accept his invitation to sit on the stone bench beneath his window, where we watch the giant ache trees pressing their crowns together as if planning their assault.

And what do you wish to discuss with me? Malachi says, his eyes embarrassed by the formality of tone I demand of him.

Having baby. How long here?

His face shows a mixture of shock and delight, but his words remain studiously neutral.

We arrived three months ago. We were … jailed for a month in the city. I take it you are … well?

Not sick. Having girl.

Now he cannot hide his astonishment. *You know this?*

Body say. Only five months prepare.

Five months to prepare for the birth?

Five months. Before queen come.

He lowers his gaze as if ashamed. *My Lady. The Queen will not touch us here. Destroying us would only defeat her purposes.*

Will come. Now girl baby. You say yourself. Will kill.

He holds a hand out to me. *My Lady. Forgive me. This is all my doing. But do not lose hope. Do not give in to despair.*

I stand. The child he planted in my womb quickens for the first time, a butterfly beating against the walls of time. Malachi is wise, but he cannot understand what I understand, cannot know the Queen as I do. He cannot imagine what it is to bring a child into the world, only to watch it die.

And so I leave him, walking back to the center of the village to gather those who will not fail me in my hour of need.

MY TIME DRAWS near.

The life within my body grows, kicks. Her limbs slide across my stomach like strange petals. She is healthy—my inner Sense tells me this—but I fear that she will come before my work is complete, that the Queen will catch her at her most vulnerable. I know no rest during the day, no sleep at night. I have so little time to spare, so much to lose.

I meet with my disciples in the Sensorium, the building that Malachi has dedicated to the core group of healers he calls the Sensorship. Malachi himself does not attend these meetings; he is not welcome. Since our last interview, I have shut him out, refused him my eyes' glance or my hands' answer. The more my belly grows, the more he shrinks, until he has no will left to contest me.

To the others, I outline my plan: a defensive perimeter to gird the village, made of living matter that will shield us from the eyes of the Queen, safeguard us should her soldiers attempt to breach it. That such an organism does not now exist, I know well: I will have to make it. To do so, I ask them to lend me their strength, to assist me when I call. To help me lay the seedbeds for the thing I conceive.

They doubt me, but perhaps they fear me too much to remonstrate. And so I begin.

The work is hard, despite all my years of training. The

Ecosystem does not readily yield its deepest secrets: how life comes to be, how one creature spawns another, like yet unlike its progenitor. That such was the means by which the Ecosystem itself came into being I am well aware, for the story of *Apis dominica* and her brood is known to all of royal blood. But to achieve what the Ecosystem achieved, to create a life that has never been upon this earth, is a mighty thing. A costly thing. A thing that requires much labor, much sacrifice, before I accomplish what I seek at last.

It starts with a vine. It drops a seed, and the seed lies smoking in my hand.

I wrap it in the shell of a stunflower to cheat Malachi's eyes. My every action comes with labored breath now, my belly a burden I carry heavily before me. But I have out-witted my adversary, succeeded before my ninemonths' time. I gather my followers, and tell them we can wait no longer.

On a moonless night, we plant my seed. We stand just beyond the village stone, wearing cloaks woven of black thread, cowls covering our heads to blind the eyes of the dark. The stump of my tongue lies useless within my mouth, but I conduct the others as they chant the words I have taught them:

House of Earth, House of Stone
Defeat our enemies
Shield us all

I stoop, being unable to bend over, and with careful hands embed my seed in the upturned soil, then shape the earth overtop it as gently as I might smooth a baby's sheets. My disciples repeat the words of the chant, over and over, their voices rising and falling like the wind. When I feel in my bones that my seed has taken root, I tell them it is enough: we can rest now. In the morning, we will return to see what we have done.

My dreams that night are of birth: my child's, my seed's. Neither enters the world without blood.

When we return at dawn, it is as I desired. Black tendrils have crept from the earth around the village perimeter, knitting themselves together to form a hedge some six inches high. I lay my hands upon the budding vines, feel their power pass like a shadow over my sight. They will grow tall and strong, immune to sword or Sense. Should the Queen cast her eyes toward us, she will not see me nursing my babe in the lonely cell I call home. Or, if she should, if she should be so foolish as to send her guards to kill the child I have borne, they will become entangled in the new life I have created, and they will die in her place.

My assistants help me stand. The hedge grows taller and thicker before our very eyes.

My Lady, one of my helpers says. Her eyes rest upon her own hands where they touched my arm. Fine black threads cover her palms like a sprinkling of hairs.

I reach for her, but my body buckles in pain. I fall as the first of the spasms catches and shakes me.

Call Malachi, I sign, before the pain wracks me again.

My DAUGHTER IS born into a village of the dying.

Malachi assists in the delivery. For reasons I can't understand, this birth tears at me as Aaron's never did. The child is healthy, and comes without complications: no excess blood, no twisting of life's cord around her throat. Yet I feel as if I am being ripped in two as she emerges slick and screaming into the world.

Her screams join those outside my window. I cannot rise from my bed, so I listen to Malachi's report.

There is plague, such as we have no experience of. It spreads rapidly, and none who was with you is without some sign of it.

He describes the symptoms: black threads emerging from the bodies of the afflicted, coating their eyes, their hair, their tongues. In the most advanced cases, these threads have thickened, the sufferers dragging them heavily like chains. The first Sensor to die—the woman who spoke to me this morning—is killed by black vines that explode from her chest, carrying a rotten stench beyond any death we know. Those nearest her are spattered with the gore, and they succumb to her malady in turn.

My Lady, Malachi says. *You must tell me what you know. You must help me to control this outbreak.*

I tell him everything. It is all for naught.

No medicine of his can halt the spread of the disease;

no spell of mine, however fervently repeated by my surviving disciples, can cripple the hedge that surrounds our village. It thickens by the hour, towering ten feet above the soil where it took root. If it continues at this pace, it will seal us all in eternal night before the coming of tomorrow's sun, what was meant to be our shield becoming our tomb.

I am too weak to rise when Malachi and those commoners who are untouched by the plague approach the hedge with torches, seeking to burn it from its bed. I lie with my child, having barely the strength to nurse her. She is ravenous, and the thought is in my mind that she will drink me dry.

Malachi returns with smudged face and hands, reporting success. The vine is vulnerable to flame, the village perimeter secured. He is preparing to return to his home for sleep when one of the few remaining Sensors arrives with word that the vines have grown anew. He sighs and rises from my bedside, torch in hand.

In time, it is decided that the village border must be permanently blackened by fire. Only repeated burning seems to prevent the vine from regaining its hold.

But the parasite is subtle, and not to be thwarted by such a simple device. Next it emerges from the cobbles beneath our feet, forcing its way into the village by routes we cannot see. Those who brush against it in passing fall victim to its touch. Malachi orders that deep wells be dug throughout the village, fires kept burning in them without cessation. The vines withdraw for a time. What they plan next is shrouded in darkness.

And all the while, the plague rages, and our people die. Those who assisted me have been buried in the village's newest addition—the plot of bare ground Malachi has designated as the cemetery—but the more recent sufferers, Sensors and commoners alike, exhibit symptoms even more extravagant than those of the newly dead. Their eyes crawl with black vermin, their mouths regurgitate lizards and frogs. These beasts spit venom in their turn, deadly to any whom it touches. When the hosts are emptied of all substance and collapse like vacant seed pods, we find that their shells attempt to take root where they have fallen, black tendrils inching from their fingers into soil or stone.

Malachi and his deputies fly to the cemetery and find their worst fears realized: where the bodies have been planted, black vines slither above the graves. There is nothing to do but burn them, and a new edict goes out from the chief healer's hand: only fire, not earth, can receive our bodies from now on.

My child thirsts. I wake, and sleep, and wake again, but it is ever the same.

Malachi calls a meeting at the Sensorium with his four remaining deputies, men and women he names the Company of the Sensorship. All are febrile with exhaustion and grief, their friends, their spouses, their children having fallen to the plague despite all efforts to stop it. In desperation, they draw up a list of ordinances by which, should any survive, the village is to be governed from this point forward. Malachi reads the new laws to me in the room where I lie with my hungry child.

There will be no more rituals such as that which you performed, he says, and his eyes burn at the memory of who first taught me the power of that ritual more than ten years ago. *The healing profession will be confined to essential tasks only: caring for common illnesses, assisting in births, preparing bodies for the fire. Meanwhile the Sensors....*

He pauses to wipe a hand across his eyes, whether in fatigue or sorrow I no longer have the capacity to tell.

The Sensors are too few to care for the management of the village. Another system of rule will be instituted, a governing body of Wardens to oversee daily affairs should order be restored. The surviving Sensors will retain responsibility for supplying the village with sustenance and fuel, but a new Sensor corps will be trained to take on an additional burden: that of defense.

Against queen? are the only words I have strength to sign.

Against the wild. We do not know when this outbreak may be contained, nor whether it may recur. The Ecosystem is not what it once was: new beings have been born of this organism, and we must be prepared to fight them. The next Sensor corps will be armed for this task with all the powers and weapons we can muster.

My eyes, so long dry from my daughter's endless draining, fill with tears. *Over then. No more peace, no more love.*

No more than we can afford.

I gaze at him, and it seems to me that he has become an old man overnight, as if his dreams were all that kept him young. My cousin the Queen could not have succeeded better had she killed us all.

Take Aaron, I say of a sudden. *Good boy. Strong. Will make best Sensor.*

My Lady....

Take him, I sign, and turn my head away. *Save village. Forget Delilah.*

He rises from my bedside, but he does not leave. He reaches out and touches my cheek, and if I could feel anything, I might feel his love for me. After all this, he is still the man he was, though never again can he show his true face to the world.

Your child, he says. *Our daughter. What is her name?*

Eva, I sign.

He nods as if in approval. *A very old name. It means "life."*

Need that now.

He smiles, turns to go. I wish my hands could call out to him, but they remain as still as stone by my sides.

Farewell, My Lady, he says.

When he is gone, I look into my child's dark eyes. She gazes back at me, and for the first time since she came into this world of sorrows, she seems satisfied. She rests, and I with her, though only one of us dreams.

WHILE MY DAUGHTER sleeps, the thing that slumbers within me wakes.

I try to convince myself that what I see are merely the shadows of the dawn growing long across my hands, my wrists, my arms. But when I rise for the first time in days and remove my clothing, the truth is everywhere: strands of black have spread across my body, their growth so rapid I can see them advance. My hair, long and tangled from many months of neglect, curls strangely about my cheeks and throat, as if it has become one with the vines that colonize my body. I have no mirror to view my face, but I know that if I could see myself, I would see that the whites of my eyes have turned to black.

With shaking hands, I remove the serpent token from my neck, wrap it in a strip of cloth. Carefully, making sure to touch only her blanket, not her flesh, I lift my sleeping babe from the bed and place her in a basket of woven reeds. The wrapped token goes into the basket beside her. I dress myself in the black robe and cowl I wore on that fatal night, and make my way across the village to Malachi's house.

I leave the basket by his front door, where he will find it when he wakes. Then I turn and make for the scorched circle that surrounds our village.

Torches burn without ceasing here, kept aflame by the

succession of exhausted commoners to whom Malachi has given the title of firestarters. The grass beyond the charred perimeter grows voraciously, having imbibed the parasite's clinging strength: *grabgrass*, the people call it. I avoid the bleary gaze of the man who guards the outskirts at this early hour, and move swiftly around the edge until I am beyond his sight. In minutes, he will reach this spot during his circuit of the village, so I must not delay.

My hand emerges from the sleeve of my cloak, my brown flesh wholly blackened by crawling threads. I reach for the nearest torch, pull it from the earth. The vines about my arm retreat instantly from the flame, but I cannot let my heart quail as they do.

I gaze at the village only once before holding the torch against the hem of my cloak and setting it aflame.

The parasite within me screams as the fire spreads. Or perhaps it is my tongue that screams: I do not know. Blackness clouds my sight, and it seems to me that my body shrinks to a hard kernel, as if the fire that sears my flesh burns away everything but that. I fall to the ground, and my final thought is that I will never rest in the bosom of the earth. I will lie like an ember on its deathbed of ashes, and my spirit will cry for release, but no sound will come from my throat except the sound of flames.

For I will be burning.

Forever, burning.

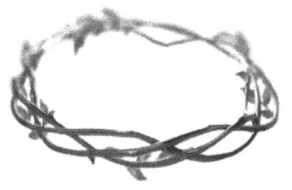

BOOK FOUR
SEED

*Perhaps the most radical act we can
commit is to stay home.*

—Terry Tempest Williams,
An Unspoken Hunger (1994)

THE DARK QUEEN'S web releases me. I should fall, but I have no sensation of falling; should open my eyes, but the vision burned into my memory squeezes them shut.

Now I know.

I know the fate of Delilah, and of the village I used to call my own. I know that the customs I'd thought to be ancient traditions were outgrowths of the plague that almost destroyed my home: the suppression of the healers, the creation of the Wardens, the scorched circle, the firewells, the burning of bodies, the rebirth of the Sensorship as a Brotherhood of warriors. What grief and shame Malachi must have suffered at the death of his queen, the death of his dream! And so he and his followers erased all history of the outbreak, spoke the lost queen's name no longer. On themselves, they exercised an even sterner judgment: bringers of plague, they would never again allow themselves to touch another's hand, share another's bed. Abandoned and bereaved, they would give up their attempts to forge a peaceful compact with the Ecosystem, and turn instead to open warfare against it.

And I know too why the lost queen returned. When I first saw the vision of my great-grandmother in the brood chamber, I saw only her face, not the pain written across it. I didn't know that her tightly closed mouth hid a wound only a queen could inflict and not even a queen could heal.

Now I know the truth: to secure her own power, Leonida silenced her cousin, exiled inhabitants of her city, tore her only daughter from her childhood friend. She drove the innocent to madness and death, and sat on her throne well satisfied with what she'd done. But everything she tried to banish returned—in her own time, or in mine.

You took it from me. Now I will take it back.

And yet, there's still much I don't know. I know *why* Delilah returned, but not *how*. I know that my grandfather returned to the city as well, but the mystery of his joining with Seraphina has only deepened. How could she consent to bear a child by the son of the woman her mother had so cruelly wronged? How could Aaron wish the mother of his child to be the daughter of his mortal enemy? Unless what he did was an act of retribution—forcing himself on Seraphina, compelling Leonida's line to bring forth Delilah's seed. And yet, everything I know about him tells me this can't be true: the visions I've seen of his younger days show me a man deeply in love with Seraphina, mourning her death, raising their daughter with devotion and pride. What, then, could have brought them together—what chance could have made the children of such bitter adversaries fall in love?

And what became of Delilah's daughter—the child Eva, my grandfather's younger sister? What life did she live after her mother fell, only to rise almost a century later in the body of another?

Miriam.

The memory of the girl whom Delilah's vengeful spirit possessed flashes through my mind, shocking me back to the present. I don't know how long I was wrapped in my great-grandmother's web, whether hours or days or years have passed. All I know is that when I departed for my journey into the past, the people I care about most—Isaac and Miriam, Leah and Gideon and all the others I left behind in the queen's courtyard—were in grave danger. I may have learned the truth, but the truth, I've also learned, isn't enough to protect the blameless from death.

I have to discover what's happened to my friends. I almost wish I could remain in this dream forever, horrible as it is; at least then, I wouldn't have to face what's happening now. For a long moment, I let myself retreat into the darkness, preferring a past I can't change to a future I can't bear.

But at last, I open my eyes.

THE BROOD CHAMBER lies in darkness. Though truly, after the darkness I've relived, not even the deepest of nights can hide its secrets from me.

The queen's web has vanished. Where the heavy strands filled the chamber to overflowing, now there's nothing but charred grit on the floor and walls. The only solid thing that remains is the token she wore, a feebly gleaming spiral of pink that's coated with soot like a snake's unshed skin.

I try to stand, but can't get my legs to cooperate. My body feels drained, my flesh hot, the way it does after I release a wave of angry power. Yet I have no memory of having done so, certainly not enough to burn the dark queen's web to cinders. I struggle to grasp what's happened to me, what's happened to her—and slowly, as the details of her life come back, I think I understand.

The brood chamber is the source of the queen's power, the place that connects her to the Ecosystem. When I accepted Delilah's bargain and submitted to her will, I didn't merely witness her life and death—I took her power into my own body. Which must mean I *was* the one who burned her web, reducing it to ashes with the fire that had raged inside her for eighty years. And then, when the parasite was utterly destroyed by that fire, her spirit departed, leaving me myself again, weakened but alive.

Did she know that was what would happen when she

took control of my body? Did she willingly transmit her power to me so the parasite could be exorcized at last, and her suffering come to an end?

I don't know the answer, and I doubt I ever will. All I know with certainty is that she's gone.

In the shadows at the edges of the brood chamber, dark shapes lie in a cluster. None is large enough to be my wyrm, so the poor thing must have been consumed along with the web. The figures are human, though they're so covered in ash I can barely make out their faces. I crawl to them on hands and knees, soot crunching beneath me like fine grains of glass. When I reach the first of the bodies, my eyes fill with tears.

It's Miriam, her hair filthy with the charred remains of the web, her eyes closed. She wears the remains of her wedding dress, though its creamy color is lost beneath scorched streaks. The terrible wasting of her frame under the dark queen's power has been reversed, leaving her with the young and slender figure that fell in the village gathering hall. Levi's blade no longer mars her breast, but when I lay a hand on her throat, her flesh is cold. My power blooms at our touch, and I'm conscious of everything that's fled her body: not only heartbeat and breath but the very spark of life. With the dark queen's passing, it seems I've recovered the gift of my birth, but the only thing it tells me is that Miriam is beyond my ability to heal.

Gently, I stroke her hair, feel its bounce beneath the ashy coating. I wish I could arrange her dense curls more naturally around her face, but that job will have to be left to hands more skillful than mine. I do take a thumb to the Sensor's token that hangs at her throat, wiping away the soot, restoring its shine. When we bury her body, I want everyone to know who she was, where she was from.

Next, I turn to Isaac.

He's covered in baked and blackened mud, but he's breathing, and his pulse is strong. I call on my power to heal the superficial cuts and bruises he suffered when he fell, along with the ugly scar from the dark queen's bird. When I lean down to kiss his forehead, my mouth comes away with foul-tasting grit. I run my tongue over my lips, wipe them with the back of my hand, but I feel as if I'll never be able to wash the flavor of death away.

Beulah is also alive, though the tall woman's pulse is desperately weak from the time she spent as a captive of the dark queen. Nothing prevents me from healing her; the parasite is there no longer to thwart my will. Beulah was exposed to that parasite for a shorter period than Miriam, and though her eyes remain closed for now, I know that when they open, they'll have returned to their natural brown.

My legs tremble, but I force myself to stand. With a foot, I wipe away the black residue from the center of the brood chamber until I find the depressions in the floor. Not sure what will happen, I place my feet in these marks, hold out my arms as I've done so many times in the past. I close my eyes, settle my thoughts, and reach out for the presence that has dwelt here for almost two hundred years.

Dominique, I call. *Hear me. Help me make contact.*

A breath passes over me, wafting the strands of my hair. It's followed by a deeper stirring in the chamber, a coming to life of the power that was stilled for a time by the dark queen. The golden strands of the Ecosystem tickle my ankles, tentatively nudge my wrists, as if they're fearful of being caught in the queen's web. When the feel of my flesh assures them that it's their own queen who's called, they twine about me, weave themselves into my bracelets and hair. I send out a calming wave to let them know I'm all right, then open myself fully to the images that stream into my mind at their touch.

My friends survive. Celestina's power has returned along with mine, and she's healed Gideon of his grievous wound, the others of their lesser hurts. I see Leah, as feisty as ever; Angelica, red hair flaming; Aurelia, her arm around Gideon's back while the old firestarter takes small, careful steps. The whole group of them are making their way through the ruins of the dark queen's web, which lies in sodden heaps on the courtyard. Still, it's a tough road to wade through, especially with Gideon having yet to recover his strength, and it will be some time before they reach the queen's residence.

I expand my range from the small circle of human figures to the world around them. When I do, I'm flooded by a feeling of relief so strong, my knees buckle and the golden strands have to catch me before I fall.

The Ecosystem survives as well, damaged but not undone. The power of the dark queen, once so deeply rooted in the soil I thought it could never be torn loose, has dissipated as fully as the web in this chamber, leaving only a silty deposit on the forest floor. There's new life beneath, buds and saplings striving to push through what's left of the dark queen's shroud. Bloodbirds circling high overhead scan the city with keen eyes and tell me that the last of the queen's abominations have been washed from the streets, while the natural creatures she recruited to her service have slunk or crawled or flown back to the places they belong. Sunlight bathes the birds' backs as they soar over the city, and I know that within hours, the brightness of the returning day will wither the last traces of the queen's web deeper in the forest. I think of the only nursery rhyme I learned from my mother before she died, the one I used to recite to myself during my earliest days in my grandfather's house:

> Through the forest, dark and drear
>
> Lonely hunter, home is near

And I know that the forest will mend, that it will become a home again to everything the darkness drove away.

I send out a last thought before releasing the strands of the Ecosystem.

Bury her body well, I tell it. *Bury it deep within your breast, that her wounded spirit may finally be at peace.*

Then I open my eyes and call out for the city's true Queen.

WHILE I'M WAITING for my replacement to arrive, I use my hands to sweep soot from the floor, which helps restore the room's golden glow. Still, it's going to take the labor of all the queen's maids—along with the assistance of a jackalass or two—before it's back to the way it was.

A soft moan announces Beulah's waking. She looks around confusedly, squinting against the room's gleam before settling on my face, the sight of which doesn't seem to soothe her. Having caught a peep of my grimy cheeks and sooty hair in the reflective surface of the floor, I can understand why.

"Beulah," I say, taking her hand in mine. "Do you know me?"

"Mistress Sarah," she says groggily. "Where are we?"

"In the City of the Queens," I say, before I recall that for her, there *is* no City of the Queens, time having frozen at Miriam and Isaac's wedding. "I'll explain later."

I help her stand, support her while she finds her balance. Her eyes widen when she sees the girl who lies as if sleeping on the brood chamber floor.

"Mistress Miriam," she says softly. "She must have died when … when Master Levi…." Her eyes sparkle in the golden light. "Where's Leah?" she asks, and I see that her memory of the wedding has returned fully to her.

I'm spared an immediate response when Isaac lets out

a groan and struggles to rise. I give Beulah a quick smile of comfort, then catch him before he loses his footing.

He grips instinctively. The familiar tingle spreads up my arm at his touch, followed by a cascade of sights and sounds I wish I could block out: his body drowning in the dark queen's web, his limbs jerking at the monstrous bird's bite. It's as if, with Miriam's death, I've reclaimed the deep connection he and I have shared these past months, and yet all it can show me is his pain.

He pulls away from me when he sees her, then falls to his knees at her side. His hand reaches out to touch her face, but it shakes too badly to complete the action.

"Isaac," I say delicately, laying a hand on his shoulder. "I tried to save her. But she was already gone. I think she's been gone a long time."

"I know," he says in a voice that's more like a sob. "I always knew. You tried to tell me, but ... I just couldn't accept it."

"She loved you," I say. "You must know that as well."

He looks up at me, his expression poised somewhere between entreaty and accusation. "I do know," he says. "But it doesn't help."

I kneel beside him, take him in my arms. He buries his head in my shoulder and cries without restraint, without shame. Without end, it feels to me while I hold him. I could use my power to spread healing strength through his body, but I know it's better simply to let him grieve. He has the rest of his life to heal.

I can't tell how much time has passed before the echo of footsteps makes me look up. When I do, I see that our group has more than doubled in size, with Celestina,

Angelica, Aurelia, and Gideon standing outside the door to the brood chamber. They're begrimed by the remains of the dark queen's web, but otherwise none the worse for their trek across the courtyard. Their expressions are hard to read, though I think I detect a hint of celebration beneath the respectful mourning. Saving Miriam was my quest, and Isaac's. Saving the City of the Queens was theirs, and though Gideon moves stiffly from his wound, I can tell he's ready to start the work of rebuilding, single-handed if he must.

There's a shriek from behind the others, and Leah pushes through the crowd to throw herself at Beulah. In her ecstasy at seeing her beloved alive, my friend nearly knocks the taller woman over, which gives her an excuse to wrap her arms around Beulah's waist and hold tight. I watch as the confusion on Beulah's face gives way to a look of pure bliss. The sight warms my heart, though I'd be lying if I didn't admit to a touch of envy. I feel—no, I know—that no one will ever look at me that way.

The Queen has left Angelica to place her hand on Miriam's brow. I exchange glances with her, but what I see in her silver eyes confirms what I already know. So long as the thread of life remains, there's a chance that a queen of the realm may reknit the frayed ends. Once that thread snaps, the only life that's possible is one such as Delilah's: a ghoulish existence that feeds off the life of others. Even with our combined powers, Miriam is truly gone.

Isaac must have accepted this, too. His tears have ceased, and he draws a deep breath as I help him to his feet. I kiss the salty mess of his cheeks before addressing the others. My words, though, are mostly for him.

"Her burial will be that of a queen," I say. "Her window will hang in the council house when the city is restored to its former glory, along with that of Delilah and all the queens who might have been."

"Who utters the name of the queen?" a new voice booms from the tunnel outside.

I turn to see who's spoken, and discover Celestina's housekeeper stomping toward us, her bad hip rising and falling sharply in her haste. How she made it all the way from the forest, much less down the stairs and tunnel, is beyond me. Perhaps that accounts for her expression: a scowl that looks as if she's haggling with grim death itself, and barely winning. I find myself guiltily wishing she hadn't survived the assault on the city. Or at least, that she'd stayed at the campsite where we left her.

But she's not alone. Her hand is knotted—barely, since the one who holds it is straining to free herself—with Rebecca's.

THE LITTLEST SENSOR succeeds in pulling away from the aged housekeeper and launches herself into my arms. The first true smile I've seen on Isaac's face in far too long accompanies Rebecca's ebullience. I can't help smiling myself at the girl's more than usually bubbly demeanor.

That comes to an end when she sees Miriam. She slips from my embrace and kneels beside the dead body, her face taking on the solemn look I saw earlier in the forest. No one stops her when she touches Miriam's cheek then withdraws her hand, looking at her ash-smeared fingers as if she expects some change to come over the body. She glances up, and her eyes, though filled with tears, are lit by an inner radiance I don't expect to see in a child, not even such a child as her.

The one she's looking at is the old woman, who hobbles forward to stand at her side. Rebecca reaches up and touches her wrinkled hand, and the woman nods. From one of the many bulging pockets in her apron, she removes some small object and holds it out to the girl. It catches the golden light of the brood chamber, and I startle when I see what adorns Rebecca's outstretched wrist.

It's a bracelet of black vines, so like in appearance to the parasite we've just defeated, I'm afraid it's an actual cutting from the dark queen's web. My queenly power tells me a moment later that I'm mistaken: the band is inanimate, forged of black metal that shimmers like an animal's glossy hide. Its construction and design are similar to Celestina's bracelets, and I wonder if, like hers, it's meant to recall someone loved, someone lost. But I can think of only one person who might be held in memory by such an object, and I reach out to my student in alarm.

"Rebecca—"

She waves me off. "It's okay, Sarah," she says, and I'm struck not only by the confidence but the sadness in her voice. "I know what I'm doing."

With the bracelet around her wrist, she lays her hand on Miriam's forehead. I can hardly believe my eyes when the black metal moves, wriggling like living vines. I feel the power flowing from the object, and I realize that it *is* alive, or maybe *was*, and is being brought back to life at Rebecca's command. A black teardrop forms on its surface, lengthens, and takes the shape of a seed, which Rebecca catches in her other hand as it falls. She cradles it in her cupped palm for a moment, drawing a deep breath before opening her hand fully. It's then that I see what she holds, and it's all I can do not to swat it away.

It's a stunflower seed.

The same type of seed Daniel showed me nearly a year ago in the village, when I was a freshly minted Sensor who knew nothing of my true ancestry. The same type of seed whose shell Delilah wrapped around the parasite that consumed her and nearly destroyed us all. When Rebecca opens Miriam's frozen mouth and holds the seed in two fingers above the bloodless lips, I press forward, desperate to stop it from falling.

But I'm caught from behind by someone much

stronger than myself: the queen's housekeeper, who holds me in a grip that belies her gnarled hands. An all too familiar surge of power flows from her, and my mind darkens, the brood chamber and its occupants fading from sight. All I can see are her ancient eyes, and in that moment, I know who she is.

"Eva!" I cry out. Some great resistance seems to trap my tongue, but I manage to shout to the others: "Delilah's daughter! Stop her—stop Rebecca!"

Isaac is the first to react, lunging for Rebecca's hand as it hovers over Miriam's mouth. Celestina stands slack-jawed and frozen while Angelica, Leah, and Aurelia charge the old woman. But their movements are as sluggish as my thoughts, and none of them can reach the child before she lets the seed fall between Miriam's lips.

The seed of the dark queen, Delilah.

Her daughter must have planned for this moment, readied her weapon in case of her mother's defeat. Somehow, she harvested the final speck of the dark queen's life from the field where she fell, and waited in the city all these years for her mother's return. And then, when we seemed to have won, she used a Sensor already compromised by the dark queen's power to let loose her plague once more.

Eva's hands release me. I stand as motionless as Celestina, expecting and dreading to see black vines erupt from Miriam's eyes, her mouth, her hair. The others cluster behind me, their hands on the old woman's arms and shoulders, seemingly turned to stone. Rebecca gazes up at Isaac and smiles.

Miriam's chest heaves a breath, and her eyes flutter open.

They're the color they always were, nighttime purple as deep as a sky filled with stars. They flick back and forth the way I recall from so many training sessions when she was overwhelmed by my instructions, or by her own doubts. They find Rebecca first, and the look of anxiety eases somewhat. But it's not until they find Isaac that they brighten with grateful tears.

He kneels, his hands poised in the air as if he's afraid to touch her. Then, wrapping his arms around her, he raises her torso in a careful embrace. I feel the warmth and suppleness flowing from her limbs, the steady beating of her heart beneath the Sensor's token she wears. The wound from Levi's knife has closed. I search deeply for signs of injury or illness, but there's no hint of anything amiss, no trace of the darkness I fear to find. Against everything I've known, everything I've learned, Rebecca's seed has restored Miriam, brought her back healed and whole. When I reach out to her, I feel the health of her young body, along with an outpouring of love that surpasses my words to tell.

I look away from her and Isaac lest my tears spoil theirs. When I find Rebecca's eyes on me, I kneel and bow my head before her.

"My Queen," I say.

Everyone—or everyone except the reunited couple, who can't be bothered with such formalities—follows my example. Even Celestina lowers her proud head, and ancient Eva settles stiffly to a knee to honor the one I called for, without knowing who it was I called—the city's true Queen.

Rebecca lets us stay like that for a moment before she places a hand beneath my chin, lifting my face to look at her. She smiles placidly, but for me, who knows the queen's bargain and the queen's burden, there's a sorrow behind the smile that I doubt will ever fade. I think of Dominica's mournful eyes that used to look out over the city from the council house window, and my heart breaks at the realization of all this child has given.

"It's okay, Sarah," she says in a voice for my ears alone. "Eva explained everything. I'm ready now."

Realization dawns on me at her words. "It was you I dreamed of," I say. "Not Dominique. You've been coming here."

"It was both of us," she says. "Eva brought me here to begin the training. She showed me how to make contact, how to relive Dominique's life. I saw what needed to be done, but for the longest time I was too afraid to do it."

And how were you brave enough now? I want to ask her. *How did you know that your strength, your will, wouldn't fail?*

Instead, I merely smile, and lean forward to kiss the young Queen's cheek.

Isaac stands, Miriam in his arms. The others are a step behind, myself included. Only Rebecca remains on the floor, her head cocked as she looks up at the big people who surround her. I see that she's slipped down from her knees to a reclining position, with her legs scissored to the side and a single arm supporting her weight. I reach out to her with my healer's power, and I realize at once what I should have known all along.

I kneel beside her again. She smiles and wraps her arms around my neck. I lift her gently. Gideon will have to design a new throne for her, something to help her keep her body upright. Maybe something others can carry.

For now, I bear Queen Rebecca from her brood chamber in my arms, and she lays her head against my cheek as if it's the softest of feather cushions.

THE CITY MOURNS for a week. That's traditional when a queen dies. Life doesn't stand still—there's too much to be done—but it does slow down as we pay homage to Delilah, and to all who were lost in this needless war.

Today, however, is a day to look ahead. A day to celebrate our victory, though it came at such great cost.

I've never attended a coronation, my own ascent to the throne having been decidedly on-the-fly. The bells ring out at midday from the council house, which stands tall despite broken windows and a few last traces of arachnard web. The joyous sound echoes through the city lanes, shakes the pavestones. It's accompanied by the cheers and whistles of the citizens who've gathered to watch as Rebecca is borne up the council house steps. The streets are as clean of dust and rubble as can be hoped. To add a touch of color, Celestina sends silverbloom petals spiraling into the air above the processional. For my part, I've asked a flock of bloodbirds to circle overhead, their russet wings cutting sharp figures against the teal blue sky. Our efforts aren't what they might have been had this day not come at the tail end of a war, but we've created enough beauty that Rebecca is all smiles in her litter of flowers.

Gideon is one of the bearers—and, of course, the designer—of the carriage on which the young Queen sits: a chair supported by poles, with a strong back and firm bolsters for its occupant's comfort. The old firestarter stands at the front right corner with his beard braided and a new eye-patch in Rebecca's favorite color, pink. I hold the bar across from him, while Aurelia and Isaac take the rear. Old Eva walks in the very back, her presence signifying the new Queen's lineage: from Dominica to Divina to Delilah to Eva, then down three generations to Rebecca, last of the line. When I look between the two of them, Eva and her great-granddaughter, I think I see a trace of the old woman's strong chin in Rebecca's girlish face, a hint of Delilah's restless spirit in Rebecca's wide, dark eyes. It still amazes me, though, that the last heir of Delilah lived among us for eight years, and none of us ever knew.

But after all, why should I be surprised? Delilah's name was never spoken in the village following the plague she introduced. Looking back, there were signs that Rebecca belonged to the lost queen's lineage: her ability to Sense the black vines long before anyone else, the ease with which the queen possessed her when Rebecca merged minds with the bloodbird. It was only thanks to Eva's lessons, however, that she learned who she truly was, and what power had been granted her.

Another cheer goes up as Rebecca waves to the onlookers from the top of the council house stairs. She's wearing the serpent-token I retrieved from the brood chamber, one of the city's artisans having set the symbol in a necklace of black metal to preserve it. At her wrist, the living circlet gleams in the afternoon light. The crowd waits impatiently while the members of the Queen's processional enter the council house, with Eva taking much longer to climb the stairs than is to anyone's liking. Then the common people stream inside, far more than the room can comfortably hold, but no one is going to be barred from witnessing the ceremony on this day of all days. Buildings that have stood for centuries have been toppled; friends who have lived beneath the Ecosystem's exacting rule all their lives have been parted never to see each other more. But today, for the first time in months, we look toward the future with hope in our hearts.

Rebecca smiles and waves again as we set the litter down on the dais at the head of the room. Faithful Gideon picks up the child who's nearly become his adoptive granddaughter and places her on what is perhaps his most ingenious contrivance: a wooden chair with strong circles of metal on each side so the littlest Sensor, now the littlest Queen, can transport herself without the use of her legs. She gave up a lifetime's worth of running and skipping when she healed Miriam, forfeiting a part of her physical life to restore another's. She explained to me what Eva told her, though I'm still astonished to learn of this new thing in the Ecosystem.

"The seed came from Delilah's body," she said. "From a vine that flowed with her own blood. But when she created it, she was filled with so much hurt, the thing she grew knew only how to lash out. That's what happened when the seed was planted again: the black vines tried to finish what Delilah started eighty years ago. But it doesn't have to be that way. Eva taught me how to grow a good seed. One that heals, not one that kills."

"But your legs…" I said.

"The Queen can't heal without sacrifice," she said. "You know that. You've given up a lot, too, haven't you, Sarah?"

I nodded, and blinked back tears.

"But how did Delilah's seed come back?" I asked, trying to work the scratchiness from my throat. "The last thing I saw in the brood chamber was her death. How could any part of her have survived to be planted again?"

She smiled. "Ask Eva. She tells the story much better than I do."

I'm going to have to wait until after the coronation to have that talk. Eva's busy in the days leading up to the ceremony, and the only one she'll share anything with is her great-granddaughter.

Now the old woman takes the two stairs up to the dais, each step of hers an eternity of anticipation. When she reaches the platform, she waits another long moment before turning to face the audience. I can see how heavily she's breathing, and I wonder what happened to the Eva who so effortlessly restrained me in the queen's brood chamber. Then she raises her hands, and her voice rings out over the hushed crowd, as strong and clear as the waves of power that flow from her.

"All my life, I have lived in the shadow of the rupture that divided this city from my former home," she says. "I was born of that rupture, daughter of a queenly woman and a gentle man who sought to mend a great evil only to fall victim to it. For many years, I have awaited the time when we could be reunited once more: when a daughter of the village could sit on the throne of the city, and the warring among those who share a single history and a single sorrow could come to an end. Today, with the crowning of my great-granddaughter, Queen Rebecca"—she pauses to cast a smile on the child, who beams back—"the day I have dreamed of for so long has finally come to pass."

At a signal from Eva, Rebecca's friend Zipporah steps forward and ascends the dais, bearing a pink cushion on which a black circlet rests. The old woman takes up the crown in trembling hands, and I see that it's shaped exactly the same as Rebecca's bracelet, except two small jewels are set side by side among the vines that overlap in front: replicas of the Sensor's token and healer's charm that have passed through my own hands, insignias of the two factions that come together in one person today. Eva stumps behind the wheeled chair—the audience leans forward in their benches as if to will her faster—and holds the crown high before lowering it onto Rebecca's brow. Then she circles to the side of the chair, kisses her great-granddaughter's cheek, and faces the crowd once more.

"I give you Queen Rebecca!" she announces in a voice that carries against the vaulted ceiling. "Long may she reign!"

"Queen Rebecca!" the crowd responds, and the stone walls echo the sound of cheers, laughter, and stomping feet. Rebecca smiles through it all, her eyes shining. Until, that is, Zipporah whispers something in her ear, and she bursts into a fit of giggling, a child once more.

With the Cathedral and the library reduced to rubble, we have no indoor space large enough to hold the celebration that follows. We settle for an open-air party in the new Queen's garden, which Rebecca has adorned with pink flowers grown by her own small hand. Food isn't what I'd call abundant, but using our combined powers, Celestina and I have restored the city's gardens to working order, so no one goes hungry. For entertainment, we have the songs of birds selected for a minimum of raucousness. Dusk falls, but the party goes on, flameflies dancing in the air at Rebecca's command to provide a soft and enchanting light. That suits Celestina and Angelica just fine, as the two go about making perfect fools of themselves with their quite public displays of affection.

I seem to be the only one in attendance without a partner, so I stick to the shadows, watching the others as they talk and laugh: Michael and Luke exploring the grounds, Aurelia and Gideon deep in conversation—no doubt trading warriors' tales—while scores of well-wishers cluster around the youthful Queen. Leah clings to Beulah's arm as she steers her around the garden, and I laugh to see how cleverly my friend has cloaked her insecurities under the mantle of protectiveness. I try not to let my eyes stray too often to the bench where Miriam and Isaac sit, the two of them holding hands and locked into a private world the hubbub can't penetrate. When I fail, I focus on how beautiful Miriam looks, with her hair braided through with Rebecca's flowers and her lavender eyes drinking in her beloved's face.

This is what I wanted, I tell myself. To save her, even if that meant I was sure to lose him.

Full night has fallen by the time Rebecca frees herself from her admirers and wheels up to me along one of the garden lanes, already adept in her special chair.

"Sarah!" she chides. "You haven't talked to me all day."

"You've been busy."

"I know," she says, and her eyes glow with excitement. "Can you imagine?"

I smile back, though I wonder whether, after this day is done and the hard work of ruling begins, she'll need my counsel as she did when she was training for the Sensorship. Maybe I can teach her to read, so she can consult the books old Malachi found when he served at her great-great-grandmother's side.

As if detecting my concerns—but of course she can, for she's the Queen—Rebecca speaks in a hushed voice. "Don't worry," she says. "I won't be alone my whole life. I'm going to be the first sitting queen to get married."

I smile. "Who are you going to marry, little hydra bird?"

"Not *now*," she says, giggling. "Though Caleb's kind of cute. And Noah."

"How can you tell them apart?"

"Easy," she says. "Caleb's the one with dimples." Then, as is her habit, her face turns serious. "Why should queens be kept from marrying? Why shouldn't we be able to care for the Ecosystem *and* for ourselves? When the time is right, I'm getting married."

I think back to Daniel's words at Miriam and Isaac's first, almost doomed wedding: *None of us, be the gifts of our birth what they may, should dwell beyond the community of human love and sorrow.* "I'm sure you will, dear one," I say to the girl before me, and plant a kiss on her fresh young cheek.

But my eyes can't help wandering to the place where Miriam and Isaac were sitting. I find that place empty, the bench basking in a pool of moonlight. Was this the same bench, I wonder, where my grandfather and grandmother met for their forbidden trysts? I hunt the grounds, but I'm unable to spot the couple anywhere else in the garden. I try to be happy for them, but my heart is a stone, and its weight is the tale of my whole life to come.

The Queen smiles knowingly, and reaches out to comfort me as only her touch can.

THERE ARE THREE weddings today. One for the village. One for the city. One for the union of Sensors and healers. There might be a fourth soon. Gideon and Aurelia draw me aside before the first of the nuptials to tell me they've taken up housekeeping together. I'm thrilled, and I wish them—old as they are—a lifetime of happiness. In my secret heart, I wonder why I always seem to be the last to suspect when love takes root and grows.

Leah and Beulah join hands first, and my best friend sobs like a child when Queen Rebecca solemnizes their vows.

Celestina and Angelica follow. The former queen blazes like a gemstone of ebony and silver, but Angelica is no slouch herself, with her red hair piled high and her skintight green dress worn off her shoulders to showcase her tattoo. She plants a kiss on her beloved's lips that would curl a fell-cat's fur.

Miriam and Isaac approach the dais last. His limp is gone, her fragility erased thanks to Rebecca's early-morning ministrations. Their clothes are plain, cut in the village manner. Seeing them dressed so takes me back to days long past, when I walked with my grandpa through the lanes of stone, full of a child's nervousness and excitement. As they speak their vows, I lay aside my own cares and open myself to their joy, and I discover something I've never felt in quite this way before: the two of them have become whole at last, cured of every hurt by the power of the other's hand. I've known such love in my life, it's strange it took me so long to learn this. By the time the two of them chastely kiss and turn to face the cheering throng, I find that the heaviness in my chest has given place to a certain buoyancy, and I'm able to bring my hands together in good earnest, and smile and cheer with the rest.

Miriam descends the dais and walks up the aisle arm-in-arm with the boy we both loved. When she reaches my place, she leans over to kiss me.

"Thank you," she says simply, her eyes glossy with tears.

Isaac smiles at me, that's all. Then they pass up the aisle together and are lost to my sight in the crowd.

After, when the revelry is done and the wedded couples have departed for their separate residences, I sit down for my talk with Eva. I've not had much time to work out the family tree, but my grandfather was her older brother, so she's my great-aunt, and Rebecca some species of cousin. Whether Miriam is a branch of that tree or not, I'm eager to learn.

The old woman settles into a chair by the Queen's fireplace, in the same room where Aurelia told me of my grandfather's mother. The days have been warm since the dark queen's death, but Eva calls on the maid to light a fire and stoke it until it's roaring. As I study the woman across from me, there's no doubt in my mind—and, more, in my body—that my great-aunt is failing. She seems to have shriveled in a mere couple of days, becoming less the strapping warrior who mastered me in the brood chamber and more like the picture I carry in my head of wizened old Malachi, her father. How much longer she'll live now that she's accomplished her end, I can't fully say, but I fear it won't be long enough to watch her great-granddaughter grow to be a woman.

It'll probably be long enough for her to answer my questions, but I jump into them without delay just in case. "When did you come to live in the city?"

"When I was seventeen," she answers, somewhat

hoarsely. She clears her throat, but that doesn't help much. "I had given birth in my sixteenth year to my sole child, a daughter named Tamar. Rebecca's grandmother. I knew nothing of my mother, having learned only that she died when I was born. But when my own daughter arrived, something happened that I could not explain."

She pauses, and I begin to see what Rebecca meant. The young Queen is too excitable to build the drama, but Eva knows how to tell a good story.

"I saw visions," she resumes after a moment. "Waking visions of a woman with flowing black hair, garbed in a cloak of matching black. I couldn't see her face beneath the cowl she wore. The visions were so real to me, they blocked out the world when they came, like a cloud passing over the face of the sun. They were at their most vivid when I was nursing Tamar, and I feared that I was going mad. I sought out the village healers, but they could do nothing. Or so I thought. In fact, they did something for which I cursed them at the time, and perhaps should have cursed them more in the days that followed."

"They told Malachi," I say.

She frowns, and I make a promise to myself not to steal her thunder again.

"They told Malachi," she confirms. "He called me to him from the home I shared with my husband and child. Now mind, he was never much of a father to me during the days I lived under his roof. He was distracted by the upkeep of the Sensorship, and moody whenever I sought his time. He would not touch me, which I thought odd but could in no way contrive to raise with him. Now he seemed fearful, more fearful even than I. He questioned me closely about my visions, and after I told him every-thing, he divulged the secret he had kept from me all my days. A secret he'd worried I might uncover on my own, through the power of the queen's touch, if ever his vigi-lance wavered."

"So you were," I start, then bite my tongue.

"I was incensed," she says, while her eyes dress me down. "I was a young mother, and to learn what had become of my own mother—that she might have been queen—that she was wronged, mutilated, and exiled from her home to die in despair—and that the whole had been hidden from me, the child for whom she died—well, I was incensed," she repeats, more grumpily than convincingly. "Ere I departed my father's hut, vowing never to return, he gave me my mother's token as if in apology for all he had withheld, but I swore to myself that I would not be satis-fied with such a sop, and would reclaim her lost birthright if I could. But how?"

She glances at me to see if I have anything to add. I sit on my hands and smile back pleasantly.

"So I left the village," she says, nodding in approval. "Not at once. I spent a year learning my mother's history, from the moment she was born to the day she died—not from my father, whom I spurned on the rare occasions he crossed my path, but from the earth itself. I discovered in that year that I had only to ask the ground, the cicatrix, the trees to whisper her tale in my ear, and it would come to me. This was power indeed, and I took it in hungrily, as hungrily as my child drew milk from my breast. I had no idea why this power had slumbered in me so long only to awaken now, but I knew that it was my mother's power, and that it was the power for which she had died. I knew, too, that her spirit still lived somewhere, for I heard her voice most clearly when I neared the edge of the stone circle. For a solid year, while my husband slept, I bundled my child at my breast and scoured the blackened turf surrounding the village, taking care always to dress in dark clothes and to slip away whenever the threshers drew near. I dug deeply beneath the charred soil, for some instinct told me that what I sought lay buried there, beneath years of burning and reburning. And at last, I found it: I found my mother's seed."

I nod vigorously, urging her to go on.

"I could tell at once that this seed came from her body," she says. "That it was of her blood as surely as I, and that, when she died, it was all that remained of the woman she had been. I could tell, too, that it was a thing of great and terrible power—a thing born of her desolation, and kept from becoming a pestilence to us all only by the repeated burning of the ground in which it lay. I knew that, if I was to advance my plan, it could not be done by replanting this seed. So, with some regret, I buried it again, and departed the village that very night, leaving my year-old daughter behind."

"You did?" I say, startled out of my schoolgirl manners. "Why?"

"Because I was headed for the City of the Queens," she answers sharply. "Alone, I hoped I might escape Queen Leonida's notice, or, if she discovered who I was, forfeit only my own life, not my child's as well. But when I arrived, it was as if fate had arranged for my coming. For it was there that I met Seraphina."

"Mm-hm," I say, as innocuously as I can.

"Seraphina, the Queen's daughter," the old woman goes on, her voice gaining vigor as if she's reliving that long-ago encounter. "I had not heard of her—I saw Aaron little enough in those days, and he never spoke her name— but when I came within her presence, I knew at once who she was, and what she had been to my brother. During the first year of my residence in the city, I joined the Queen's handmaidens so that I might twine my heart about her daughter's, and in time, I heard the girl's secrets from her own lips. And then, at the conclusion of that year, I knew the time had come."

"But didn't Leonida know?" I blurt out, unable to contain myself any longer. "Didn't she realize who you were?"

She crosses her arms, and for a minute I think she's not going to answer. *Never interrupt crotchety eighty-year-olds*, I say to myself. *Especially those with a grievance against you to begin with.*

"Queen Leonida did not suspect," Eva says in a low growl. "For I used my powers to blind her eyes, just as she had used hers to take my mother's tongue."

She talks on, while the fire dies and the room grows dark, no maid appearing to rekindle the hearth. In time, she's nothing more to me than a voice issuing from the darkness, invoking days no less dark. Listening to this woman of almost unspeakable power tell her tale, I wonder why she did not simply wrest the throne from Leonida and place herself upon it. But then it comes to me: the rift between us was caused by all that's worst among our kind, by Leonida's lust for dominion, Delilah's thirst for vengeance. Grieved though she was at her mother's fate, Eva longed to heal the wound that had brought her into this world the only way it could be healed: by love.

"I returned to the village at the close of the year," she says, "and told Aaron what I had discovered. At first he would not believe me, but I showed it to him through the eyes of the Ecosystem—showed *her* to him, the woman Seraphina had become. I told him I had learned of ways to convey him quickly to the city, through underground passages only urthwyrms traveled, so that he might visit his old playmate and return before he was missed. Still it was risky, and we could not contrive to bring him to her more than once or twice a year. But I assured the two that, whenever Aaron should visit his childhood friend—now his beloved—I would cast such a spell over the Queen's eyes that the secret entrance to her garden, though dug at the order of Leonida herself as a means of escaping the city should the need arise, would remain beyond her sight. Seraphina was furious at her mother for the acts she had not understood as a child, and so she willingly embraced my deception. And it was effective: not even in her brood chamber did I permit Leonida to penetrate the night in which I enfolded her. Oh, how I exulted then that I could wield such power over her wicked mind!"

She pauses, and I listen to her nearly silent breathing, as if she's become one with the darkness around her. I wonder if this is the reason the Ecosystem seemed so muddled when I asked it to show me more of Seraphina and Aaron's meeting—why it showed me the pregnant Delilah leaving the city instead. Could it be that it was trying to show me the unsuspected child in the lost queen's womb, the child who would later draw a curtain over its eyes and Leonida's alike?

"In time, as you know, Seraphina gave birth to my brother Aaron's daughter, and died that same night," the old woman goes on. "Then it was that I feared all my pains had been for nothing, and I spirited him and his child back to the village by secret paths Leonida did not know. Whether the Queen ever learned how she had been duped, I cannot say. I kept watch over her in the city, and drew a veil around her so thick I hoped no ray of light could peek through. But for all that, I could not prevent my mother's final prophecy from coming to pass: the girl whom my brother loved did indeed suffer great pain ere the end, and Leonida was indeed withered by the sting I planted in her bosom, and died at long last a broken and miserable creature."

Again there's a pause. An image jumps into my mind of a white-haired hag whose blue eyes bulge from a face as pale as a skull. I shake my head to clear away the vision, but it won't depart until a wave of power from Eva makes it fade into the darkness.

"Aaron raised the girl, your mother, to follow in his footsteps," she continues after a time. "I visited him now and again—him, and my own grown child, now raising a daughter of her own—but I always returned within a day's time to keep watch over the doings in the city. For years, your grandfather and I debated whether, despite the mother's death, his daughter might not grow to sit on the throne. I insisted that it could be done, but Aaron was wary, and his grief at Seraphina's death not quick to pass. In the end, he argued for a middle course: that we might strive to resurrect the prestige of the healers in the village, and in so doing end the war among our own kind."

"Really?" I say. "I thought my grandpa … well, that he distrusted the healers."

"His first allegiance was to the Sensorship," she answers. "But he believed he had found another who might help heal the breach without challenging the Sensors' power. A newly appointed Warden, deeply devoted to the welfare of the village, and eager to distinguish himself in its service."

"Daniel."

"You know your history," she says with the hint of a smile. "At Aaron's bidding, I gave the young Warden my mother's token, and taught him some of the simple songs I had heard her spirit whispering on the wind. I made him swear never to reveal his activities to the Sensorship lest, this time, they destroy the line of healers root and branch. Of the ritual that produced the plague, I of course said nothing, nor did I breathe a word of the seed that rested to that day deep beneath the earth. In the end, alas, all my devices were undone: Aaron's daughter fell in love with one of Daniel's recruits, the Sensor Abraham, and began training secretly with Daniel—Chief Warden by that time—while my mother's seed was discovered, though by what means I have grown too old and weak to learn."

I say nothing to that, but I note in her quavering voice what I saw in the firelight: she is far from the woman she was in her prime. "Then you don't know how Miriam was…." *Infected*, I think. "Chosen?" I say.

"If you ask whether the girl is any family of mine, the answer is no," she says. "But how the spirit of my mother came to manifest itself in her body, I cannot guess."

I'm disappointed, but she gives me no chance to probe further before she lets out a heavy sigh.

"It may be that the death of my mother's enemy was what finally stole my strength," she says. "While Leonida lived, I had reason for anger; when she died, I had cause for little but remorse. In the days that followed, I lost the ability to foretell, much less control, the outcome of events. I did not guess that Estella would turn the city's wyrms to her own service, so that neither I nor my brother could readily travel between city and village, and I surely did not imagine that your father Abraham—Gabriel—would call for the mother of his child, thereby sealing her doom. After that tragedy, I hastened to the village one last time, only to hear from your grandfather's lips that he could no longer abet a plan that had cost him both his beloved and his only child. With a heavy heart I returned to the city, and here I have remained."

"You never went back?" I ask.

"Never," she says. "I lost all contact with the village, even with my own flesh and blood. Word reached me years ago, in a vision it may have been, that my father had left the world that had blasted all his dreams. But I was as shocked as any when Celestina sent her mother's wyrms against my former home—even more shocked when, against all hope, that calamity brought the girl Rebecca to the city. I could do no more than introduce her to her birthright while you sat upon the throne, but so soon as you departed for the mountains, I knew I must act. I hastened my great-granddaughter's training in the woods beyond the city, taught her of the seed that can kill or cure. To the Ecosystem, I swore a solemn vow: that the one I raised to take up Delilah's scepter would seek no vengeance, utter no curse. She would live in the Ecosystem as the Queen is meant to live—as its daughter, humble and wise. And so it has come to pass. For the last child of my mother's family *is* wise, and long after I am no more, she will live to mend the hurts her ancestors have done."

Her voice falls silent. I can't even hear her breathing, and I have a moment's fear that with these final words, her life has departed indeed. But when I reach out with my own small share of queenly power, I find that I'm wrong: she's still there, unspeaking and unmoving in the dark, a piece of the past made present. Like my mother's token, my great-grandmother's charm, Eva is a part of me now, and will be until night enfolds us all.

There's one last question I need to ask. "You're the one who's been blocking me, aren't you? You're why I couldn't communicate with Rebecca or see some of the things I asked the Ecosystem to show me. Why I couldn't even see *your* power until you used it against me in the brood chamber."

"I did not know you," she says. "True, you are a child of Delilah's line, but you are also Leonida's seed. You were but a babe when last I saw you in the village, and I could not be certain what rights you would claim for yourself should you defeat the one you called the dark queen. I could not take the chance that you might stand in the way of my great-granddaughter's ascent to the throne." She pauses, releases another sigh. "I am an old woman, and my time was short. Forgive me. Leonida's enemy I might have been, but like her, I was seduced by the power in my blood."

I rise and move to where she sits, feel the strength that remains in her like the last embers of the fire. To my question about restoking the blaze, she answers that one of the maids will be along soon. I don't know what impulse makes me lean down and kiss her wrinkled cheek, but when I do, she lays a hand on my face and returns my kiss. I leave her sitting in her chair in the darkened room, and I say to myself that this woman who's outlived so much pain and sorrow couldn't possibly be as frail as I fear.

But again I'm wrong. When I return to the Queen's residence the following day, it's to discover that Eva died in her seat by the empty fireplace the night before.

TIME PASSES QUICKLY now that we've so much to do. Mending the gully my wyrm opened before the Cathedral is a monumental task, rebuilding toppled structures another. The Cathedral and library are beyond our power to repair, but we use their ruins for smaller buildings. Stone by stone, the city rises anew. Some of the stones are salvaged for the cemetery, the markers left fire-scarred and rough-hewn in reminder of all we've won and lost.

There will be no tombstone for Eva, however. We find instructions in her apron pocket, written in an unsteady hand—she learned to write quite late in life—providing for her body to be cremated, then returned to the village and scattered on the plain where her mother died. Once Rebecca stops crying long enough to issue proclamations, she approves her great-grandmother's last wish, along with my request to be the one to bear Eva's remains to their final resting place.

I'm not sure why I volunteer. Maybe it's merely an excuse to avoid Isaac, whom I see from time to time shouldering his share of the workload. But I think it's more than that. I've been growing restless of late, feeling as if I belong elsewhere, not in this foreign city where I served so briefly as queen. Teaching Rebecca her ABCs is rewarding enough, yet I can't help believing there's more I'm meant to do with my life, some answer I'm meant to find, even if I don't know what question I've been asked. The Queen has counselors aplenty: Gideon, Aurelia, Michael. I won't be missed.

I can't, however, leave at once. The Ecosystem appears stable so far as Rebecca can tell from her brood chamber—Gideon carries her down the stairs for the time being, though he's working on a ramp for her wheeled chair—but she's unwilling to take a chance with the city so newly cleansed. One of her first queenly acts, therefore, is to commission scouts to explore the woods, starting near our borders and expanding in an arc toward the village. I'm an obvious choice for this work, and Celestina would be, too—but she balks at being separated from Angelica, who's working with Flora and the twins to refurbish the healers' clinic. Personally, I feel that the former queen and her spouse could use a break from making dopey eyes at each other, but Celestina convinces Rebecca that her healing powers are needed in the city, and so I'm paired not with her but with Miriam.

I laugh when the Queen tells me. I have no objection to Miriam's company, but Rebecca's edict reminds me of Esther's from months past. The girl-queen even furrows her brow in an apparent attempt to emulate our lost Chief Sensor's scowl, which makes me laugh even harder. I drop a polite curtsy—I've become quite good at them, having learned that they go a long way toward covering up what one must leave unspoken—and head off to prepare for my rendezvous.

The first morning, Miriam meets me at what used to be the lofty front gate to the City of the Queens, though at present it's little more than a way-station for the heaps of stone being carted into and out of the city. In the few times I've seen her since her wedding day, I've noted that she's taken to wearing dresses, while someone—my guess is Celestina—has been tutoring her in the fine art of face-painting. Today, though, she wears a short brown shift similar to her Sensor's outfit of old, and her face is freshly scrubbed, her violet eyes framed by natural lashes. The only thing different about her is that she's trimmed her hair and wears what's left in a single braid upon her shoulder—the less, I presume, to remind Isaac of her days as the dark queen.

"Shall we go?" I say, and she nods. Together, we speed into the woods.

"What are we looking for?" Miriam asks once the city vanishes behind us.

"Anything suspicious," I answer. "Creatures we haven't Sensed before, remnants of the queen's web. Are you okay?" I add, seeing her shiver.

"I'm fine," she says. "Just a bit edgy."

I let that go, steer our conversation in other directions.

As it turns out, there's little to do *but* talk, for we meet with nothing untoward the entire day. The forest is no *edinnu*, that dream-world of perfect tranquility Daniel described on the day our village was lost—there are still venomous plants, aggressive animals, whispering trees—but there's nothing we can't handle. The worst we find is that some species I'd counted on to last forever, such as the shy, tree-hopping quetzals, seem to be gone for good. As the day unfolds, we talk of all manner of things: the young Queen's first week of rule, the glassmakers' progress on the council house windows, the other cities that might lie beyond this one, waiting to be found. The only thing we don't speak of is him.

Days pass in this fashion, a week, two. We develop a routine, and a rapport. Miriam's hair no longer tells us if anything's on the verge of breathing its last, but her skills as a Sensor haven't been dimmed by her own near-death experience. The skittishness of the first day recedes, and I feel safe to pose the question I've wanted to.

"Were you scared?" I ask while we lunch in a shaded grove, pigdeer and warhogs rooting nearby.

"I was lost," she says. "There was so little of me left, and it wasn't strong enough to fight her."

"You *did* fight her," I say. "Just like you fought to stay alive in the cave of the urthwyrms. You're a lot stronger than you think."

She answers only with a smile. A curious pigdeer approaches to eat from her hand, but it scampers away when we rise to our feet.

"The Queen has asked me to work with her," Miriam says. "On a new program to train common folk in the Sensors' arts."

"How wonderful!" I say, though in truth, the proposal was mine. I'm glad to hear that Rebecca has taken me up on it. "You'll be perfect."

"I had a good teacher," she says, and though I fear she's too kind for my deserts, I leave it at that.

Within three weeks, Rebecca calls us in from the field, satisfied that the woods are safe. I gather my belongings that night—there's not much, just a water flask, a knife, and the urn that contains Eva's remains—and stuff everything into a haversack for the road. All that's left now is to say my goodbyes.

I'm up early the next morning. Leah nearly crushes the life out of me with her hug. When she lets go, I see Beulah behind her, holding two-year-old Huldah in her arms. My friend tells me they're adopting the little girl, which brings tears to my eyes.

"Be safe," Leah tells me. "Don't go fighting all your battles on your own."

"Who's going to fight them with me?"

"Send a bird," she says before kissing my cheek. "I'll come running."

Then it's off to bid farewell to the others: Gideon and Aurelia, Celestina and Angelica, Michael and Luke. Every parting is another heartstring snipped from my chest. My consolation is that they're all so happy, so full of hope for the future. As I whisper my blessing on each of their homes, I wonder if I'll ever be able to say the same of myself.

There's only one visit left. I shoulder my bag and make my way across campus to Miriam and Isaac's house.

It sits on the periphery of the city, far from any other structure. Nearing it, I wonder if it was the site that Malachi chose for his secret studies—the house where my grandfather was cured, my great-aunt conceived. When I see the extensive garden that spreads behind their back door, I'm sure of it. Angelica told me that the students used to play games here, something with a pig's skin and a gold post, whatever that was. But the field where they played has become this garden, and Malachi's lonely hut will soon be reborn as a community gathering-place, where Miriam and her students will be free to unravel the mysteries of the Ecosystem.

And I know, though she said nothing of this in the forest, that Isaac will be working by her side. As Sensor and healer, they'll strive to restore the dream for which so many in my family have given their lives.

He's out in the field when I open the gate to the front walk, and he waves to me before hastening over. I'm determined to keep the tears inside my eyes on this visit, but the mere sight of him striding toward me, looking so much like the cocky boy I first met on the village commons, just about scuttles that plan.

He holds out a hand to usher me into his home. The tiny house is silent, and when I look around, there's not a shadow of its second occupant. "Where's Miriam?" I ask.

"The Queen called for her," he answers. "She'll be back in a few minutes."

"Is everything okay?"

"They're finalizing plans for Mimi's job," he says. "But there's something I needed to talk to you about alone."

My heart senses enough danger to quicken its pace. "Isaac, I don't think—"

"It's nothing like that," he assures me. "It's about Mimi."

"Is something wrong?"

"She's fine," he says. "But I wanted to tell you this privately. Before you leave."

"I'll be back," I say. "It can wait."

He looks at me hard, and I see that he still knows me, maybe better than I know myself. "I think I should tell you now," he says. "Just in case."

We sit on the wooden chairs that have replaced Malachi's reed mats. It's a small room, and with Isaac's long legs, I feel cramped, even caged. His eyes are troubled when he finally gets up the nerve to speak.

"I've never told anyone this," he says. "Not even Mimi. I know I'll have to tell her eventually, but I thought maybe, well…."

"You'd try it out on me first?" I quip, then realize what that must sound like.

He smiles in a strained way. "I'm sure you've wondered where the seed came from," he says. "The one that gave birth to the dark queen. Eva didn't know, right?"

I shake my head.

"It was me," he says, sighing deeply. "When I first started training with Daniel, I was always digging around in the dirt outside the village, trying to find something that would impress him. I was just so excited to be uncovering the Ecosystem's secrets, and being a thresher, I had a chance to search in places no one else got close to."

I imagine this younger Isaac, flushed with the importance of his new job, eager to please. "Where did you find it?"

"Beneath the charred circle," he says. "It was buried under what must have been three feet of ashes and dirt, and I had no idea what it was when I dug it up. I showed it to Daniel, and he said it was a seed from a stunflower— what used to be called a sunflower before the coming of the Ecosystem. He said people back then grew them all the time on their front walks, and that they stood for joy, for happy homes. That gave him an idea when Mimi and I got … when we set a date for our wedding."

"Daniel planted it," I say. "As a wedding present to you and Miriam."

"Yeah," he says. "Some present, huh?"

"You couldn't have known," I say. "When you gave Daniel the seed, you couldn't have had any idea what it truly was. You were just—"

"Being stupid," he says. "As always. Believing I knew best, and causing trouble for everyone else. Except this time…."

He buries his head in his hands. I can see it now: the seed replanted in the grabgrass beyond the charred circle with Isaac and Miriam looking on, Daniel speaking a few words of blessing even as the black threads begin to creep through the soil and work their malign power on the nearest Sensor, giving her the uncanny ability to Sense the dying. And then, when she nearly died herself, the parasite took over the body it was given, and Delilah reentered our world. Reentered it, and nearly brought it to an end.

But I also know that can't be the whole story. Delilah could have destroyed us all if she'd chosen to, but she didn't. She was brought back to life after nearly a century in the grave, and her outrage was all the greater for that—so great, she tortured the two men who'd forced this hellish half-life upon her. She wanted to stay dead. And so, when she held me captive in the brood chamber, when she could easily have slain the great-grandchild of her enemy before joining me in death, what she wanted even more than revenge was for Leonida's heir to become the bearer of her story. To *know* her, and her grief, so that she might never be forgotten again.

I kneel beside Isaac's chair, coax his hands from his face. His tears tell me of the impossible choice he's been wrestling with since the day he met me in the throne room: whether to kill the woman he loves, or watch her cause the deaths of the others he helped expose to Delilah's wrath. I exert all my queenly power to quiet the torment in his heart, but I know it's not enough. That healing will be for another to bring, if it comes at all.

"You tried to make it right," I tell him. "You risked your life to make it right. No one could ask more."

"But if I'd never fooled around with that thing in the first place...."

"We can't go back," I say. "We can only try to make a better tomorrow. For Miriam, and you, and everybody."

He nods, tries to smile, fails miserably.

"I have to be going," I say. "And you have to tell

Miriam. As soon as she comes home. She'll forgive you. She"—I tilt his head so he can see me smile—"she loves you so very much."

He lets out a sigh, loud and long, as if he's trying to expel all the ghosts of the past. Then he stands and walks me to the door. I'm on my way out when I see Miriam opening the gate, hurrying up the flower-lined path.

Her face shows no perturbation to discover me here. Cautiously, I reach out to read her mood, and I find her thoughts peaceful, her love for Isaac as strong as the day he first sauntered into our training session. I find as well that she's got news for him, private news she's rushed home to share with him alone. It's too early for her to detect in her own body, but Rebecca could, as can I.

She hugs me at the doorstep. Contact with her skin confirms what I felt from afar. My tongue itches to congratulate her, but my better self chides me not to spoil her secret. I kiss her forehead instead, and she beams.

"You'll always be welcome here," she says. "No matter how long you're away."

I gaze at Isaac, who's got an arm around her shoulder. He looks as if he's about to say something, but changes his mind and merely smiles.

"Be well," I say. "Remember that I love you both."

Walking down the path, I can't help grinning when I picture how Isaac's going to take the news. I turn at the end of the walk, see them nestled against each other. They raise a hand and wave. I blow them one last kiss, then set out across the City of the Queens for home.

IT TAKES ME a week to reach the village, more time than it might, but I'm in no hurry. I imagine myself following Eva's path, my steps forming a bridge, however small, between city and village. Maybe one day, that path will be walked by others, even if, by that time, I'll have moved on again.

The sky's faded to dusk when the forest opens to reveal the site where the village used to stand. In the dim light, I see that the dark queen's hedge has vanished, becoming nothing more than black dust to add to the charred circle under which her seed rested for so many years. Strangely, the palisade of trees her wyrms planted to defend her stronghold has disappeared as well, which makes me wonder whether the trees were part of the inner architecture that held the Armegaddon together. The wall of earth and stone the wyrms built up around her lair has sunk down to nearly nothing, just a few scattered blocks jutting from the earth like broken teeth.

I step out of the forest onto the blackened sod, reach inside my bag for the jar that holds Eva's remains. A warm wind spreads the ashes to earth when I tilt the container. As they fall, I speak a few words that might be a spell, or a prayer:

House of Earth, House of Stone
Heal my people
Grant them peace

There's no answer from the surrounding woods, only the soft sigh of the wind. I raise my head to the open sky, see that a single star has appeared in the empty black gullet of the night. It's but a pinprick, far too weak to cast back any inch of the darkness. Still it holds my attention as I stand upon this plateau where life meets death. When I was a child, returning from Sensor lessons with my grandpa and staring up at the night sky, I thought of the stars as torches or firewells that kept back whatever evil creatures floated through the impossibly vast Ecosystem above my head. Though I've since learned from my reading that the stars are just like our own sun, I find their ethereal pixie-lights so beautiful I can't help imagining that whatever worlds revolve around them must also be more beautiful than mine, worlds of light and laughter where no danger lurks. In the darkest of days, I've often thought I'd like to go there, to leave this world and its fears and cares far behind.

But now I have another thought, and maybe it's only my uncertain future that brings it to me, but I think it's right: *There are Ecosystems there, too.* Each world is its own Ecosystem, ancient and all-powerful, whirling around balls of fire I'll never know. And all of those spinning Ecosystems are knitted together into the far larger one that spans the sky, each a part of the whole.

I stand, and stare, and as the night darkens, a thousand

stars I couldn't see before crystallize overhead, populating the sky as if each star has given birth to a hundred twinkling children. Behind or within this nursery of stars, I see a faintly glowing band that both *is* and *holds* the starlight, the way an ember on the hearth both is the flame and bears the flame within it. My breath catches as I gaze, enraptured, at the galaxy, and I feel—though I can hardly Sense—the millions of lives that might be, could be, must be unfolding within their own separate Ecosystems. I lift my hands to the stars, and it seems as if my brown skin swims in fields of light.

There is no *edinnu* here, or anywhere. Daniel tried to bring it back long before we were ready for it, or long after we had let it go for good. But that doesn't mean I can't use my hands to heal the only home I'll ever have. In my heart, I know it's going to take a long time, maybe all the time I have to give. Yet I know too that this is my charge. To live in this world, and prepare the ground for a future where everyone can walk without fear on the lonely, lovely earth.

I kneel in the soil. I plant a seed.

THE END

HISTORICAL NOTE

In the City of the Queens, it became conventional to utilize the dating system of BCE (Before the Coming of the Ecosystem) and AD (Anno Dominica), which marked the crowning of seven-year-old Dominique Dawson. Due to the upheavals that attended the Ecosystem's rise and the consequent loss of records, precise dating (both BCE and AD) was not always possible. Thus the following is an approximate timeline of the major events recounted in this chronicle. Since there is no year AD zero, calculations of time that span the BCE/AD divide are made by adding the total number of years on each side and subtracting 1.

50 – 12 BCE:	Collapse of worldwide bee populations
12 – 7 BCE:	Creation of *Apis impunita* colony by chief researchers Reginald Dawson and Meredith Cowley-Dawson
7 BCE:	Birth of Dominique Dawson
7 – 1 BCE:	Dissemination of *A. impunita* genetic material
	Rise of Ecosystem
AD 1:	Dominique crowned Queen Dominica I
AD 1 - 55:	Rule of Queen Dominica

AD 23:	Birth of Demetria, eldest daughter of Dominica
AD 28:	Birth of Delphina, middle daughter of Dominica
AD 33:	Birth of Divina, youngest daughter of Dominica
AD 55:	Death of Queen Dominica
AD 55 – 90:	Rule of Queen Demetria
AD 58:	Birth of Delilah, daughter of Divina
AD 60:	Birth of Leonida, daughter of Demetria
AD 64:	Birth of Malachi
AD 82 – 94:	The Great Rupture
AD 82:	Death of Divina
AD 83:	Birth of Aaron, son of Delilah
AD 83 – 93:	Delilah and Malachi explore alternative paths of healing
AD 86:	Birth of Seraphina, daughter of Leonida
AD 90:	Death of Queen Demetria
AD 90 – 153:	Rule of Queen Leonida
AD 93:	Delilah, Malachi, and their followers exiled from City of the Queens
AD 94:	Birth of Eva, daughter of Delilah and Malachi
	Cataclysm in village claims the life of Delilah and other exiles
	Aaron begins training as Sensor under new rules of military preparedness
AD 100:	Aaron invested as Sensor
AD 108:	Birth of Daniel
AD 110:	Birth of Tamar, daughter of Eva
	Eva inherits Delilah's token from Malachi

AD 111:   Eva relocates to City of the Queens
AD 112:   Aaron's first visit to City of the Queens
AD 128:   Birth of Abraham
AD 131:   Birth of Sarah (the elder), daughter of
             Seraphina and Aaron
             Death of Seraphina
             Sarah (the elder) brought to village
             by Aaron
             Abraham begins training as Sensor
AD 134:   Sarah (the elder) begins training as
             Sensor with Aaron
AD 135:   Eva passes Delilah's token to Daniel, who
             begins to explore the way of the healers
AD 139:   Birth of Estella, great-granddaughter
             of Delphina
AD 142:   Daniel becomes Chief Warden, expands
             secret healer training program to
             include Sensors
AD 143:   Abraham begins training as healer
             with Daniel
AD 145:   Abraham invested as Sensor
AD 147:   Sarah (the elder) invested as Sensor,
             begins training as healer with Abraham
             and Daniel
AD 153:   Death of Queen Leonida
AD 153 – 173: Rule of Queen Estella
AD 155:   Birth of Isaac
AD 156:   Birth of Ruth, daughter of Sarah (the
             elder) and Abraham
             Sarah (the elder) expelled
             from Sensorship

Abraham flees village for City of the Queens, where he is renamed Gabriel by Queen Estella

AD 157:   Birth of Celestina, daughter of Estella
            Birth of Miriam

AD 158:   Death of Sarah (the elder)

AD 159:   Ruth begins training as Sensor with Aaron, who renames her Sarah

AD 166:   Birth of Rebecca, great-great-granddaughter of Delilah

AD 168:   Death of Malachi
            Aaron becomes Chief Sensor

AD 171:   Isaac begins training as healer with Daniel, discovers Delilah's seed
            Miriam and Isaac pledged in marriage

AD 173:   Ruth (known as Sarah) invested as Sensor
            Miriam begins training as Sensor with Ruth (known as Sarah)
            Death of Queen Estella
            Death of Aaron

AD 173 – 74: Rule of Queen Celestina

AD 174:   Rule of Queen Sarah
            Death of Gabriel
            War of the Queens
            Rule of Queen Rebecca begins
            Marriage of Miriam and Isaac
            Death of Eva

BESTIARY

Due to the unstable character of the A. impunita genome, the planetary Ecosystem gave rise to innumerable emergent species, both plant and animal (and continues to do so, with a steady background of mutation punctuated by bursts of heightened mutagenic activity). The following list, therefore, represents only an infinitesimal fraction of the total number of species within the constantly evolving Ecosystem.

Ache tree: deciduous tree with leaves that cause dizziness and disorientation

Angerconda: constrictor reaching thirty feet in length

Arachnard: arachnid lizard

Armegaddon: monster created by the dark queen resembling a winged, many-headed dragon

Badflower: plant in the mustard family whose scent causes irritation of the nasal passage

Bald evil: large, powerful bird of prey of the northern mountains

Berserkflower: collective name for any of a number of spitting or biting wildflowers

Bitter retch: plant in the pea family that produces
bleeding ulcers when ingested

Bloodbird: vampire bird, apparently descended from the
common American robin

Blurjay: passerine bird whose feather patterns
induce disorientation

Bogsand: species of grabgrass, abundant in marshy areas

Braindigger wasp: wasp that paralyzes victims with bone-
piercing stinger; also known as a horrornet

Breach tree: deciduous tree with peeling white bark that
causes skin irritation and inflammation

Cardivore: carnivorous bird of the passerine family; also
known as a cardinull

Carnary: carnivorous songbird, small and brightly colored

Carrionbou: herd animal of the frozen north; scavenger

Charmeleon: small, rainbow-colored reptile with heat-
producing glands beneath its skin

Chicanery: herbaceous plant that disseminates parasitic
seeds in the flesh of animals

Chimaera: predator of the northern mountains possessing
leonine, caprine, and serpentine features

Choken: flightless bird whose barbed bones puncture the
throats of predators

Cicatrix: winged insect that travels in massive swarms

Clawshoe rabbit: rabbit of the far north with long, clawed
hind feet

Crocodont: crocodilian with multiple rows of retractable/extensible teeth

Dragonfly: swamp insect capable of producing small gouts of fire

Drake: scaly waterfowl with venomous breath

Dreadwing: carnivorous swamp bird with black body and red wing markings

Eelfish: snakelike freshwater fish with powerful jaws

Fearkat: small, rodent-like animal that lives in large colonies

Fear tree: coniferous tree with prehensile branches

Fell-cat: wild cat, lynx-size

Fire-tailed hawk: bird of prey whose feathers produce intense burns

Flame ant: colony insect that utilizes a chemical pheromone to attract and consume prey

Flamefly: flying insect that signals mates with bioluminescent abdomen, hot to the touch

Flamingull: pink-colored shorebird, rumored to combust upon capture

Frogbull: large, horned frog

Gash tree: desert tree with projectile spikes

Ghastly bear: ursine predator of the woodlands

Ghosthawk: any of a number of birds of prey with the ability to camouflage themselves in wooded areas

Glassgrass: sharp desert grass, capable of penetrating flesh

Gnoose: feathered, flightless quadruped

Grabgrass: clinging grass capable of pulling bodies underground for consumption

Grassharrower: jumping insect whose mating song induces intense pain and hallucination

Great Horned Howl: nocturnal bird of prey with sharp, bony protuberances above prominent eyes

Grossquito: flying insect whose bite produces painful abscesses

Gryphon: giant bird in the condor family, with a wingspan of over fifteen feet

Harm tree: deciduous tree with roving roots that emerge to penetrate and ensnare prey

Hellion: giant shorebird with a long, serrated beak

Hexlox: coniferous tree that devours prey through digestive pustules

Histeria: poisonous thorn bush that causes madness and death

Honeysickle: flowering plant with barbed berries

Horrornet: stinging hornet (see also braindigger wasp)

Huntingbird: fast-flying, sharp-beaked bird that feeds on plant nectar and animal blood

Hydra bird: predatory bird that uses vestigial second head to misdirect prey

Jackalass: donkey-like scavenger

Jekyll: dog-like scavenger

Juggernut: deciduous tree with tough, scaly branches and projectile seed cases

Killdeer: deer whose flesh acquires the venomous quality of the plants it consumes

Leprous tree: deciduous tree adapted for swamp living; similar to mangrave

Mangrave: swamp tree with animate roots and limbs

Maul tree: deciduous tree known for bright red leaves covered with spiny stingers

Molusk: blind, burrowing mollusk

Pain tree: coniferous tree that uses intoxicating scent to lure prey and poisonous needles to produce asphyxiation and death

Pandalion: maned feline with black-and-white fur

Pigdeer: small antlered deer

Poison arrow frog: brightly colored amphibian that spits venom thirty or more feet

Poisonrose: poisonous rose bush

Preying mantis: insect capable of clutching birds and small mammals in grasping claws

Prowler monkey: carnivorous monkey that emits a deep, throaty attack call

Quetzalcoati: feathered arboreal marsupial (currently believed to be extinct)

Raspberry: bush that produces partly indigestible berries

Ravener: carnivorous crow of the eastern desert

Rhubhard: poisonous bulb

Sawgrass: sharp-edged swamp grass capable of amputating human limbs

Scaramander: forest amphibian with toxic skin

Sharkbug: carnivorous insect distinguished by prominent thoracic "fin"

Shredder tree: aromatic tree, lethally intoxicating to many animals (including human beings)

Shrew-cat: burrowing feline with long, pointed snout and sharp teeth

Shriek: small bird of prey that attacks in huge flocks

Sickenmore: deciduous tree with limbs capable of telescoping inside the trunk to capture prey

Slickworm: moth larva known for regurgitating cloth-like matter

Snailsnake: slug-like snake with venomous mucus membranes

Snatching turtle: swamp reptile that pulls prey into its shell for dismemberment and consumption

Soil-serpent: venomous snake that nests belowground in shallow, sandy soil

Stab beetle: insect with pincers whose bite-force per square inch equals that of a terror wolf

Stabbing nettle, projectile: poisonous nettle capable of shooting barbs fifty or more feet

Stunflower: carnivorous plant that paralyzes flying prey

Swallowtale: poisonous butterfly with brightly
colored wings

Terror wolf: pack hunter of the northern mountains

Tricky vulture: flightless bird; scavenger

Tyrantula: one of a class of furry, venomous spiders
measuring ten or more inches in length

Unicorn beetle: insect with modified single pincer that
injects numbing venom, fatal to small prey

Urthwyrm: giant toothed worm of the eastern desert; also
called a borer or landprey

Vampire bee: blood-sucking insect, bat-size

Virago creeper: climbing vine capable in its mature form
of ensnaring large mammals

Warhog: spiny warthog

Water lilith: swamp flower that drains vital fluids from its
victims upon contact

Watermite: carnivorous swamp insect that attacks in
colonies numbering in the millions

Wilderberry: edible berry that produces hallucinations if
over-consumed

THE LINE OF THE QUEENS

In the year following the War of the Queens, Queen Rebecca ordered the restoration of the council house windows. The oldest two windows—those depicting Dominica and her three daughters—were painstakingly reconstructed from memory, while new windows were installed to represent not only the past rulers of the city, but other women of queenly blood who had not sat on the throne during their natural lifespans. The latter included Delilah, the lost queen; Eva, daughter of Delilah; Seraphina, daughter of Leonida; and Sarah (the elder), daughter of Seraphina. At Queen Rebecca's bidding, the images of these women were paired with those of their own generation who had ruled in their stead, including the cousins and bitter rivals Leonida and Delilah; Estella and Sarah (the elder); and Celestina and Ruth (known as Sarah). In the case of Seraphina, both her lover Aaron and her confidante Eva were added to her window to signify the reconciliation of the warring lines.

Though Rebecca herself was too modest to request this, a single window was devoted to her as to Dominica, thereby memorializing the two girl-queens who had brought peace to the Ecosystem and the city.

The following artist's rendering depicts the council house windows as they stood during the reign of Queen Rebecca.

HOUSE
OF
EARTH

HOUSE
OF
STONE

HEAL
MY
PEOPLE

GRANT
THEM
PEACE

DOMINICA

DEMETRIA

DELPHINA

DIVINA

LEONIDA

DELILAH

ACKNOWLEDGMENTS

Now that I've brought the Ecosystem trilogy to a close, I'd like to thank those who played a part in its origin and development:

My agent, Liza Fleissig, and my editor, Christa Yelich-Koth.

The three writers who introduced me to the world of indie publishing: Louise Cypress, Stephanie Keyes, and Kat Ross.

Jessica Khoury of Lizard Ink Maps, for the gorgeous drawing of the Line of the Queens.

The creative team at Damonza, for bringing my imagined world to such vivid life.

Riverstone Books, for hosting each of my three launch parties.

All of the authors who have been so instrumental to my growth as a writer, including those I know personally and those quoted in my epigraphs.

My readers, whose faith in the stories I tell means the world to me.

My wife and children, who understand why I need to tell those stories.

And last, my father, who died at the age of eighty-nine while I was working on this book. Though he never had a chance to read it, his presence is there in every word.

ABOUT THE AUTHOR

Joshua David Bellin has been writing novels since he was eight years old (though the first few were admittedly very short). A college teacher by day, he has published numerous works of fantasy and science fiction, including the two-part Querry Genn Saga (*Survival Colony 9* and *Scavenger of Souls*), the deep-space adventure *Freefall*, and the short story collection *Ten Tales of Terror and Terra*. The Ecosystem trilogy—*Ecosystem*, *The Devouring Land*, and *House of Earth, House of Stone*—is his latest foray into speculative fiction. In his free time, Josh likes to read, watch movies, and take long hikes in Nature with his kids. Oh, yeah, and he likes monsters. Really scary monsters.

To find out more about Josh and his books, visit *https://joshuadavidbellin.blogspot.com/p/contact.html* and sign up for his newsletter. He promises not to send it to you more than once a month!

joshuadavidbellin.blogspot.com

ALSO BY JOSHUA DAVID BELLIN

Ecosystem (Ecosystem Trilogy, #1)
The Devouring Land (Ecosystem Trilogy, #2)
Survival Colony 9 (Querry Genn Saga, #1)
Scavenger of Souls (Querry Genn Saga, #2)
Freefall

www.ingramcontent.com/pod-product-compliance
Lightning Source LLC
Chambersburg PA
CBHW011443170626
46816CB00008B/2500

* 9 7 8 1 7 3 2 1 8 5 9 6 8 *